BRICK, LIME AND MOONSHINE

BRICK, LIME AND MOONSHINE

for the love of a lake cabin . . .

VICTORIA VENTRIS SHEA

Dedicated to:

Our Parents and Grandparents
for their love and perseverance

Cheer up, laugh, be gay. It is surprising how much we can get along without if we only have love, love and a home and family.

Lots of Love to All, Grandma Ida

The memoir chapters (written in italics) are true.

They are the author's reflections of her lake cabin, a cabin which will become important to the story and connect the past with the present.

A Life's Work

I know the soul of this place, every inch, rock and shingle, every dust mote, every spot where the sun's heat comes through the morning windows to warm my bones.

I walk outside and sit in Mom's "Coffee Camp," pull her orange and brown scarf tight around my neck against the chill. The Canadian geese near shore sound like unhappy donkeys with their hee-haws and honk-ee honk-ee's. Our cat Andrew purrs across my legs and investigates the fallen leaves.

It seems my entire life has been contained within this lake cabin, a place where memories of family are kept, where love abounds. Saying goodbye feels impossible.

I first saw the cabin as a child. It was a brown box, anchored to the crest of the hill on the southwest end of Loon Lake north of Spokane. People there were called "cliff dwellers." There was nothing but empty space below the door on the water side of the cabin where a deck had never been built. I worried that someone would walk out that door enraptured by the aquamarine view and break their neck from the fall. The only warning of danger was a tall, skinny fir tree about ten feet out from the cabin.

On a rock foundation, the cabin had a hip roof and a wall of screened windows facing the lake. Inside were the bare essentials—a large room with layers of "The Spokane Daily Chronicle" glued to the walls for insulation, a burgundy enameled woodstove at one end with broken panes of mica that leaked golden firelight into the room. No water, but a sink against one wall and a hand-dug well ten steps out the back. Hand over hand, the cleanest, sweetest, coldest drinking water in Eastern Washington could be brought up for a drink from a bucket. The outhouse further up the hill was a two-holer, though I don't remember sharing.

By the time we bought it, dark wood paneling had been installed inside. A homemade cabinet of varnished fir held three fluted glasses that were pink with cherries etched on their bottoms. A small, rough deck had been constructed outside that dangerous door. For my family and me, the cabin became our refuge, and the lake was a languid sponge that slowed down time and soaked away all our worries.

When I was ten, Dad leaned the heavy twelve-foot wooden ladder against the side of the cabin on top of an old wobbly blue table which was leveled on the hillside with chunks of firewood under the table legs. He asked me to climb to the top. I was to paint the upper eaves under the hip-roof a hopeful forget-me-not blue to cover the final bit of old brown. Clumsy, afraid of heights, it seemed like a tall order.

The youngest of his four daughters, I was probably the closest to a son that he never had, but this was much too high and way too wonky.

"You'll be as safe as a babe in your mother's arms," he urged, bracing himself against the ladder. Rusty, our cocker spaniel, wagged his stubby tail as if he agreed.

I wasn't that encouraged. Still, if there was one person I trusted, it was my Dad. Slowly, I crawled up, knees trembling, grabbing each rung like a cry for help, a partial bucket of paint swinging from a hook on my belt. The ladder didn't move.

Frozen at the top, my nose flattened against the wall in front of me. I imagined the ladder pulling away from the wall, could nearly feel the impact of my body smashing into the ground. I willed my clenched right hand to grab for the paintbrush, but unable to look down, I knocked the bucket instead and heard "ker-plunk splat" as it hit the ground.

The ladder didn't move.

Dad held it steady as I inched my way back down, shaking like a car bumping over a waffled road. Rusty came back around the corner; his short blue tail flicked paint from side to side. The twinkle was in Dad's eyes. "The eaves, Vickie, not the bushes . . . or the dog," he laughed, "though it is a pretty color."

Dad never scolded. Instead, he would tell us girls how much he loved us. "I never built a bridge or anything permanent," he'd say. "No legacy, nothing to leave behind in this world except my girls. Make me proud of my life's work."

I always tried to make him proud since he only seemed to see the good in me. "And remember, Vickie," he promised, "if you ever falter, I'll always be here to help you up again."

He died when I was 19, but he had taught me the comfort that nature and a few melodies could bring, like the ones he'd depended on during his rough beginning. A few tunes had been a good distraction while he'd ridden the rails to look for work. "The woods" was his favorite place. He sorted out life's little troubles there like blue paint splattered on a hillside, and he appreciated nature's treasures, even in a tiny twig.

We sat in the sun against a log, and I began to recover in the warm *whisper of air that swirled up from the lake. Dad sang "love's old sweet song" as he whittled, transforming a young, supple stick into a tiny, fragile flute. He asked me to play it. I blew carefully, sliding the core in and out of its bark. The delicate notes came smoothly, gently. Satisfied, he stood up.*

"Come on Vickie, I think you can hold the ladder for me this time."

I wasn't sure that I could, except that he trusted me to do it, and I was awfully glad that he wasn't asking me to go up there again. So I held it with all my heart. From the ground I could hear his whistling as he painted the eaves blue. Encouraged, I called up to him, "You're as safe as a babe in your mother's arms!"

"I know," he chuckled.

His name was Joe.

PART ONE

Perseverance Moonshine

Inland Pacific Northwest

1889-1932

In His Mother's Arms

Midvale, Idaho 1922

Joe stared into the popping bonfire over his plate of biscuits and gravy, locked in the memory of a different big fire when he was four years old. His family said he was too young to remember, but he did remember. His toes curled in his boots from the cold wet as if he still stood barefoot in slush, clutching his baby blanket. Shadowed figures hurried about, voices raised, screams and stifled cries came and went. Scooped into his mother's arms, he was carried above her stretched belly to the safety of the neighbor's homestead.

It had been scarlet fever. His parents had burned formaldehyde to fumigate the house, and the fire had spread, burning everything. He could still smell the caustic twang, like burnt pickles. The neighbors had been saints to take them in, them and the scarlet fever.

Too much pain had come too fast. Joe's mother, Alice, had already lost three children before their house burned, her own mother had recently given up the ghost, and despite her desperate prayers, Joe's eight-year-old brother Hartzel, her eldest son, had not survived the fever. The neighbor had offered the old Elly homestead on his property, and Alice had given birth to her last baby there. Vera had lived only one day, and the difficult delivery was serious. It had taken Alice two weeks to regain consciousness and nearly a year to get back on her feet.

She had wondered how tender her four-year-old's heart would become after being around all that loss and her long illness. Joe had spent much of that winter curled up next to her on her sickbed, listening to her heartbeat. She'd told him that he helped her, so he had stayed, his pudgy hand patting her arm now and then. As her health had begun to return, she'd read the Bible to him, *"The Lord is near to the brokenhearted and saves those who are crushed in spirit."* It had been the doctor, a drunk, who had finally gotten her out of bed. He'd told her that if she didn't get up, someone else would raise her children.

The memory faded from Joe's mind. He wiped up the last of his sausage and cream gravy with a biscuit and stood to straighten his back, running his fingers through his cropped, straight dark-brown hair. It had been a long day with the six-foot cross-cut saw, the misery whip. He felt the misery in his arms and legs, and in his back. Like the others, he had called it a "sawing bee" at one time as if it were some kind of frivolous fun. Now he knew better, he'd known ever since he'd gotten big enough to handle the whip.

Waves of *Red River Valley* came from inside the barn, his older brother James Roy playing the fiddle, and Joe turned to see bodies in there moving with the beat. He realized that his younger brother, Tommy, had been talking at him about something.

"Those folks dancing in the barn there aren't too smart," Joe interrupted. "They'll be sorry tomorrow."

Tommy sat, poking the fire. "I was telling you about the foot-race I won yesterday . . ."

"Stupid, really," Joe grumbled, rubbing the tender calluses on his hands. "Work all day, dance all night. They haven't got any sense."

Tommy smiled. He knew that Joe could not resist a dance. His eyebrows raised as he talked to the fire, "I even won two bits and next time . . ."

The music changed to *Wabash Cannonball*, a snappier tune. "That's great, Tommy, you *are* pretty fast. Aw nuts! I guess I'm as stupid as they are." Joe shook his head and wandered off toward the barn.

He knew there would be more work tomorrow, several families cutting wood together, and the following week the whole crowd would move to another farm until every farm in the group was set up with firewood for winter. The women and girls constantly cooked to feed them all. Joe and his brothers and sisters would need to keep on milking their fourteen cows twice a day and drive them to pasture and water, take care of the horses, pigs, and chickens.

Fall harvest would be handled the same way, neighbors helping to gather the bounty and have fun doing it, an added gift of the harvest. The neighborhood boys would walk behind the horse-pulled wagon, husking corn from left and right, throwing the ears against the bang board to fall into the wagon like the beat of a work song. What wasn't sold fresh would be put into the corn crib to dry, then it would be shelled and ground for feed, the cobs used for fuel in the kitchen stove. Apples and other fruit would be picked; potatoes, onions and other root vegetables would be dug and put into the root cellar. The canning would continue throughout the season whenever there was more food than they could eat or sell or trade, and leftovers were thrown to the pigs.

Neighbors worked together for winter butchering, too, processing and curing their meat. A hog would be killed and hung to bleed, then put on a platform to scald and the hair would be scraped away. After the innards were removed, it would be taken into the house in a washtub so Alice and the other women could remove the leaf lard. Some side pork would be put into a barrel of salt brine, and bacon and hams would be hung for smoking in the smokehouse along with the sausage that Alice would make in tubes she sewed from old flour sacks. Joe's mouth watered at the thought.

Spring was birthing season and planting season. The earth would be turned, releasing its smell of promise, and the pulse of life on the farm would continue by the grace of God.

Joe had always loved to dance. He'd learned his love of music, along with his quietness, from his father. Everything seemed rhythmic, the ax splitting wood, milk squeezed into a bucket, the gallop of a horse. He sidled on up to a cute young neighbor, hands on his hips. Her curly auburn hair bounced with the beat, making him smile, and his legs didn't feel quite so tired anymore. His lanky body moved naturally to his brother's fiddle as his father called the square dance and the round. "Do si do," and Joe promenaded his partner around the floor, holding her hands with their arms crossed one on top of the other.

When the music stopped, lumpy blankets were spread over mounds of straw, and exhausted farmers sent thanks to the Lord for their good day and good neighbors before falling asleep, knowing there would be work again in the morning. Within minutes, they were already dreaming about the strong, hot coffee that would be there when they woke.

Unassigned Lands

Oklahoma Territory 1889

Joe's people were a hardy sort. Originally from England and Wales, his parents and grandparents settled in Oklahoma Territory twenty years before he was born. They were part of the mad scramble for homestead property into "unassigned lands" previously set aside for the Plains Indians. They'd joined the big race, farmers, cowboys, and old soldiers waiting for the go-ahead gunshot to find and stake their claim.

For six years, Joe's father, John, toiled on his family's chunk of hard work in Paradise, Payne County. He was satisfied with their progress until he met Alice, the preacher's daughter. She was a bit shorter, patient and kind, a good listener if he ever chose to say anything, and sweeter than he imagined a woman could be. She loved the Lord and had a six-year-old daughter, Julia, her husband having died after six months of marriage. Alice helped John feel grounded, surer of himself; and on Christmas Eve, the brown-haired, blue-eyed, and slightly serious couple held hands as they were married by her father, Elwood.

Their first house was a soddie. John busted sod into strips a foot wide and four inches thick. He laid two rows side by side, grass-side down, lengthwise for the first level, then crosswise for the second level, then lengthwise again and on up. A sycamore log served as the ridgepole, its slight curve creating a whimsical roofline.

The house was one room, fourteen by sixteen feet. John laid the sod up around the door frame and the window frame, drilling holes in the frames to drive wooden pegs through and into the sod. As the sod settled its weight above their only window, the glass broke; and Alice, who tried to see the positives in life, had to admit that she was a little disappointed about that.

Despite mud dripping in after a hard rain and snakes curling up in her cupboard which was an apple crate pegged into the wall, she gave birth to their first child in that house, a beautiful little girl with peachy cheeks the color of the red Oklahoma dirt. They named her Ruby, their precious gem. Alice was watchful over Ruby. The day she saw an orange-striped ribbon snake slither toward her baby wrapped in a blanket in the yard, she bludgeoned it into mush with a hatchet and left it as a warning to others.

Even so, illness took baby Ruby at only three months. Brokenhearted, John built a little pine box. Alice's father prayed her tiny spirit into the Lord's hands and helped bury her under the black walnut tree behind the house where Alice could rest and visit. John often joined her there and held her hand, not being the type who found it easy to offer words of comfort.

"I know you're hurting as much as I am," she said, patting his hand. Ruby's death had stolen her strength and she used what little she had left to push the words from her mouth.

They raised cotton and corn, planting the corn in rows forty inches apart so a horse and cart could get between them; and after the first frost, bundles stood in sheaves grouped across the field like skinny hats before being shucked and dried. Local Indians made themselves at home then, sometimes asking, sometimes taking, always accompanied by an elder in a calico shirt, turquoise beads around his neck.

As the cotton fields broke from green-brown seeds into a sea of white puffs, Alice helped with the harvest, pulling a nine-foot sack down the rows with a strap over her shoulder until her leather gloves got thin. Then she wrapped her fingers inside the gloves and kept going, twisting each puff of cotton out of its sharp spikes.

There were household chores too: cooking, canning, baking, laundry, mending, and there was love. John was in awe of Alice as he watched her fluid movements in the kitchen, knowing that she could keep going as long as he could and somehow still feed him with kindness and encouraging words despite the difficulties of her day. More children came: Elwood, named after her father; Grace for the Grace of God; and John, named after his father. Baby John lived only one month before joining Ruby under the walnut tree.

John thought a long time for words that might comfort them both when baby John died. "Love is a difficult thing," he finally said as he held Alice under the tree. It seemed so inadequate, yet she sobbed into his chest, and he held her tight.

"It is," she cried. "It really is."

Enticing stories called folks further west for land and opportunity, "a western paradise, yours for the taking" and whoppers like "dumplings fall from trees in Idaho." Alice's parents went, her father having been called to lead a church there. John wanted to go too, but Alice held back. She couldn't leave her babies under the walnut tree and take her family on such a difficult trip, knowing too well how fragile life could be.

The morning she saw the Kickapoo elder walk to her children's graves and solemnly place a bit of corn there, turquoise beads swinging from his neck, she felt able to go, knowing their graves would not be forgotten. She and John put their faith in the Lord and headed West in their wagon, a long, arduous trip, suffering through malaria and typhoid along the way. When they finally made it to Alice's parents in Genesee, Idaho, Hartzel was born. Joe was still just a twinkle in his father's eye.

A Gateway

Counties were formed when land was opened for homesteading, and when railroads laid track, train stations and towns were created. John found a job as a section hand on the Spokane-Palouse rail-line in Farmington, Washington, a town of five hundred people near the Idaho border within the spectacular views of the undulant Palouse prairie. The family lived in an apartment inside one end of the train station where afternoon shade was provided by tall grain silos.

Farmington sat alongside the tracks in a green fertile valley dotted with clusters of pine in the distance, the tip of Steptoe Butte showing above rolling hills to the southwest like a protective watchtower. The butte had been originally known as Power Mountain to the local Indians, then Pyramid Peak to settlers.

John was a section hand. He spent his days digging and pounding out broken or rotten rail ties and driving in spikes to keep the new ones in place on his seven-mile section of track. He thought about Steptoe Butte as he stood to stretch his back. Folks said you could see two hundred miles across the prairie from up there. He wondered if that was the power that had named it Power Mountain in the beginning.

The train station was a busy place for shipping wheat and lentils and a trading post for the Coeur d'Alene Indians who stormed in on their ponies, giving Alice and the children a fright, then settling on a grassy spot on the other side of the tracks. The hobos and drunks who hung around the station worried her more. She couldn't abide by drunks.

Alice gave food to those who were hungry if she could. *He who is gracious to the needy honors Him.* She saw how they eyed the caboose when it temporarily sat at the station, lovingly calling it the "Accommodation Car." On occasion, she let someone stay the night in their apartment and offered a bit of work so they wouldn't feel like it was charity, a little weeding or dishwashing, filling the wood box or sweeping. They always seemed a bit lost, and so she offered what comfort she could.

"How are you getting on, Mister?"

"Missing my family, Ma'am. Feel guilty 'bout leaving them behind to look for work."

"I can imagine," she said, patting a shoulder. "Would it help if we prayed together for you and your family?"

Eyes filled with tears, heads bowed, and they prayed for protection and a job, and a little help and guidance, and to see their families soon.

"Thank you, Ma'am. The road can be pretty lonesome sometimes."

A well-mannered man named Leon appeared at Alice's door with a tumble of brown curls on top of his head and a round boy's face that any mother would love. He looked thin and weak.

"I would appreciate a brief respite from the hardships of the road," he said.

She let him stay several days, treated as part of the family. He used his rest time to write in a small notebook. One afternoon at the kitchen table, he poured his too-hot coffee into the saucer to drink, and Alice sat down to ask about why he was on the road.

"I'm a hobo," he shrugged. "We're different from bums and vagrants. We follow a code of ethics, travel cuz we're looking for work, *always* looking for work, and sometimes we need a little help," he smiled.

When he left, he was fed and clean and had some sandwiches to take along. Alice found a beautiful black necklace and a thank you note torn from his little notebook with a simple sketch of a cat. "This necklace is the only thing I have to give as a 'thank you' for your kindness. It belonged to my mother. The cat picture is how I found you. It tells that you are a kindly lady." She recognized the cat from the picture scratched on the front post of the train station, and she wasn't sure if the cat picture was a gift or a curse.

Years later, Alice would see his picture in the newspaper, Leon Ray Livingston, also known as "A-Number One." He had helped create the picture code so hobos would know where they were welcome or not, barking dogs and the like and had written twelve books about living on the road, including a memoir of his travels with eighteen-year-old Jack London, the author.

While repairing his section of track, John paid attention to the trains moving through. Beyond that was the constant huffing of horses and grinding of equipment as farmers plowed and harvested their fields in the valley. It was a stunning place, so green and fertile it could have been from Heaven. He had never seen such abundance. After pounding in a spike, he stood to watch the wind churn through copper heads of wheat. He breathed in the rich, sweet smell of the fields, and his heart bent. He wanted it, he *needed* to have a farm of his own.

The idea of leaving the security of a paying job with a home felt selfish, but he couldn't see raising his family in a railroad station. He wanted his children free to run about, safe on their own property, healthy and strong.

James Roy was a bundle in Alice's arms the day that President Teddy Roosevelt stepped off his seven-car train at the station with his entire entourage. It was pure excitement. The group walked at a brisk pace a quarter mile down the track and back, Roosevelt's voice booming as they went. John and Alice had never seen so many men dressed in vests and suits, watchchains bouncing and overcoats swaggering.

From the back of the train car, Roosevelt leaned out across the railing to speak to the crowd that had gathered.

"What a beautiful valley!" he said, waving his arms. "I love the West. Have always loved it. It's a gift to see it and a gift to be able to meet you folks. Living here, surrounded by all this frontier, well it's a testament to American character; and I aim to keep as much of it frontier as I can. Tell me now, folks, what's on your mind these days?"

He'd already designated five new national parks and was on his way to Spokane and then Seattle to speak to four hundred thousand people and see his sixteen battleships during their world tour, the Great White Fleet.

The town buzzed after his visit, as if his enthusiasm had been contagious. John was enthused too. Knowing that the leader of the country was a boisterous outdoorsman who cared about farmers was all the fuel he needed.

Within a few weeks of hearing about the promise of homestead land in Middle Valley, Idaho, John left Alice and the children with her parents and travelled south, joining four other families for the two-hundred-mile trip. His wagon was pulled by two horses, household goods clanging as it went, leading a milk cow, a calf, and a skittish colt named Prince that was bottle-fed.

The wagons rolled slowly along the Snake River and over the trail along the Salmon River, through mountains and valleys, forest and sagebrush, cactus and wildflowers. He'd never seen such beauty before. The rim of Hells Canyon rose five thousand feet out of its base and widened beyond sight. He heard the raspy *chuk* of the chukar partridge and the eagle cry, watched bighorn sheep and mountain goats climb steep rocks and saw elk grazing and drinking at the river. Where the trail got rough, the travelers engineered the wagon wheels over rocks and steep places, and through soft, muddy grass.

He found a sea of sagebrush and claimed it, sending a letter to his father-in-law Elwood to ask for help. Elwood came on the train, and together they hauled lumber from Cambridge eighteen miles away and managed to build a rough cabin and a small barn before the first snow.

Leaving the livestock with neighbors, they started back through Whitebird Pass on horseback, talking of how wonderful it will be to bring the family in spring. When an early blizzard hit, snow falling fast and thick, blinding them, they continued for a time, hoping it would blow through, but climbing to higher elevations didn't make sense.

"We've got to turn back!" Elwood hollered, looking for John through the falling snow in front of him. "We'll never make it!"

John heard him and came back around, his eyebrows and eyelashes loaded with white. "I was thinking the same thing!"

Together, they retraced their tracks as long as they could, watching them fill with snow. The horses trudged doggedly, heads hanging low, no longer sure of their footing. They lost direction for a time until they were graced with the outskirts of Cambridge and were nearly frozen by the time they found their way to the cabin.

Snowed in, little food, not much wood cut, unable to get out to hunt, it was the goodness of neighbors and the few squirrels and wormy rabbits they could snare that kept them alive. The neighbors could only spare so much, also being new to the area, and they had planned on having the milk cow for their children for the winter, so John left it there. He didn't have any feed for her anyway.

"This is what we old-timers call 'rough'n it,'" Elwood said as he rocked in Alice's chair next to the fire. "We'll be alright."

John, whose backside had been to the fire, turned to warm his hands. "I've dreamed about having my own farm for a long time," he said, shaking his head, "but for the life of me, I can't remember this winter ever being part of the dream."

Joe would be born on this property five years later.

The Lake Cabin in Spring

Loon Lake, WA

Spring is when the geese return to the lake to leave their fragrant calling cards. They poop on all the docks, especially the new plastic ones which are warmer, and consort with their girlfriends and boyfriends, making a noisy honking racket that gets faster and faster until it stops. Then it starts up again. The air is cold and clean and smells like new fish.

There was always clean-up to do after winter. It was an annual event to light a big bonfire of forest debris resulting in enough coals to heat chili and roast hot dogs for lunch. Hot, gooey marshmallows for dessert.

As a child, I claimed my sleeping spot in front of the warm wood-stove. My bed was a rusted metal roll-a-way with a feather mattress covered in pink ticking that came with the cabin. In the morning, boiling pitch spit about three feet from my face as Dad fed the fire, waking me to see orange and yellow flames flickering. The sweet tang of pine smoke created my cocoon.

Closing my eyes again, I scrunched down into my red flannel sleeping bag among all its little blue cowboys and stayed, loving it there.

I was vaguely aware of the rumble of the 7 a.m. freight train running north toward Springdale up the track on the other side of the lake.

Coffee began to perk, quietly at first then pop, pop-pop louder until with a clang, someone removed it from the stove, grabbing me back. The smell of morning coffee, rich and fresh, filled the air and the heavy iron skillet clunked onto a burner. The sting of freshly caught fish hitting hot grease told me that Dad had made a catch. There would be chunked potatoes sizzling next to rainbow trout.

My mouth watered; stomach rumbled. Pulling jeans and jacket over pajamas, I stepped into shoes, laces flick-flicking across the wood floor as I shuffled for the door. Outside, I headed up to Mary's. A crisp morning, I turned to see the lake in full view. Doug fir and giant ponderosa pine edged the quiet expanse of water, alive with tiny lightning bolts, reflections from the morning sun. White-flowered trillium, blue lupine, and waxy kinnikinic blanketed the hillside. The lonely fir tree close to the house on the water side had gotten taller, its top poking above the roofline where wispy smoke climbed from the chimney. A shrill "tut tut tut" scolding from a protective squirrel warned me to move along or he would pelt me with cones.

In the outhouse, I sat my bum onto the frigid toilet seat next to the Sears catalog then hurried back to join Dad for breakfast. He would need a mid-morning fishing partner. I thought about the newspaper clipping on the bulletin board at Granite Point Resort across the lake that we'd seen: a 30 lb. mackinaw that someone had recently caught. We'd stared at that picture together for a long time. He would want to troll deep with his "jackaloyd" lure to pull the sun's reflection down into the dark, to the big fish. I was willing to scale that big fish with Dad's jackknife. He was whistling when I got back down to the cabin.

Sweet Home

It was a quarter section, a 160-acre piece of land thirteen miles east of Midvale between the Weiser River and Crane Creek, mostly sagebrush fields with hills of pine in the distance and snow-topped mountains beyond. The family arrived to see the tiny cabin waiting for them with a loft where the children would sleep in a bed fitted together like toes in a shoe, enveloped in the warmth from the woodstove below.

Midvale may have been called the sheep capital of the world at the time, except the territory was overrun with white-tailed jack rabbits that ate entire crops, everything green including the roots, a plague of varmints. A female could produce a litter of eight every 32 days. Walking through the sagebrush stirred up hundreds of them, long ears flapping as they ran. In summer, they hid under sagebrush umbrellas to escape the heat of the day and flooded throughout the valley to feed at sunset.

Local authorities had put a bounty on bunny ears ever since 1882, five cents a pair. They said it was Idaho's "Manifest Destiny" to get rid of the rodents. Couldn't sell the ratty fur or the meat in bulk since it was stringy, full of worms, and folks worried about "rabbit fever" from the poison they'd tried to give them. Communities started annual "bunny bopping" events, men and boys armed with clubs on a rabbit drive, wanting to avoid the expense of ammunition. It became a common activity on Sunday afternoons. Eventually, they were hunted on Thanksgiving mornings as good sport before the traditional family dinner, clubs and shotguns only.

Like all farms, there was never a shortage of chores. The children helped John and a crew of neighbors grub out the sagebrush where it was tallest since the ground was most fertile there, a good area to plant. Big pieces of sage were put aside for firewood. While Alice and the children planted fruit trees, gooseberries, currants and a garden in potatoes, onions, carrots and turnips, John and some neighbors hitched up a couple of draft horses to plow for planting wheat, corn, and beans.

John embraced his new life like a type of addiction, dripping with sweat as he tilled the ground, turning the earth. When he stopped to take a breath and look over his fields, he imagined his wheat seeds sitting in the ground as it warmed, waiting for the next rain to spark life. He hoped it would soften the tightness in his gut, seeing that first bit of green, knowing that he could feed his family from his own land by the grace of God.

When harvest finally arrived, the first wheat was shucked, threshed and winnowed by hand, beating the stalks and tossing the grain from big, flat baskets into the air to lose the last of the chaff. Beans were trampled on a tarpaulin, the chaff blowing away in the wind. The corn was fed to the pigs. Anything that needed to be dried went onto the roof. They got the root cellar dug just in time for their first harvest from the garden.

Even before the United States entered World War I, the government had asked farmers to grow more wheat to support our Allies, guaranteeing the price to be at least $2 a bushel through the war. So farmers turned up more ground. It was the patriotic thing to do.

John cleared and plowed and planted and was eventually able to purchase some help: a header to clip the wheat heads from the stalks. Then he bought an old threshing machine that beat the seeds and husks away. Finally, with easy credit, he secured a loan to get a combine and more horses to pull it. They hauled their grain to Midvale to sell. John and Alice had their working farm.

As the community grew, Alice and John took on more responsibilities. Their cabin became a post office where the mail was collected, and Alice sold stamps out of a little desk near the window. George, the postman, came twice a week and became part of the family, often staying for a meal or leaving with a sandwich or biscuits or icebox cookies to sustain him on his travels.

Midvale folks voted to make liquor illegal in their community six years before their state of Idaho did, which was ten years before national Prohibition. Since John had been deputized to keep the peace in and around the farms, he was thankful they'd gone dry, hopeful that it would make his job easier without drink being involved.

With his neighbors, he built the Sweet Home schoolhouse at

Crane Creek, three miles from their home. It was a one-room subscription school, each family agreeing to help pay the salary of the teacher. There were eighteen students, first through eighth grade, a pot-bellied stove and an outhouse.

In winter, the children walked to school over the frozen fields; and despite their mother's protests, they skated on the solid creek at lunchtime, ruining their shoes. Once old enough, they rode horseback, two to a horse, though Buck would dump them in protest when he felt it was too cold to leave the barn. If the snow was deep enough, they hooked the horses to their homemade sled and wrapped themselves in blankets with a hot soapstone tucked inside.

On a hot, lazy August morning, John was off with the team to get water. Alice wore her loose cotton house dress which draped to her ankles, bare feet feeling free on the cool wood floor. She hummed as she cleaned up the breakfast dishes, knowing she belonged in this place, in her own home, feeling her roots beneath her feet as she listened to the *pop, pop* of the neighbor boy's 22 in the distance, practicing with his new gun.

Eight-year-old Elwood was out to collect eggs from the chicken coop and heard his friend practicing. He pulled his hat down close to his eyes and squinted for protection against the bright morning glare to look for a good stick. Then he walked to the neighbor's field, stirring up the sagebrush as he went, getting the rabbits to run out into the open for something worthy of target practice. The spicy scent of sagebrush haunted his nose.

Alice was tending the little ones, getting them dressed for

the day. Abruptly, she noticed silence and realized that Elwood should have been back with the eggs long before. Her breath grabbed. Screeching for Jesus, she busted out the house running full out, six-months pregnant, her apron flying behind. She found him sprawled in the dirt, a red halo growing into mud. Dropping to the ground, she scooped him into her lap, holding him there, rocking him like she always had from the time he was a baby, crimson filling her apron. Love could heal and she poured her love into him, but he was limp in her arms. Truth waited and she pushed it away, refusing it. She denounced it, but it came with her soul anyway, erupting up through her throat and into her screaming wail, echoing off the hillside.

After his burial, Alice spent many a late night in her rocker, John cleaning his tools or guns or carving toys near the fire to stay close. Eventually, she was able to shake her head and say, "I miss my boy something fierce" with a quivering chin.

John got up to squeeze her shoulder. "An accident is different, isn't it? We didn't see it coming, didn't get to say good-bye, tell him we love him." Then he headed to the barn. It had been the hardest thing he'd ever said.

She kept young Elwood's hat with the bullet hole and the dried blood. She couldn't give it up, hung it on a peg inside the door as a reminder that every moment should be lived with kindness and faith, impossible to know if it might be your last. John didn't need reminding. Elwood had been his eldest, the boy John had imagined to be a man one day, a son he was already proud of. His son's face stayed with him, the freckles and large front teeth. John took on a far-away look, a distancing that never left.

In time, through prayer and faith, Alice forgave the neighbor boy and even loved him because he had loved her son. *Give your burdens to the Lord. He will carry them.*

Emma Louise was born three months after Elwood's death. Joe came two years later in 1910. It was the year of the Big Blowup, one of the largest forest fires in American history. It had been the driest year in anyone's memory, and in a matter of hours, fires in eastern Washington, Idaho, Montana and southeast British Columbia became firestorms shooting flames hundreds of feet in the air and moving faster than a horse could run. Trees were sucked out of the ground and turned into flying blow-torches. It sounded like a thousand trains going over a thousand train trestles as it came. In two days, five towns were leveled, including the eastern third of Wallace, Idaho. Its smoke created daytime darkness in New York, and its ash fell in Greenland.

Like everyone else, John and Alice feared the flames and grieved for those who were lost. They also thanked the Lord for their healthy baby Joe, that the fire had stayed nearly three hundred miles north of them, and that they were able to weather the drought.

Tommy was born two years later, and two years after that, scarlet fever took Hartzel. He was eight years old, their oldest boy at the time. Alice was pregnant with Vera, her last baby. Vera lived one day. Of Alice's eleven children, six lived beyond childhood, which was not unusual in those days. Her daily prayer was that her remaining children and their children and those who came after would know the Lord, that they would live good, long lives and that they would feel secure in the love of family.

Matched Mules

Midvale, Idaho 1917-1922

The United States entered World War I the spring of 1917, and farmers were encouraged to turn up even more land to feed the troops. Mother Nature provided a bumper crop, and John was proud to purchase a matched pair of mules for the farm. They were dignified, knew how to pull together, sure-footed on nearly any terrain. He loved those mules as much as he loved his farm. Joe and his siblings were told not to go into the barn if the mules were there since they'd kick anyone behind them, and it could be deadly.

Like gossip, word spread about those impressive mules. It was a wicked day when John saw a stranger ride up to the barn.

"What can I do for ya Mister?" John asked.

"I heard you got a matched pair of mules," the man said, lifting his hat without introductions. "I was sent to buy them for the war effort overseas." He showed some paperwork. "What'll ya sell 'em for?"

John shook his head. "Not for sale."

"I've got authority to take 'em from ya if I need to. You might as well name a price," the man shot back.

John felt his blood boil. *Like to see ya take anything from me*, he thought. "A hundred dollars each then," he said, knowing it was well beyond the price of any mule, hoping the amount would somehow keep him from losing them.

"Done! Along with the harness."

John's mouth dropped. He was shocked, wondering how he would manage without his mules. They were dependable, needed every day, and he'd learned to rely on them.

"They need to be kept together as a team," he said once he'd recovered enough to speak. "They won't be worth their feed if they're not together." Too downhearted to watch them go, he hadn't thought to say how they could kick.

Dances were the best reward for the constant demands of the farm, and the chores needed to be done first.

"Who you gonna dance with tonight?" Tommy threw an armful of cut sagebrush into a pile as he and Joe grubbed out a section of ground for a neighbor. They were moving fast so they could go to the community dance at the school.

Joe shrugged and went back to swinging the mattock, a combination axe and hoe, a grunt with each swing like the beat of a song, breaking out chunks of root from the ground. Sweet, spicy sage aroma made his nose run and he blew it onto the ground, his finger pressed against one side.

"Who you *want* to dance with?" A bit shorter and stockier

than Joe, with sand-colored hair and a slightly broader face, Tommy wanted to talk.

"None of your business," Joe breathed with the swing. "Even the old ladies like to dance, you know."

"You got money to buy a box lunch from some girl tonight?" Tommy threw brush faster, catching up with Joe's swings and bent over to grab the next bunch thinking it had already been cut just as Joe's ax came down onto his head.

Joe felt the softer impact under his ax and saw Tommy fall, blood running into his face. "Oh gayd!" he cried. Adrenaline pumped as he dragged Tommy's dead weight home, praying and crying, telling him to stay alive. Frantic, finding no one around, he poured turpentine into the gash, the only remedy he knew.

Tommy's screams announced his consciousness as Alice arrived from the barn. All that blood and Elwood's death flashed at her, but she didn't show it. Silently she prayed as she cleaned him up and glued the cut closed with pine pitch. Turning to Joe who was pale-faced and hugging the doorjamb, she squeezed his arm. "He'll be okay, son. It was an accident."

Tommy didn't sit for long. He insisted that they go to the dance despite his head hammering. The whole family went. He didn't remember any of it. He didn't remember that there had been some drinking going on, that a fight had broken out between farmers and how his father had intervened and collected all their guns. He was confused about his mother making extra biscuits the next morning until all the neighbors came by to get their guns back.

In summertime, Alice's father came to visit and called together the believers and the seekers for church. They came from several counties, having heard about his revivals. Horses with buggies or wagons, and cars lined up at the school, men dressed in their best bib overalls with the mud kicked off their boots. The ladies wore hats, one filled with cropped turquoise peacock feathers, the peacock lady; everyone knew her. When her birds screamed, her neighbors thought a woman was being murdered.

"In the shadow of your wings, I shall sing for joy!" Singing was easy in church since people were already full of music. "Praise be to God the Father of our Lord Jesus Christ," Elwood began, "the shepherd of our souls."

"I am the vine, Jesus said, remain in Me and I in you. The Lord wants us to be joyful, brothers and sisters. Do you want to know Joy?"

"Yes!" Children jumped from their seats. They'd been to revival before.

"Stand up! Lift your hands! Open your hearts! Say, show me the way, Lord Jesus!"

"Show me the way!" The peacock feathers began to sway.

Hands were up, waving to Heaven, and Jesus was invited into opened hearts. With the *halleluiahs* and *amens* and the Spirit rekindled, they wound down singing, *"What a friend I have in Jesus."*

Joe had never felt the need to jump or cry *halleluiah*. He'd always had a quiet relationship with Jesus, knowing that his parents had prayed for him even before he was born as well as for those who would come after him. He felt the Lord close, a constant companion. Revival made him think he could never be a preacher, not an evangelist anyway.

Folks settled down for a picnic after church. A baseball game and a footrace competition drew attention to Tommy since he was athletic and ran like a bullet. There was ice cream to make, sugar and cream in a tub, chunks of ice sawn from a big block with salt in the outer tub, churning with a hand crank. Fresh sweet berries or ripe peaches that dripped juice from elbows with every bite came from the orchards in Indian Valley. Sometimes there was pie; Joe loved pie.

Worthless Wheat

After chores, the boys went to a ranch nearby where they could have little rodeos, learn to rope and ride calves, try to ride the wild horses. Joe did well, especially with the horses, and the ranchers encouraged him to enter the bronco contest at the fair nearby, even offered to pay his entry fee.

At the Cambridge Idaho Fair, with borrowed chaps and spurs, Joe willed his twelve-year-old body to relax into the saddle of a small Appaloosa born to buck. It was a hot day. He said a quick prayer, "Please Lord, keep me whole," and wiped his damp hand on his shirt before wrapping it with the rope that would become his anchor. He leaned back, lifted his heels above the horse's shoulders keeping the spurs turned inward and raised his left hand in the air.

First jump out of the chute, the horse stiffened his front legs and kicked his back legs to the moon, fully extended. It bucked left and right, and twirled around, kicking like crazy. Joe rode the beat, could feel the beginning of each move, predicted the action. Eight seconds seemed a long time, the horn sounded, Joe reached out to the pick-up man and dismounted just as his horse turned and kicked once more, cracking Joe's leg.

It took a minute for him to put weight on it after he went down, feeling the leg vibrate under the pressure. He was stoic about it, though, only a grimace on his face as he ground his teeth against the pain, embarrassed about getting hurt *after* his ride. Hobbling to the back of the family wagon where he could watch the other riders, he realized that he'd had a chance to win except with no second go-round, there would be no purse for the family, and no easy pay-back for the neighbors. He felt like he'd let everybody down. Tommy delivered his hat, and he pulled it low to his eyes.

A few cowboys came round to console him. "You done good, Joe. Better luck next time."

Joe showed them his easy smile and shrugged. "Need ta prac-tice get'n off, I s'pose."

As the wagon pulled away to find a doctor, every jerk and bump shot pain up into his groin. He looked at the swelling and bruising that had already begun on his leg and laid back to hide under his hat, realizing what a son-of-a-bitch his chores would be now.

November 11, 1918 was Armistice Day, the Great War had ended. Those "boys" had a hard time getting home. They gathered in France where they were taught a trade while they waited for a boat. Some traveled on seized German ships to get back to the U.S. The reception was joyous when they finally arrived, plenty of respect, parades and flags waving. They got off the ship with only a few dollars in their pockets; and the nation became so caught up in mourning for the dead and the "never forget" message, that our returning men, who *wanted* to forget and recover from their injuries, both seen and unseen, were the ones who became forgotten. Instead, they were left feeling guilty for having survived.

With World War I finished, farmers were finished too. There was an abundance of grain all over the country and the government's guarantee on price ended, so it was practically worthless. Joe's father had taken the risk of a down payment on equipment to increase production, but the more the farms produced, the more the price dropped. A few dry, hot years, tired soil and those damn hungry rabbits didn't help.

John knew that being a farmer had changed him. After fourteen years, he'd learned to take life as it came. There was only so much a person could do when depending on Mother Nature. He took on that "wait and see" attitude, and it settled over the rest of the family like sticky pollen. Patience and prayer became as necessary as rain.

He had always talked with neighbors about weather and money, but now they nearly whispered about the need for rain as if saying it aloud would acknowledge how desperate they all felt. The homesteads began to fail, and neighbors began to move away. John knew the end was coming. He couldn't pay his bills and bank loans. He was broke and would be forced to file bankruptcy like the others.

Alice had seen it coming too, though John had tried to protect her from it as long as he could. This place was her life. She had friends here. It was her home. Three of her children were in the Eastside Cemetery here. After their decision to leave, she spent the night in her rocker near the window, trying to grab hold of what was coming . . . homeless. She listened to the familiar click of her rocker and the creaking of her house as it cooled, the fall evenings getting chilly now, and she recited scripture in the dark, tears streaming down her face. *Search me, O God, and know my heart.*

By the time her emotions were purged, she was exhausted, and orange warmth was rising from the horizon behind their barn. It was in that moment that she made the decision to be positive because it did no good to be anything else. She would be an example of strength for her family and wrap herself in faith because if she worried, her family would worry too. She made a strong pot of coffee and got ready for a difficult day. The children would need to be told.

They didn't talk about it much other than to reassure the children the best they could: "We'll get to see family. You'll make new friends. It's an exciting adventure." But nobody believed it. Leaving was something they needed to do, so they did it, focused on the tasks, postponing the melancholy. In the next few days, Alice and the family canned all the chickens, turkeys, fruits and vegetables that she had jars for and packed up everything that had been dried.

On that final morning, tears wet John's face as he grabbed a handful of soil. He smelled the inherent promise of it and watched it fall to the ground along with his dreams. The children said goodbye to their few friends who remained with downtrodden faces and did their final chores to care for the livestock.

Then they left it all for the bank, stopping for a last visit at the Eastside Cemetery to say goodbye.

They were headed to Utah, the first time that Joe and Tommy had ridden a train. As it picked up speed and Alice knew there was nothing more she could do for the moment, her eyes closed and her head began to bob. The pulsing rumble of the train delivered memories of another time when she'd ridden the train as a young widow from Kansas to the 1893 World's Fair in Chicago. She'd seen the devastation of the cyclones from the train window, the straw blown into the sides of trees, making them look like pincushions. At the fair, she'd ridden the giant Ferris wheel 260 feet into the sky, walked on the movable sidewalk, ridden a gondola down the canals. It had been the beginning of picture postcards and souvenirs--such a fun, optimistic time of new things. Focusing on the landscape outside the train window, she knew what lay ahead would not be fun, but she was determined to be optimistic.

Winter Cabin

Loon Lake

Cold air coated my throat and froze the fuzz inside my nose. I pulled my burgundy scarf up over my face, hat down over my ears and told the gray sky that it was too cold for more snow. My boots made a loud crunch with each step like a bite into a thick potato chip. I stopped walking to look around and listen. The woods were dead silent.

Dad, my sister Cathie, and I had come to the cabin to see if it was still standing. The narrow dirt road hadn't been plowed beyond Larson Beach Road, so we walked the quarter mile in. Dad carried a shovel over his shoulder, knowing we would need it to clear the doorway if we wanted to get inside. Ever since he'd installed a steep metal roof over the original shingles, the snow slid off, dumping a mountain in front of the door.

It felt even colder inside the cabin than outside, each breath creating a white cloud. Dad got a fire going in the woodstove and started shoveling off the deck while my sister and I frolicked, slid, and tumbled down the hill in a world of white. The frozen lake had melted in sun enough to refreeze with a smooth surface.

My skating wasn't pretty. It was more like riding a scooter with my left skate and pushing with my right. I travelled forward, though, and having been told that the ice was nearly two feet thick, I skated with my eyes closed until I turned to see how far I'd gone. The cabin was a blue dot on the hillside above the blue dot of the tiny boat house which leaned a bit to the right.

The great challenge was climbing back up the hill to the cabin in deep snow. Nothing to grab hold of, I swam and crawled through the crust and needed to stop and lie on my back to rest every few feet, vowing to never do it again. Looking up at the cabin, I saw our lonely fir tree, silent and strong near the deck, its trunk being pelted with snow from Dad's shovel. I wondered if he might throw me a rope so I could climb up over the steepest part of the hill just below the crest. I wondered if we even had a rope. A crack of yellow light broke through the gray sky, sending a new gush of energy and pushed me over the crest.

Having brushed snow from my coat and pants, I stomped my boots before going inside, hoping for some warmth. Still, tiny white crystals clinked to the floor and didn't melt, and I swept them up before leaving to avoid puddles during the thaw. I knew that when I opened the door again in spring, I would be greeted by that lovely, musty sweet smell of earth and granite and wood that I absolutely adored.

Chasing the Rainbow

Utah and Washington 1922-1924

Their comfort came from the Lord; their strength was from the family. They lived in a tent outside Manti and harvested potatoes. They worked the sugar beet fields. Joe seemed to pay more attention to his mother than usual, a hand on her shoulder or a glance at her face to see how she felt, perhaps remembering a time from years before when she'd told him that she needed him, that his being near had made her feel better.

The guys herded sheep while Alice and Tommy stayed with Grace who was married now. The job was on the high plains of the Wasatch Plateau of Sanpete County, more millionaires there per capita than anywhere else in the country. It was partly due to John Seely who had bred his sheep with the Rambouillet from France, creating a strong, healthy, obliging animal that produced far more wool than any other, Merino wool.

Joe was fourteen when he served as cook, moving the camp wagon wherever it was needed as the sheep grazed, a ranch hand bringing food to them once a week. They kept their hats pulled down and their collars pulled up against the fierce winds of the high plains and drove the herd to water every evening with the help of a couple of dogs from the ranch. Joe loved to watch the dogs move the herd like experts, keeping them together.

It could have been lonely except that they had each other. At night, the tunes began to play, James Roy with his fiddle and Joe with his jaw harp, which brought the herd in even closer. James Roy played a quiet solo the night a curious lamb was bit on the nose by a rattlesnake. Joe thought the lamb would be a goner. He stayed with her throughout the night, massaging her throat and dribbling water into her mouth, talking quietly, keeping her calm. By morning, she was on her feet although a little wobbly, his new best friend.

Poverty was a constant that squeezed the air from John's chest. Every job was temporary and hard to find. Without a choice, he did like so many others and rode the rails to find work, taking the two boys with him. Joe was fourteen years old, yet tall for his age, when they wrapped their bedrolls with canvas, hoping for protection from rain. They were heavy-laden, pockets stuffed with jerky, burlap bags full of dried beans and rice, enough bread for the first week.

John knew about hopping trains from his time at Farmington, how inexperienced guys who didn't wait for an open car sometimes stepped onto a ladder on the outside, thinking they could hold on. By the time the train snuck up to top speed, it was going too fast to get off. Sometimes they were speeding across bridges, over canyons and rivers, and through tight tunnels and the dust and soot and asbestos from the brakes blew in their faces and it went on for hours, and sometimes they fell off and died.

He found an empty grain car and watched from behind a shed for the highball signal that the train was ready to go. The wheels began to turn, and he hollered for the boys.

"Come on now! Watch out for the wheels!" They ran alongside the train, and John pulled himself into the car first. "Give me your hand!" He pulled Joe in. Then James Roy, running full out, flew in on his belly, both of them yanking on his arms.

They hunkered down into a corner shadow until the train began to rock at full speed. The boys' eyes were wide when John told them they could crawl out from behind their bindles. They saw that several other men had joined their ride; and as they talked amiably about the prospects for work and places to go, Joe relaxed.

Inside the boxcar, the thumping of the track presented a rhythmic beat, and music was inevitable. No one seemed to mind when they played. James Roy pulled his harmonica from his pocket and cupped his hand around it, starting them off. Joe plucked the trigger of his jaw harp against his teeth, moving his tongue and opening his mouth for different sorts of twang. If someone with a banjo or fiddle joined in, they'd play "Chicken Reel," and everybody stomped along. Life seemed fine while the music played, and it didn't cost a thing.

There were a lot of guys riding the rails, two million family men, farmers, factory hands, bank clerks, store owners, veterans, all broke and wearing their hardships like clothing. For the most part, they trudged ahead, filled with false hopes since jobs seemed to be rationed like food, but false hopes were better than no hope at all.

Young Joe found himself sensitized to the miseries around

him. He saw those men who had lost limbs or brain matter to the war or who had succumbed to addiction. It seemed to have an iron grip on them. Some had the shakes so bad that he couldn't understand how they'd gotten onto the train. Some had trouble controlling their hands, feet, legs. *Jake legs* they called it, debilitating effects of drinking Jake, a drug called Jamaican ginger. They drank it to get the 80% ethanol it contained.

At one stop, when they got off the train, two angry men dressed in dirty baggy suits grabbed John. "You! Hand over whatever you got," one said.

Joe reacted like a hornet, jumped onto the man's back, smashed his hat against his face to blind him and bit his filthy ear while James Roy shoved his bindle stick into the gut of the other man and they got away. From then on, their awareness of people around them was sharpened, knowing they could become victims to those who were desperate. Whenever they had any money, it was taped to John's back.

Still, Joe admired the courage and optimism he witnessed in the community of men. Despite getting thin and needing to add cardboard to their shoes, they sometimes referred to their situation as "chasing the rainbow," sort of a hopeless attitude, yet with a positive outlook. "I'm not poor, just broke." A realistic outlook would have done them in. And he appreciated the humor they often wrapped around their stories like cotton around a thornbush, making them easier to hear. "My family's so poor, the flies have to carry their own lunches when they come to our house."

Hobos had been named ever since the Civil War, the returning boys were "Homeward Bound" and looking for work. Now, twenty years later, they had organized into their own "Tourist Union" with a Code of Ethics and a Hobo Court. If they saw a traveler with a knot hanging from his neck, a "monkey's fist," they knew the guy was in good standing with the code and could probably be trusted.

Several times they joined a Jungle camp, a place to wash and rest. It was usually in the woods near a train stop and with water nearby. There was a fire in camp during the day for cooking the community meal. Anyone who wanted to eat had to contribute wood for the fire and food for the pot. John added a few handfuls of rice and beans, and Joe had some wild onions he had pulled along the way. There was also a pot for boiling clothes to kill cooties, a clothesline, and a mirror for shaving, though Joe had no need for shaving.

The first time they decided to boil their clothes, Joe knew his father would dunk him in the river no matter how cold it was, having heard that he "stunk like something dead." In a private spot, with his back-up clothes ready, he stripped and stepped into the water to his knees, one hand pushing air towards his father.

"Let me get in by myself," he said. "Just give me a minute." It *was* icy cold.

James Roy came alongside him on his toes. "Oh," he said, "It's so cold!" and he tackled Joe into the water. "It's called 'taking the plunge,' brother," he said later. "It's the only way."

A few weeks later, a dunk into a frigid river felt good, the only way to get clean.

The Code required they respect the law and railroad operators, and if unable to find work, to at least practice a skill or craft. It said that a hobo should never get stupid drunk because their behavior made it harder for the next guy. Code of Ethics Rule #13 was about watching out for child molesters. Older guys would mentor young ones, teaching them how to stay alive in exchange for sex. The Code described these "wolves" as the worst scourge on earth, and hobos were expected to turn them over to the authorities and encourage runaway children to go home.

The campfires were put out at dusk to avoid the railroad guards who were hired to protect strikebreakers and to stop hobos from hopping onto trains. Sixty-five hundred hobos were killed that year, either by accident related to the trains or by "yard bulls" with their clubs. At one stop, so many men came out of the woods as the train began to pull away that the brake-man didn't try to stop them. He just shrugged and waved them on, calling "All Aboard!"

Gift from Heaven

Montana and Washington 1925-1927

Like a gift from heaven, they found work plus room and board on a big ranch in Havre, Montana. Havre was known to be rough at the time, only ten years since being named "lawless" by the Chicago Law and Order League. They named it "the worst of the sixteen cities visited." Still, John thanked the Lord that he'd be able to send money back to Alice in Utah. Among other jobs, they rounded up cattle and broke in wild horses. It was with the horses that Joe wanted to be. To him, it was more about helping them adjust to domestic life than breaking them. He admired their spirit.

In the bunkhouse at night, they listened to the local stories that were told over their poker games. Havre's well-loved gentle outlaw, "Long George" Francis, had been one of the best horse trainers, rodeo riders and ropers in the country and they said he'd had style, a six-and-a-half-foot tall cowboy in a fancy Alaskan beaver coat. He'd been generous to his friends and had had a few enemies. It was probably true that he had found newborn calves "with a long rope," but he had been convicted of horse stealing and given six to ten years in jail. The missing horse had been found dead and mutilated *near* his property which was mysterious since he'd been known as a horse lover. An abused horse in the area that was missing could often be found on Long George's ranch where it would be receiving care. Some had called his good deeds "interfering."

He had also loved a schoolteacher who lived in the hills out of town; and before going to jail, he had received permission to see her one last time. It had been late Christmas Eve when he had loaded gifts into his automobile and headed out to see her despite a Montana blizzard blowing in and the temperature dropping. He never got a chance to make his delivery or to see his love. His car was found the next day off the road. His body was three miles away with a broken leg. His throat had been cut. Somehow the authorities had decided that he'd done it to himself.

Joe met Marie Gibson "World Champion Cowgirl Bronc Rider" at the ranch. He admired her. She'd learned rodeo from Long George himself since she was sixteen, and she was good at it, needed to be since the prize money was how she fed her kids. She was no-nonsense, practical; and she kept winning.

"You need to have patience and to watch the horse," she told Joe. "If the horse's nostrils flare, eyes stare, eyelids twitch, or if she starts to sweat, she's stressed."

He started with halter training, brushing and patting her head, then the bridle with the least restrictive bit. Before he tried the saddle, he'd lean on her while brushing, always talking and singing, using a heavy blanket first. The tricky part was wrapping her back and belly to get ready for a cinch.

Finally on her back, if she bucked, Joe stayed on, calming her down. If she was smart and slow to spook, he trained her for smooth transitions between gaits, leg signals, and even rein backs to bring a higher value to the horse.

When the ranch foreman saw Joe's talent with horses, he suggested that he ride one of their racehorses at the Hill County Fair in Havre. The fair was a big deal in the county: 4-H and livestock competitions, auctions, a carnival with a Ferris wheel, rodeo, including one for kids, agricultural booths, lots of food competitions. The keenest contest was the Havre Brewing and Malting Company competition; they offered a cash prize for the best bushel of malting barley.

Joe was excited to ride in the derby. Nothing seemed as important as he began to train, riding Flying Don every chance he got, a tall chestnut thoroughbred with a thick white stripe from between his eyes down to his muzzle. Flying Don needed a good warm-up, he was slow to start, yet he had tremendous speed once he was ready; and he hated getting mud in his face. He was a bit high-strung but wanted to please.

Joe pushed Flying Don to his limit every time he rode, spending the rest of his spare moments grooming the horse, telling him how fast he was and keeping him exercised. Two days before the race, Joe gave him a bath and trimmed his tail. Flying Don knew a special day was coming. He was relaxed and ready and looking for a race.

On race day, Joe was intimidated by the size of the crowd, the noise, the activity all around, and mostly concerned for the horse. He led Flying Don around the mess of people and onto the track. The loudspeaker blared. Blue and yellow banners whipped in the breeze in the stands. Flying Don huffed his breath; his eyes darted. Joe stroked his neck, "You're okay, boy. All these people came here to see you win today. It's okay." When the owners waved, he held up his hand and tried to look confident.

Mounted, he looked calm in the saddle though his stomach churned. He'd said his prayers first thing that morning. Clouds were moving in and rain drizzled. He was reminded of his ride on the bucking Appaloosa and that feeling of letting someone down threatened to spook him. He tried to empty his mind, think of the horse like Marie had taught him. At the gate, the horses were tense, and it was contagious.

Off the line, Flying Don was slow, falling behind the others. Joe hovered over the saddle, knowing it was what the horse needed. After the first five strides, he squeezed his knees together and leaned further forward, exaggerating the horse's reach, encouraging him to stretch out. Flying Don went, running smoothly from behind, claiming a path between horses, passing one after another after another, until only four remained in front. They entered a wet stretch of track and mud kicked up into the horse's face. Joe moved Flying Don around and ahead, out of the spatter and gave a few kicks, waving a strap near the horse's face—their special signal. Flying Don went full out, finishing in second place as the crowd screamed.

He was the youngest jockey that year, and he introduced a horse with potential to race. At the end of the season, he hated to move on with his family, but the local jockeys who saw him as competition were okay with it.

James Roy was hired by the Inland Empire Paper Company in Millwood, eight miles east from Spokane in the Spokane Valley. It was a budding community named after an agreement between the mill and the Woodard family who were the original land-owners. John helped build houses there while Joe and Tommy attended West Valley High School. The predictability of the routine that came with attending school and the steam whistle that blew at regular intervals from the papermill was a comfort to the whole family. Even the putrid sulfur smell from the mill was welcomed as a sign of progress and employment.

Joe had just graduated from high school when the mill laid off workers, but they were lucky. James Roy's boss gave him a tip about potential jobs in Potlatch.

It was the story of so many lives. Tommy stayed with relatives to finish school while the family left, hoping for work. There were no social programs like unemployment compensation, Medicaid or even Social Security. The only help for the unemployed came from community relief programs and the Salvation Army. It didn't matter. Like many people then, John said he would rather starve than take a hand-out.

The Dignity of Work

Charles Weyerhaeuser was the first president of the group who represented the Potlatch Lumber Company on the Palouse River. It was a steam-powered mill, producing 350,000 board feet of lumber in a ten-hour shift. With over 100,000 acres of western white pine, it was the largest white pine mill in the world when it opened for business in 1906 with five hundred employees. William Deary, a Canadian lumberman, was general manager. The mill itself consisted of thirteen connected buildings and a 65-acre drying yard.

Full of hope, Joe stepped off the train with James Roy and his parents and saw the giant mill on one side of a tangle of tracks.

"What a monster!" Alice said, grabbing ahold of John.

It looked intimidating, sprawled out in the valley with long tentacles. The enormous five-story building was topped with a vented roof ridge that ran the entire length, and several large dormers sat on top at one end which was built over the Palouse River. On the other end of the building, a long roof covered the drying kilns, extending the building even further. White steam climbed in the air, swirling around a tall, black, silo-shaped burner for wood waste that stood behind the main building, accompanied by several smokestacks. They could see logs travel up the conveyor chain high into the building for the first cuts, hear the squeal and roar of the big saws before the cut logs continued down for the smaller cuts, smell the pine resin floating in the air.

On the other side of the train tracks and station, more than two hundred little family houses climbed in rows up the hillside like cogs in a machine, Residence Hill. People moved about everywhere like bees caring for their hive, people with jobs, people with purpose, with homes, living their lives. It looked good. It felt good.

Optimism arrived like a splash of fresh water when each of the men was hired: John to help maintain track, James Roy to start with the green chain, and Joe to learn machinery maintenance. When they were told that a company house would be provided, Alice bent over and wept into her hands.

"Thank you, Lord," she whispered. She had become so very tired, staying strong and positive ever since they had lost their farm in Midvale; and now, at last, this was a place she might be able to call "home," at least for a while.

Clearly, Potlatch was a company town, named the Chinook word for a celebration of goodwill and gift giving. It had all the essentials: two schools, a hotel, two churches, a bank, a post office, a big general store, an opera house, a community center with an athletic club and the Potlatch Brick Company which was one of two in the state at the time. The company also had two bunkhouses, two boarding houses, a lot of outhouses, and a cook house, not to mention the facilities provided at the logging camps. No liquor was allowed, and even though the men loved to gamble, it was forbidden in the bunkhouses. The company said so.

The family's house was on Residence Hill with all the rest. It had three rooms with a covered, corner porch, a parlor with a window on the roadside, a large kitchen with a wood cook-stove, and one bedroom. It had been built in a hurry with green lumber from Palouse River Lumber Company, wood that had twisted and shrunk as it had dried over time, leaving evidence of multiple repairs and patches around the windows, doors and flooring. Further up the hill, the houses were nicer. Large, two-story homes with three or more bedrooms and wrap-around porches sat atop Knob Hill where the managers lived.

At The Merc, the Potlatch Mercantile company store, Alice found she could get $20 credit because of the family's employment. Wide aisles were packed with everything anyone could want for their home and happiness: food, tools, furniture, clothing, shoes, everything. She bought a nice roast and the basics, bread, milk, butter, ice, some potatoes, onions and greens for a good dinner. As she left, she saw a sign that the company would buy fruits and vegetables if she could grow them, and she said a prayer that she would be able to stay long enough to do that. When she got to know her neighbor, she learned to get a big sack of produce on Saturday nights just before closing at a reduced price.

From home, Joe walked several blocks downhill to the largest building at the base of the residential area, the Community Center. It was an impressive two-story building with a full basement and a huge wrap-around porch. He felt lucky to have access to it. There was a full-size basketball court, several lounges and club rooms including an Athletic Club, office space, showers, locker space, and there were tennis courts outside. It seemed pretty top-notch to him.

In the Athletic Club, he warmed up by skipping rope with alternate feet and thought about the first time he had seen boxing up close. He had loved the footwork and how quick the boxers had been, something he thought he might be able to do. Switching to skipping with both feet together, he replayed in his mind his talk with his mother.

"You should become a preacher like your grandfather, Joe. You have the constitution for it, son."

He shook his head as he continued to skip. *I'm not much of a talker, mother.*

"But why boxing, son?"

Because of years of feeling powerless, of being in places where I could get beat down and no notion of how to defend myself. To feel some kind of control over my life. And I like working out with the guys. Please don't worry, mother. I'm highly motivated to not get hit.

He laughed, thinking that his answer might have been the longest speech he'd ever given; she must have known it was important to him. His father had been secretly sparring with him to help him practice. Even so, he felt a little unsettled, never having gone against his mother's advice before. He continued with shadowboxing and practiced his footwork: step forward with the left and drag the right; back with the right and drag the left. Jab, pivot, hook, jab, pivot, cross.

"I'm a lover, not a fighter," he always said. *Try to think like a fighter*, he told himself.

A trainer motioned him over to practice his right uppercut on the heavy bag: pivot, drop and swing up, quick recovery. Then the speed bag, more shadowboxing, and some sparring practice. Gloves up to cover his face, elbows close, stepping back for space, in for the jab and a cross. Some weightlifting, pull-ups, push-ups, sit-ups. Finally, some good stretching, slowing everything down. He stood on his head, allowing gravity to quiet his mind.

A Lover, not a Fighter

At the end of a wintry workday, the cold dry air had sucked all the moisture from the snow. The air was still, no breeze to make goosebumps down a collar or up a sleeve. Joe's father introduced him to a group of Greek co-workers. "These guys aren't allowed in the Athletic Club, Joe," he grimaced, a pain spearing his stomach. "They love boxing," he gritted his teeth. "You could learn a lot from them. Not much English, though."

Joe nodded, smiled at them, wondered why his father grabbed his stomach, but his eyes lingered on the grinning hungry-looking guy with balled-up fists.

"You interested in trying a match with them, son?"

Joe's eyebrows rose. "How sure are you that they won't kill me?"

John doubled over.

"What's going on?" Joe asked, putting his hand on his father's back.

"Aw, nothing. Been fighting a bad stomach for days. I'll

manage through it. Don't worry about it." He straightened up, his face a waxy sheen. "They're good guys," he continued. "I work with them every day. You might learn something that will help you out since you're so bent on boxing." He doubled over again, and Joe put his arm around him.

"Let's get you home for now." Joe said and waved to the group.

Alice had been concerned for John. He'd had no appetite for nearly a week. That evening his fever heated the room, and he began to vomit. She was scared and put cold cloths on his forehead while Joe went for the doctor. He was back so fast that Alice wondered if she'd blacked out and missed the passing of time. "You hardly left!"

"I skied. It's downhill you know."

Her eyebrows squeezed together. "You don't have skis."

"Well, I've got *one*," he shrugged. "That's all I needed, I guess."

The doctor shook his head, explaining that John's appendix had burst, probably days previous, and he'd started a serious infection. Alice grabbed Joe's arm, remembering that even Houdini had died from complications of appendicitis.

"It's a mystery to me how he could keep working through all that pain," the doctor said. "He'll need to be in the hospital for weeks, if he survives."

Joe put his hand over his mother's. He knew she couldn't allow any thoughts of losing John. The world would be impossible without him.

Tommy arrived on the train from Spokane. With his outstanding skill in athletics, he'd earned a full scholarship with room and board to Whitworth College, the pride of the family. He was home to see the Saturday night fight at the Community Center, proud of his big brother.

The crowd was ready for entertainment, clicking their jaws with their neighbors about odds and bets like hungry coyotes. Management men from Knob Hill and some of their wives wearing feathered hats were there to watch in a full house.

Joe hoped he was ready for the real thing, a Saturday night fight with an audience. The Newcomer! He wondered if he was nuts.

In the locker room, the volunteer trainer wrapped strips of gauze three times around his wrist and hand and between his fingers, securing it with tape. Joe closed his fist, feeling the wrap tightening, keeping all the joints in place. Then the gloves.

He stayed warm, practicing his footwork, keeping his body loose, trying to wipe the "I'm gonna die" look from his face. *I asked for this,* he told himself. "Stupid," he mumbled. *How much warm-up is too much?*

He saw his father looking frail where he stood with his brothers close to the ring. After two weeks, when the doctor had said "you'll live," John had gotten out of bed to see his son box. Recognizing his opponent—a cocky, red-headed block of a kid from the company with an easy smile and a short temper, Joe willed his body to stay relaxed and quick, his greatest strength.

He stepped into the ring and tried to look like a boxer: knees slightly bent, head tilted into his gloves, left glove slightly out front. He hoped no one would notice the subtle trembling in his legs. He told himself to breathe and felt the mat solid under his feet. At the bell, he stepped back to avoid a punch and delivered a jab at chin level like a hammer followed by a quick left uppercut, stepping back just in time. After some dance moves, a slamming left hook hit him in the side of the head, knocking him back, nearly off his feet. He shook his head, trying to clear his vision, a roaring in his ears, and he kept dancing, avoiding another punch. He came back, head down with a quick jab, right uppercut, left hook, right cross as the spit and snot flew, sending his opponent onto his butt. Joe danced again, staying light-footed as his opponent got up, shaking *his* head this time.

In the second round, after a series of exchanged hooks, blocks, and crosses, Joe didn't think he could last much longer. He stepped in to deliver an uppercut liver punch with an immediate hook to the face, bringing his opponent down. Unable to grab a breath, it was a technical knock-out. As the referee lifted Joe's hand into the air, he looked down and was shocked to see his own blood spreading like a red flag across his sweaty chest and stomach as it ran from his nose. Twirling like a ballerina, he passed out, landing on the mat next to his opponent.

The next afternoon, after a strong cup of coffee, some Watkins liniment and church, he was back in the ring. Now that he'd won, he supposed he'd be expected to fight another match. The Athletic Club had taught him how to box, and he would continue for them and help train others too. It was a way of giving back.

Alice examined the print on the feed sacks at the Merc, hoping to find a pattern that appealed to her. Settling on little blue flowers, she made the purchase of four bags, hoping to have enough to make a dress, and thinking she could use old plain feed sacks for bloomers. She wore the new dress for church the next Sunday, but John stopped her from walking out the door.

"Alice," he said, "did you know that you've got a sign on your backside that reads '100 Lbs. Net Weight'? He laughed harder than he had laughed in a long time.

"What?" Alice slapped his shoulder, horrified as she rushed back into the bedroom to turn her bloomers inside out, not sure if she was laughing or crying.

In church, John's shoulders shook now and then, lips slammed shut, eyes glistening. Alice knew he was seeing her bloomers in his mind and that she'd never live it down.

Joe encouraged his horse to a trot as he rode towards Palouse which was two miles inside the Washington border. He kept to the side of the muddy road and maneuvered around bunchgrass because of the automobiles that sped by, honking as if they knew nothing about horses. The road wound between rolling, green-velvet hills of spring with the blue mountains in the background. A few head of sheep ran along the road ahead of his horse until they veered off into a pasture. He smiled to see the lambs, remembering the lamb he saved in Utah when he was camp cook.

It was a seven-mile trip to Palouse, to a confectionary where he could buy sweets for Mother's Day. He arrived just before closing, a little bell tinkling as he opened the door. Sugared air surrounded him. A long-legged, brown-haired, sultry girl with the darkest eyes and a dimple in her chin looked up from her counter and locked eyes with him, smiling. He went rigid, eyes glazed, he absent-mindedly removed his hat, squashing it against his chest.

"Hi," she grinned, waving at his trance.

"Howdy."

"What would you like?"

"Mmm?"

"Can I get something for you?"

"Ah . . . my mother," he stammered. "Candy."

"Oh, for Mother's Day? We have special variety boxes all made up. Would that be okay?"

"Mm," he hummed, nodding.

She wrapped the box in brown paper and tied it with string, then handed it to him, accepting the money he offered. He watched her hands move to avoid her eyes, hoping his brain might kick in soon.

"Is there anything else?" she raised her eyebrows.

He shook his head.

"Okay then. Thank you for coming in," she smiled.

He seemed hesitant to leave.

"What's your name, cowboy?" she asked.

"Joe." He backed out the door, stumbled over the threshold, picked himself up and got back to his horse, oblivious of the chuckles around him. As he rode away and the dark eyes and dimpled chin began to fade from his mind, he realized that he'd meant to buy his mother's favorite, chocolate covered orange sticks.

Chocolate Fudge

Loon Lake

A healthy field of wheat along the highway on our way to the cabin would cause Dad to pull over. Mom would cut enough for a bouquet. At the cabin, stiff stalks bobbed with heavy heads in an old fruit jar on the kitchen table.

She loved the lake and the cabin, the lack of chores, the quiet, the trees. Being there gave her time to enjoy the birds and their singing. She would sit outside on her "coffee bench" most warm mornings, and on chilly nights or wet days when rain beat on the metal roof like God was talking, she played Solitaire or read in front of the woodstove, Reader's Digest or her favorite, Gone with the Wind.

Wildlife was an attraction, both good and bad. We'd walk through the woods above the cabin to see the black bear that visited the small community dump. Sometimes we'd find skunks instead. She loved the birds until they ate all the cherries off her tiny tree. She wrapped the tree in wire netting, but the birds still got in. Threatening them with the broom and posting me under the tree with a squirt gun of ammonia water didn't help.

She stood on the deck and poked unshelled peanuts into the bark of the lonely tree for the squirrels until a blue jay flew around and around after the squirrel who ran with nuts bulging his cheeks. The morning that the blue jay woke us too early for nuts by tapping our metal roof and the squirrel ran out of the cold woodstove and up Mom's arm, leaving little black paw prints, she was done. No more nuts.

When the weather was blistering, tiny sunfish nibbled at her toes in the water as she held onto the dock ladder to cool off despite being afraid. Her brother had drowned, and she'd never learned to swim, so she was more of an alarm than a lifeguard when she watched me splash around in the water.

Mom was a spitfire and a catch. Her eyes were brown and could flash to ebony if she got mad. She loved a little mischief in people. We could hardly eat cherries or watermelon at the lake without a pit- or seed-spitting contest. She was known to throw a dinner roll to company, bouncing it off the wall; and she served extra food to the football players in the cafeteria at West Valley High School in exchange for their smiles, though it may have been a request from my uncle Tom, the coach.

A little disagreement between us led to the best chocolate pudding fight at the dinner table, flicking spoonsful like miniature catapults. Her aim was better than mine, hitting my face and hair. I got her white cafeteria uniform. We laughed like fools, made all the better by the horrified look on Dad's face, "Hey now, somebody's gonna get hurt!"

He was her youth potion. When he wrapped his arms around her, she giggled and became a silly, flirty girl again, sparkles in her eyes. She taught us to love and respect him. "Remember, your father's word is his bond. His reputation is everything, and you need to live up to it."

I wish I had known her longer. I was 28 when she died. I would have told her how strong she was, how I admired her for loving Dad so fiercely, how she amazed me as she recovered from breast cancer and radical mastectomy. I would have asked her how she managed to go on after the death of my sister. I would have asked her to give up her grudge against God, the grudge she'd had since she was 18 years old, watching her own mother spit up clots of blood as she died from tuberculosis with no money for medical help.

Shopping downtown Spokane with Mom was a special event that included a bus ride since she could "only drive a tractor." With make-up and hair fixed and sometimes wearing a hat from one of her hat boxes, her heels clicked down the city sidewalk like someone in authority. Our special treat was to have hot-fudge sundaes under the clock in The Crescent.

She went through the clothing racks in a flurry, looking only at the labels as if she knew the designers personally. After putting some back according to price, I gained a wool suit, burnt orange, the nicest outfit I'd ever had. She also sewed our dresses and darned our socks.

Dad nearly prayed for pies. She made great pies. Chocolate fudge candy was her specialty at the cabin. If it didn't cool fast enough, she would stand outside, stirring the big pot held in the crook of her arm. She also made perfect peanut brittle and those puffy fluffs, divinity. We made popcorn balls together for Halloween and pulled taffy as a team.

I asked for her thoughts regarding my future, and she told me I could do whatever I put my mind to—not the help I was hoping for, but it gave me confidence. She could talk to anyone, entertain them, exaggerate a story to make it better, and I loved her for it. She suffered from cancer in the end and her pain sucked away my memories of her happy, feisty, loving life until I wrote this poem:

Is it Mama's face that you see in the mirror?

Her worried expression, your eyes, a tear?

Her pain and struggle those last few years?

Remember her youth, the sparks in her eyes.

They're there on your face near those tiny laugh lines.

Biting a Dirty Palm

Palouse, Washington 1925

Helen rode her pony Blackie bareback between wheat fields over the rolling hills of Palouse, auburn highlights in her chestnut hair winking in the wind. It was her favorite thing to do. Laddie dog came too, her black and white border collie running behind until he was distracted by something to chase.

A little time to herself was hard to find. She was alone and free on Blackie, free from chores for the moment, free from her father's demands and her mother's expectations, free from the hired-hand's friendliness. She stopped to watch the breeze massage its way through the field, hear the shushing song of wheat kernels brushing against each other. Her spine relaxed. It smelled like home, like earth and health.

"Hey Helen!" the hired hand called. "Wanna earn two bits?"

"Doing what?" she asked.

"Just climb up here on the tractor with me and bite the palm of my hand," he said. "I bet you can't do it." He held up his dirty, greasy hand.

A quarter was worthwhile money. "Show me the money first," she said. Seeing it, she climbed up, grabbed ahold of his hand, and not wanting to think about it too much, went in for the bite. But she couldn't do it. Her lips smashed up against his hand and she couldn't get her teeth into his palm. She tasted the slimy filth from it as he laughed, spit a few times and tried again, but she couldn't do it.

"Maybe you should practice some and try again another day," he laughed.

Next thing she knew, he was fired, and she was expected to drive the tractor herself.

She was the second child in a family of five, and her older sister, Marie, was learning to be a seamstress like her mother. Her two brothers were too young to be of much help, so she didn't mind being treated like a boy. Anything outside, driving tractor, milking the cows, even cleaning the stalls was better than sewing. Everybody needed to do something.

Her father Clarence had been proud to be a wheat farmer in Palouse for years. His fields had hummed with activity at certain times like stops on a clock. Extra farm workers had come seasonally, and he had constantly hired new men during harvest. They'd slept on straw and sacks in the fields and sometimes crews had changed overnight. It had taken many trips to haul all that grain to the warehouse since they could get only twenty-five sacks into his wagon at one time.

He knew how things could change, having experienced several years of the stinking smut like so many other wheat growers. His fields had turned black with a stench like rotting fish, and he had dusted it with copper carbonate but couldn't completely cover every kernel. In the end, he had burned his fields. The following season, the black smut had returned. In a last attempt, he had planted Ridit, a hard red winter wheat that was resistant to smut, and it had saved him. The grain had been tough, so he'd replaced it with Albit the following year, a softer version.

During the War, Clarence had used his warehouse receipts like so many other farmers as collateral for easy bank loans through the Farm Loan Act to purchase new equipment and "Win the War with Wheat." All kinds of government expectations had followed. The Food Control Act had banned the production of distilled spirits from any grain that was used for food. Women had been encouraged to sign pledge cards to follow Herbert Hoover's guidelines in the home to make "victory bread" using 20 percent grains other than wheat and to grow "victory gardens." Menus in homes and restaurants were to be restricted: "Wheat-less Wednesdays," "Meatless Tuesdays," "Sweetless Saturdays."

A year later, when one-fourth of all American production had been diverted to the war effort, when farmers had been sup-plying 70 percent more wheat than normal in order to feed the troops, the war had ended and the demand for wheat had bot-tomed out along with the price. With more supply than demand, warehouses had filled up and sacks of grain sat along railroad tracks for miles like soldiers without a cause while Clarence's debts had grown.

He had tried to hunt more often. Everyone had, and it hadn't been long before the local deer had been hunted out, gone from all their watering spots in the valleys of Palouse. He had traveled further and longer by horseback than ever before, resulting in a few birds for his effort and the gnawing thought that chores couldn't wait.

As he'd walked the wheat field, its smell of prosperity had turned sour to him, all that wheat and nowhere to sell it. He remembered sitting against the barn and looking out over his fields, his chin on his knees, feeling exhausted, knowing that something needed to change.

That was when he'd sold some of his property including their little farmhouse; it had been enough to settle his debts. He'd kept the barn so he could grow wheat on the land that was left and had moved the family into a house in town where he could think about ways to diversify. It was a modest, two-story hall and parlor house, two rooms wide and two rooms deep with a front porch and a small barn just south of Main Street.

Helen's mother Ida had easily fallen for Clarence. He was a handsome flirt with a shock of brown hair hanging freely over his forehead, a dimple in his chin, and an easy, open-mouth laugh like the end of a good joke. She'd been attracted to his daring, mischievous, wide-eyed enthusiasm for the future. "What's the worst that could happen?" he would ask and distract her with a squeeze, a kiss or a twirl before she could answer. It had felt like his attitude could overcome anything, that they would always be happy together. She wasn't entirely sure that she could trust him, though.

Ida was tall and proud, respected in the community as a good seamstress. She was glad to live in town because it enabled her to be more involved in the community and the town had electricity. If she could get an electric sewing machine someday, her work would be so much easier. Since money was scarce, she sometimes received payment in the form of food, chickens, rabbits, or used clothes. One of the schoolteachers often paid for sewing with her own used clothes which meant that Helen and her sisters would get her remade dresses to wear to school.

Helen was especially proud to wear her teacher's sage green coat with the Peter Pan collar, a collar that her mother had turned over to hide worn spots. When she outgrew it, her younger sister Mickie would wear it, then it would pass to another family until it was pretty much worn out.

The comment they hated most was, "You'll grow into it," meaning "it" was much too big. They'd be wearing the same old thing for years, and even before they grew enough that it fit, they would hate it and would hope it would tear or become hopelessly stained or would get lost; and when they finally grew into it, they would get something to replace it that was much too large. It was in the interest of "getting your money's worth."

Ida had named Helen after the 1912 film, "When Helen Was Elected," about a young wife who was encouraged to run for mayor against her husband who was also running for the same position. Helen won the election. Then they discovered she was not old enough to hold office. Ida had wanted Helen to be unafraid of making a difference in the world, to know that she could do whatever she wanted in life, even as a female.

Temperance and Moonshine

Palouse, Washington 1914-1927

Women had finally won the right to vote in state and local elections in Washington in 1910, three years before Helen's birth and after fifty years of perseverance by women like May Hutton of Spokane. Washington was the fifth state in the nation to do so and helped inspire the suffrage amendment to the U.S. Constitution which was enacted ten years later. The prohibitionists had supported suffrage too, knowing that women's vote would be needed to outlaw liquor.

In Washington, women could also serve on juries and hold public office. Ida felt it her moral responsibility as a voting citizen to be informed, to express her opinion and to be a good role model for her children. "You will receive the respect you deserve by the way you behave," she told them. "Look and sound like someone ready to advance their station, work hard, and it will happen."

For years, she sewed everything from doilies to house dresses for bazaars to support hospitals and war veterans sponsored by the Ladies' Aid Society. She was a member of the Palouse Xenodican Club, "Hospitality Club," ladies discussing conditions of the town while doing their hand sewing. When her neighbor suggested they create a library for the town, she thought it was a great idea, books being a sort of treasure.

Ida helped collect books for their library by going door to door for donations, happy to talk about the necessity of literacy and how townsfolk needed to be informed. The day they moved the books from storage in the Episcopal church and down the street to city hall to create the library, they had a nice inventory. She carried a stack of books while Helen trailed behind pulling a wagonful, and others came behind her. Ida called it their "Parade of Knowledge" and made sure that literature on the evils of drink was there as well.

Clarence wasn't afraid of taking chances or breaking rules even though his father and grandfather had been honorable members of the military. His grandfather had been the Major General in charge of transporting Lincoln's body to the Whitehouse after his assassination.

His father had fought with the Iowa infantry in the Civil War. He'd been eighteen years old when he had been captured and sent to Andersonville Prison at Camp Sumter with thousands of other Union army prisoners. Most were dressed in rags and kept in the open without shelter or sanitation. 45,000 prisoners went through the gate during its fourteen months of operation and over 13,000 died there from starvation, disease, and tainted water. Maybe it was the lingering shadows from his father's nightmares or perhaps it was his cocky, entrepreneurial nature that wouldn't allow him to follow the mold. Either way, he broke it.

Idaho had been in debate about the potential of liquor laws since 1909 and had settled the issue by not taking a stand, by letting each city and county make its own decisions. As soon as it had become illegal in various places, booze had become especially popular. Clarence noticed that customers had been crossing state and county lines to get it like church goers on a Sunday.

Washington State passed an initiative against making and selling booze in 1914. It was a warning, not enforceable; and even though Washington and Idaho declared alcohol to be the demon's elixir through the vote two years later, Washington folks still had access. They could import liquor from other states if they had a permit, and Spokane County was generous, issuing 34,000 permits to its 44,000 registered voters.

Clarence felt that when opportunity presented itself, a man would be a fool not to take advantage of it. With the bottom dropped out of the wheat industry, he thought of his family's old recipe called Perseverance, and he had all that wheat that didn't have much value anymore. He was good at sales, and he thought that sampling his product might help take the sting out of hard times.

He set up shop inside the barn with the only access being through a low hole from the pigsty, hoping that fumes from the pigs would disguise gases escaping from the still and that he wouldn't burn down his barn. Gathering empty bottles from outside the dance halls after dances on Saturday nights became a regular routine.

"I can't stand men coming around in the middle of the night, tapping on our bedroom window for a bottle of your Perseverance," Ida told him. "I don't want you waking up Mickie when she's dead asleep to crawl under our bed to get the stuff."

"She's the only one small enough to fit through the hole under the floor without moving the bed!"

"I don't care! It's dark and scary down there and she should not have to do it. Especially in her nighty!"

"Well dress her in pants for bed, then. I'm trying to make a little money here. You've got to sell when the customer wants to buy, gawd dammit!"

Ida knew a lot of people made moonshine, her family made good corn whiskey back in Iowa, but she didn't think they sold it. Selling it was against the law. If he got caught, Clarence would go to jail and ruin their reputation. How would they feed the family then?

The third night that Clarence rousted Mickie from a deep sleep in the middle of the night to crawl down into the dark, damp crawl space under their bed in her nighty, Ida heard her daughter's whimpers, and that was it. The next morning, she declared "war" and officially joined the Temperance Movement.

She hadn't slept a wink, wondering how they would manage if she convinced him to *stop* making moonshine. Still, she confronted him in the morning.

"You listen to me, Clarence. Our children will NEVER be involved in your moonshine business in *any* way. Do you hear me? I mean it! Find someplace else to store your liquor."

"Well, my dear. You are being self-righteous and preachy and frankly, a nag. I'm just trying to keep the family fed, you know."

"Well, I think you like it too much," she said. "And you're on your own."

Women's Christian Temperance groups had been active in Washington State for more than fifty years, the first having been begun by Reverend George Whitworth who also founded Whitworth College. Ida made a small donation and pledge to join the Whitman County chapter: "I hereby promise, God helping me, to abstain from the use of all alcoholic drinks, including wine, beer, and cider, to employ all proper means to discourage the use of and traffic in the same." Ida wasn't sure that all members used "proper means." She remembered seeing Carrie Nation when she had visited Palouse at the Eslick Bar in 1910 and had delivered a piece of her mind. Carrie was known to make her point by swinging a hatchet and breaking chairs.

Despite her pledge, Ida chose to ignore the keg of spicy cider that sat on her back porch. Cider had been a family tradition for as long as she could remember. There was a limit to how many apples could be stored, used or dried without making cider.

Dark-eyed Girl

Thirty-three states were already dry when Temperance became Prohibition throughout the nation effective January 17, 1920, with the 18th Constitutional Amendment, "the manufacture, sale or transportation of intoxicating liquors ... is prohibited." It was enforced by the Volstead Act.

Nothing was said about owning, buying or drinking those beverages. People were allowed to drink whatever they already owned in the privacy of their own homes, and the well-to-do had plenty. They'd had a lot of warning and time to stock up. Basements in neighborhoods like Browne's Addition and on the South Hill in Spokane were full of liquor.

In the beginning, the American Medical Association supported Prohibition, stating that there was no medicinal use for alcohol, even though whiskey had been prescribed for any kind of stress since, well, the beginning of whiskey. Two years into Prohibition, however, when the stashes of the wealthy had begun to dry up, the AMA changed its message, creating the Referendum on the Use of Alcohol. It stated that liquor could treat twenty-seven conditions including diabetes, cancer, asthma, snakebite, lactation problems and old age, and was available only through prescription. A lot of prescriptions were written then. Sixty-five new pharmacies opened in Seattle within three months. Clarence told Ida that he was supporting the medical profession and helping his community heal from their ailments.

Ida remembered the battle against liquor before Prohibition. It had been fierce. *The Palouse Republic* had reprinted part of H. W. Grady's 1887 speech that he'd delivered in Georgia: "Liquor is the mortal enemy of peace and order, the despoiler of men, the terror of women, the cloud that shadows the face of children, the demon that digs graves." The Temperance group had sponsored writing essays and speech contests in school about the harmful effects of alcohol and cigarettes. The Anti-Saloon League had had a billboard campaign that had made her shudder, the most powerful one being of a Model T with the Grim Reaper standing in the backseat, black hood and scythe lurking over the head of the driver, "Death Rides with The Drinking Driver." Now she fought against liquor in her own home.

For Helen, her father's moonshine enterprise opened the door to a new life. She'd always had a sweet tooth, and when he arranged for her to have a job at Jess's Confectionary after school and Saturdays in exchange for bulk sugar for his still and a small wage, she spun around like Laddie with a happy tail. She learned to make every kind of candy and licked the pans if no one was looking: fudge, divinity, penuche, pralines, taffy, peanut brittle, all of it.

With her re-made clothes and her mother's guidance, she received more admiration at the confectionery than she had ever experienced before. She and her girlfriends began to think about fashion and dances and having fun.

Helen's father was already in the doghouse for making hooch, so he decided to raise a few fine roosters too. Good money could be made off fighting cocks if he had the best. His pride was a big Miner Blue. Blue had a flamboyant, iridescent blue-black tail as proud as his enormous cockspur, and he attacked anything that moved, including Laddie dog. After a few horrifying attacks by the flapping, stabbing hurricane, Laddie learned to stay away.

Clarence trained his birds for fighting, antagonizing them with a stick until they fought back. He put their food outside their cage, so they needed to push their heads between wires to eat, which strengthened their necks. He tossed them up into the air, making them use their wings, and encouraged them to walk up steep ramps to strengthen their legs. He hosted cockfights behind the barn during his wife's regular club meetings on the other end of town, and he made a killing off Big Blue.

Ida noticed local changes that came with Prohibition. The lemon extract at the grocery story was chronically sold out. People were drinking it for the alcohol content. Her sewing customers asked for larger pockets to be sewn into the inside of their jackets, pint-size or even quart-size for carrying their drink. When the neighbor, Mrs. Keller, was arrested, Ida was shocked. Mrs. Keller had been collecting $10 per week for her service of taking in young girls to protect them from immoral women. At the same time, she'd made 174 quarts of beer in her home. Ida shook her head, wondering what else her neighbors were capable of, what they might do to make money when it was hard to come by.

Could morality be legislated? That's what the debate about Prohibition boiled down to, causing it to be called "The Great Experiment." It was the first time that the U.S. Constitution had denied rights to citizens rather than granted them. "The end of individualism in the U.S." according to businessman John D. Rockefeller.

Ida prided herself in community involvement. Walking to the grocery, she passed two neighbors in their yards and raised her hand to them as she always had with a "Hey" as she passed. Maybe the first one hadn't heard her, but the second neighbor also turned away as if she were deaf. *Community judgment,* Ida thought. *So the word is out.* She didn't know if she could endure it and began to play a fantasy in her head about sabotaging his still or getting a divorce.

Divorce was out of the question. It was nasty business. The children would automatically go with their father unless she could prove that he was a bigamist or adulterer or impotent. Kind of difficult to prove impotence with all those children they had, and the only adultery she knew about was with that still in the barn. Besides, she still loved Clarence.

"The government is trying to kill people," Clarence told her. "I'm protecting folks from poisonous drink is what I'm doing."

Within six years of Prohibition, so much industrial alcohol was being drunk that the government required it be denatured with bitter chemicals. In response, bootleggers hired chemists to "renature" it. The following year, the government required that methyl alcohol be added which caused blindness and sometimes death. Wayne Wheeler from the Anti-Saloon League called it suicide, "To root out a bad habit costs many lives."

Clarence diversified, dusting off his old delivery wagon, "Palouse Dairy" written on the side; and with resilient entrepreneurial flair, began to promote his "Authentic Snake Oil and Other Remedies" along with an occasional bottle of moonshine if requested. "My snake oil will mollify your arthritis and bursitis if rubbed onto your joints," he proclaimed as Blackie pulled the wagon. "It reduces inflammation and pain." It was his recipe of mineral oil and turpentine with beef fat and red pepper, no snake oil. It sold well, and that was all that mattered.

He didn't mind being known as a bit of a scoundrel. Selling remedy seemed more ethical than resorting to what some farmers were doing like digging deep, muddy holes in roads so that automobiles would get stuck. Then showing up with horses to pull them out of the hole for a fee.

Big Blue was hungry early one morning and began pecking at the leather strip that closed his cage. The door flew open, and he escaped, strutting out into the yard full of mud puddles from last night's rain to find bugs and misplaced kernels of corn and grain. As the sun rose higher, he saw another rooster, a big one pecking at him from the ground. Instantly, he attacked, pecking with vengeance over and over, wings flapping like a storm as he'd been taught. Each time he stopped and looked with a beady eye, the rooster appeared again. So he attacked again, going deeper and deeper, pecking harder and harder until his throat plugged with mud, and he couldn't breathe.

Helen was up early Saturday morning to feed the chickens before going to work. She found her father's favorite rooster, Big Blue, dead in a mud puddle and hurried through the feeding while shaking her head, wanting to be gone before her father got up. Also, it was the day before Mother's Day. She liked a busy day for selling candy.

Laddie dog came around the corner as he did every morning to check on anything new in the yard. Discovering Big Blue in a puddle of mud, he stepped back, afraid. The bird didn't move. Laddie shook his head, remembering how Big Blue could attack. Slowly, with head down, he snuck forward, ready to bolt if the menace should raise its head. When he got close enough to poke the bird with his nose, it didn't move. Laddie attacked, taking revenge on his nemesis, biting, growling, shaking him until pieces began to fly away.

At Jess's Confectionary, just before closing, a tall, lanky guy with crystal blue eyes under a cowboy hat sauntered into the shop to make a purchase. He seemed more interested in looking at Helen than the candy. She asked him his name.

His eyebrows rose as if he were clearing his vision from a dream. "Joe," he said with a grin.

Dead Chicken Hanging

Palouse, Washington 1929

Going to Palouse felt like a holiday to Joe. It had been a vibrant town at one time. Truth be told, Potlatch Lumber Company was helping keep Palouse alive, yet the town still felt full of possibilities.

After the Palouse fire of 1888, all the buildings had been rebuilt with stone, brick or corrugated iron. He enjoyed looking around: the Security State Bank with its stained glass, half-round windows, the big skylight in the ceiling of the Ankcorn Hardware store, the St. Elmo Hotel with its electric elevator, the first one in the state when it was built. St. Elmo was the only three-story building in town, taller than the 600-person Opera House in the Powers Block where folks went to hear speakers and watch entertainment.

In the early 1900s, the town had had 1,800 residents served by five doctors, three lawyers, and seven churches. Before it went dry for Prohibition, there had been a brewery that had provided for at least five saloons. The police had looked after the drunken harvesters and hobos who would work a week and then come to town for a drink. Ever since the farmers went broke and the brewery and saloons closed, the town had been shrinking. There were stores for groceries and general merchandise, a confectionary, a bakery, two restaurants and of course a newspaper, *The Palouse Republic*. There was even talk of Penney coming to town.

Five bridges spanned the river in town, including F Street bridge, a source of pride in Palouse, a testament to activity and commerce, especially related to agriculture. During harvest in the early 1920s, farmers in horse-drawn wagons had lined up across that bridge waiting to unload their wheat at the Flour Mill.

There were still a few houses of ill repute clustered on the south side of the river that had originally taken care of the lonely loggers and railroad crews, fewer houses now than the original eight. Joe looked in that direction as he walked by. He could see the path across the river on the footbridge and up the thirty-two steps and the steep hill above it. He wondered how many patrons had ended up in the river considering the terrain and the condition they might have been in. That didn't hold his interest for long. His interest had something to do with dark eyes.

He knew the brick schoolhouse wouldn't be quiet for long, though it sat silently in full sun when he arrived. In the shadow of a willow tree, he used his hat to beat off the dust from his Levi's, then leaned against the trunk to wait. It wasn't long before a flicker bird began to drill on the trunk over his head and the bell sounded. A long stream of students filed out the door together like he imagined a school of fish. She came walking toward him with her long legs, laughing with a friend.

"You've got to come over and see the new dress I bought in Spokane," the friend said. "It's lavender silk with white trim, awfully cute!"

As the girls got close, Joe stood straight and tipped his hat, "Helen?"

Helen's eyes grew, then she remembered. "Joe the cowboy," she smiled. "How was the candy? . . . And where's your horse?"

"The cat's meow," he replied, looking over at her friend. "I hopped the train."

"I'm Evelyn," the friend said. "I've gotta go." She looked to Helen with question marks in her eyes. "I've gotta see a man about a dog," she laughed, walking away. "Come over later, Helen. I want to introduce you to my new friend, Maybelline."

"Maybelline?" Helen asked.

"You'll see."

"Does Maybelline know Max? Max Factor by any chance?"

Evelyn waved and kept walking.

Helen smiled, looking up at Joe a few inches taller, "How do you know my name?"

It took him a moment, those dark eyes. "I asked around. Thought I'd walk you home, maybe carry your books if you'll let me." He stretched out his hands. She smelled like sugar and peppermint.

The sun hit and hid between tree canopies in a slow rhythm as they strolled along. "What's your favorite candy?" It was the only question he could think of.

She looked at him again. "Fudge probably," she laughed. "I like black licorice . . . and peanut brittle is awfully good, too. Basically, I like candy." She felt heat in her face. *I sound like a pig.*

"What year are you in school?" he asked, hoping it was a better question.

"Sophomore year. You?"

"I'm done with school, working in Potlatch now. Live there with my family."

At Helen's house, Joe saw a large garden, a few outbuildings with the river behind, and something quivering in the shadows. "What's going on there?" he asked, nodding.

"Oh, sorry, that's our dog Laddie. My father is punishing him. He thinks Laddie killed his prize fighting cock, but he didn't. I told him so, and he doesn't believe me. He's had that stinking, rotten bird tied around his neck for over a week now. It's disgusting."

"Come boy," Joe patted his leg. Laddie came slowly, scrunching low like he was in trouble, dragging what was left of the putrid carcass between his front legs, the white fur of his neck and chest matted and brown. The stench came with him. "What's the deal Laddie? Wanna get rid of that, boy?" He pulled his jackknife from his pocket and cut the rope from around Laddie's neck, tossing the dead bird into the bushes.

Laddie was free! He ran around and around Helen and Joe, bringing them closer together as they tried to avoid his reek. Joe broke away to run behind the house, calling the dog to follow him to the river. Their commotion stirred up the chickens, and their clacking caused the goats to bleat. He threw a stick to the water's edge and grabbed the dog by the scruff of his neck, giving him a scrub in the water to remove the worst of the residue. Then letting go, he ran, knowing that Laddie would surely give a good shake and spray him with tainted water.

Helen laughed and they ran together, turning to see Laddie rub his neck and shoulders through the dirt. "Dirt's a lot better than chicken rot," she said. "Thanks."

"It's hard to love a dog with a dead chicken tied around his neck," Joe said, looking at the small barn. Helen's father stood in the entrance, his hands on his hips.

Joe walked forward. He'd been taught about the sanctity of the handshake his whole life. How it created a bond, was a statement of respect, was sometimes a binding contract. "Hi. My name's Joe," he said, extending his hand.

Clarence swayed a bit, radiating a waft of alcohol. He'd done some extra tasting of his shine that afternoon, just until the future lost its threat, and he didn't want anyone coming around. "Keep your hands off my property," he spewed.

Joe backed away, stood a moment, and turned to go. "Take care of your dog," he said gently to Helen, giving her a kind smile before he walked away.

Helen's eyes burned holes into her father after Joe was gone. Her mouth was clamped shut above her dimpled chin and she walked into the house as quietly as a rabbit.

Cutting a Rug

Palouse and Potlatch 1929

On Saturday, Joe stood outside Jess's Confectionary, waiting for the store to close.

"Are you trying to wrangle me, cowboy?" Helen asked when she stepped out the door.

Joe's eyebrows raised. "Maybe," he smiled.

"I don't see your rope."

"Thought I'd see how you were doing, that's all."

"Well, I'm doing fine. It took you long enough."

"Mm?"

"I had decided you weren't interested."

"I'm interested." *Can't quit thinking about you.* "Maybe we should go out on a date."

She smiled, waiting, eyebrows raised.

"Howz about a dance, Tootz?"

"Suites me fine, cowboy." She flirted, lifting one shoulder.

The following weekend, Joe traded his dusty work hat and clothes for a brown fedora and slightly used felt slacks and tweed jacket, thankful that he had a little money from a regular job. He was lucky to borrow his boss's old Model T Ford, a Tin Lizzy, with his promise of its safe return.

His boss, chief engineer Bob Bowling, had said he wouldn't need the car. He was trying to invent a machine to make an automated version of his Pres-to-logs, like the PrestoLog of wood, coal, and chemicals that gave off colors to show levels of heat. Bob wanted his logs to be from the mill's wood waste without chemicals, turn waste into a usable product. "Hard times breed innovation," he'd told Joe. "We need to use our leftovers." His logs would take one-fourth the space to store compared to wood, and one-third of a log was enough to cook a typical meal.

The Model T was equipped with a tire patch kit and air pump. A five-gallon can of gas was strapped to the running board. Joe pulled up in front of Helen's house and stopped the car with a careful hiccup. As he stood at the door, his breath was shallow, and he removed his hat as he met her mother and siblings. Clarence stood further behind the family, twirling a toothpick between his teeth, looking over Joe's shoulder at the car out front.

Joe nodded to him. *What kind of father doesn't shake the hand of his daughter's date?*

Helen came to the door wearing her most fashionable dress. Her mother had been a genius at the sewing machine, having combined three different pieces. She'd removed the bottom of a straight, plain gray dress and turned it into a drop-waist by attaching a pleated, navy skirt at the hip, then tied it all together with a navy and rose-patterned strip to cover the seam and used the same fabric to fancy the V-neckline, ends hanging to be tied in the front. Helen grabbed his arm and pulled him down the steps, the tie on her chest bouncing.

"Gee, you look swell," Joe said, replacing his hat. She smelled like lilac now rather than sugar. The weight of her hand on his arm made him feel responsible as he walked her to the passenger side of the car. No door to open, he held her hand as she slid onto the seat.

"Thank you, sir," she put her hand behind her head and smiled as if for a photograph, showing off the finger waves in her hair.

Joe cranked the handle below the grill and did it again, and the engine turned over. As he climbed into the driver's seat, Clarence came out and deposited two gallon-jugs of moonshine behind the seat. "You can deliver a gift to my friend Bean on your way. Helen knows the place." He pulled the toothpick from his mouth and winked with a big grin, drawing a circle in the air. "Drive around back when you get there," he said before walking back into the house.

Joe looked blankly at Helen. She shook her head and shrugged, looking down.

Joe raised his voice over the idling engine, a sincere look on his face. "I can't do hard time, you know." He was thinking of a cop turned bootlegger in Seattle who had gotten four years hard labor.

Helen stared at him, then guffawed an explosive laugh.

He grinned back. "How about you point out the direction and we get rid of this stuff before we're sorry?" he hollered.

She flamboyantly whipped her arm up like the conductor of an orchestra, and he pressed the left foot pedal, stopping it halfway down for neutral to release the handbrake. Then he pushed the pedal all the way down for low gear and increased the throttle next to the steering wheel as they jerked forward, on their way.

"Hold on!" he hollered, immediately pushing the pedal on the right to brake for a horse and buggy coming up from behind. He hadn't looked before pulling out. Thankful he had avoided the center pedal, which was for reverse, he made a mental note to park where he wouldn't need to use it. Going forward was enough to manage. Within a few blocks, he felt the chill, saw Helen tense as if she were cold, and handed her the car blanket. She took it with a thankful smile.

At Bean's house, Joe left the car running as he got behind the seat to grab the two gallons. In his rush, the jugs collided. They shattered, filling the car with illegal moonshine, blasting fumes like a neon sign. He gasped and froze, wishing he could rewind the scene in front of him, stop it from happening. Then he looked around, jumped back into the driver's seat, and pulled his hat down to his eyes as he hiccupped the car away.

"Look at your face!" Helen roared, unable to stop laughing. She wiped the tears from her eyes and kept laughing. "The horror," she cried. "It's priceless!" She tried to stop but couldn't. "It's just so funny!" she spit. "You should see yourself!"

"A memorable first date then!" Joe grinned.

Helen tried to compose herself as they rolled through town. Folks on the street seemed to turn in their direction as if they smelled criminal activity. Helen scrunched down into the seat, hand over her mouth.

"I was supposed to be a minister, you know," Joe said solemnly, looking over to her.

Helen exploded in laughter again, unable to contain herself.

"Guess that's over now," he continued. "Hadn't ever planned on being a gangster, though."

Helen sobered, seeing that he might be serious. "Drive back to the house," she said. "We can clean the car. My father won't notice."

They picked out broken glass, toweled up the moonshine, and tried to camouflage the odor with turpentine. "I hope you're better at dancing than breaking the law," Helen said, hoping they still had a date.

"Good," Joe sniffed the air. "Now it smells like *clean* moonshine. Yeah, I've been known to cut a rug. How about you, Tootz?"

The sparks in Helen's eyes gave him the only answer he needed.

The band at Sorenson's barn played everything from jazz to country music. To Joe, dancing seemed the quickest way to get to know Helen, the dancefloor his most comfortable place to do it. She was light on her feet, moving with the beat on those long legs. Her hand on his shoulder felt like a comfort, and when he fell into those dark eyes, he grabbed her tighter about the waist and they spun around the floor.

Helen had never danced with a guy like Joe before. It was smooth, safe, fun. She could trust him, on the dancefloor anyway. She was exactly where she wanted to be. And the brute stole a kiss as if he knew she wanted it, as if he'd read her mind.

A Grand View

Palouse and Potlatch 1930

Clarence was able to sell a calf for two loads of hay. He shingled the roof of a neighbor's house, helped raise the sides of a barn, but no steady work. He'd heard about guys starting fires so they could be paid to help fight the fires they set. It made his moonshine business seem darn right ethical.

He *was* ethical. He knew what he was doing. He knew how to cook off the methanol so no one would go blind, and he didn't make any of that super strong 150% proof shine that could kill a person. The Feds had been arresting a lot of rumrunners, the guys who carried the real thing across the Canadian border, so the demand for moonshine was up. It was a matter of him supplying their demand, that's all. He was providing a service, skimming the top for his most discerning customers and selling the dregs for less. He told them it was squirrel whiskey, "It'll make ya talk nutty and climb trees." The more time he spent in the barn, admiring his still and doing taste tests, the more he thought that everything would be okay.

Clarence wasn't the only one. In rural areas where an unusual amount of grain alcohol was made, grocery stores sold Peeko, flavors to add to moonshine--rye, gin, rum, even crème de menthe. Throughout the country, production of corn sugar was way up, one wholesaler alone bought up to three railroad cars of corn sugar every week. A population of 24 thousand bought 152 million pounds of Fleischmann's Yeast in four years. The Feds tried to fight back. In 1929, more than 35 thousand stills were confiscated, and 26 million gallons of mash was destroyed. It made no difference, the same effect as a bucket of water from a lake.

Clarence was proud of his set-up, a separate pot for cooking his mash so he could let it ferment for a week while he distilled his previous batch. It was a beautiful still, a slightly banged up vat with a two-inch metal leg from an old bed coming out the top which was capped with the soldered end of a tin can. A copper tube came out near the top of the leg so his savory salivation, his proud-as-a-papa prized product, could condense and run down the tube and into a bottle.

Ida was struggling. She had been stashing away bits of money from her sewing jobs the best she could, feeling sure that even harder times were coming. Stores were beginning to close, and ladies were dropping out of Ladies Aid. Plus, she had a cough that was wearing her down, causing her to buy bread for five cents a loaf without the energy to make it herself.

Helen's hours at the confectionary were being cut back and she began to work a second job after school in Phillip's department store a few hours per week. At the end of her sophomore year a friend signed her autograph book, "If you have nothing and your fellow has nothing, don't be in a hurry to wed. For nothing plus nothing equals nothing and nothing doesn't chew like bread."

Farmers had been scraping by for at least ten years before the stock market crashed in October 1929, and banks had failed before and after that event. Farmers didn't deal in stocks and bonds. They dealt in grain and livestock on their farms and did whatever they could to continue their lives and livelihoods. Lumbermen and mill workers faced reduced wages and fewer hours and lost jobs too. Those who were young had distractions, though, like falling in love and watching picture shows. Picture shows were nearly affordable if you had a whole dime.

Joe couldn't quit thinking about Helen, her joy and carefree laugh. She was like a tonic to his spirit. Once the spring thaw showed bare ground in the hills, he invited her for a ride on horseback up the Pine Ridge trail to Kamiak Butte. The trail head was five miles southwest out of Palouse, then a climb higher into the pine and a two-mile loop along the edge of the butte.

They let the horses run a bit to the trailhead, the fringe of Helen's orange and brown neck scarf bouncing off her back. Joe enjoyed seeing her on a horse. She looked relaxed on Blackie as they headed up the trail, her rear wagging back and forth with the saddle.

"Kamiak Butte," he projected his voice ahead to her. "Named after Chief Kamiakin of the Yakama tribe, the one who led the Indians against Steptoe and sent the soldiers pack'n."

"Steptoe as in Steptoe Butte," she called back.

They rode beyond the north bluff and view of the town of Palouse to the sunnier south side and the grand, panoramic view of the prairie, vibrant in various hues of green and leftover dead tufts from winter. From up there they could see dots that were farmers already ploughing their land. The birds seemed to rejoice in the warm spring sunshine. Blossoms from early purple grass widow stood in stiff clumps below them. It seemed so perfect that Joe felt the good Lord had gifted them the day.

They looped the horses' reins to a tree limb and sat on an exposed ridge of granite that had been warmed in the sun.

"Steptoe," Helen said. "The battle didn't even happen there. It was at Pine Creek. It was hardly a battle, actually, compared to what came after. You think you know something . . . and then you find out otherwise."

"Like trying to make a living in farming," Joe replied. "You'd think you couldn't go wrong--the most solid, safest thing folks could do if the weather didn't drown you out or fry you dry. We were doing pretty well in Midvale until the wheat quit paying and the bills didn't stop. It seems like nobody is sure of anything anymore."

Helen smiled, turning to him. "I know I'm happy being here with you, Joe." She leaned against his arm.

Joe swallowed, her quick comment unexpected. "I'm glad you're here," he said. He looked out over the prairie. "It looks like never-ending possibilities out there, across that prairie, if you ask me. I don't understand how so many folks can be hurting."

Helen hugged her knees. "We seem to get by so far . . . Need to find fun wherever you can, like a ride up Kamiak trail," she grinned. "Maybe you should see me more often, cowboy. You know, to help keep you out of the doldrums."

He wrapped his arms around her, and *she* kissed him. Of course, he kissed her back, and he got to know her quite well on that private, warm slab of granite with the grand view.

Letters from Joe

Palouse and Potlatch 1930

April 13: *Dear Helen, Palouse*

I was so downhearted I didn't get over to see you last night that I went with the gang to the bootlegger's well. If I ever do that again, I should be shot. I used to be sort of a gentleman once. I think I'll try it again for you if you want me that way. I hope you think enough of me to answer my letter. Please write. Adois! Joe, Potlatch

Joe knew he was falling for her. He'd told her that her letters were better than any medicine for the blues. Being in love was wonderful. It made him want to smile and joke and dance; and he dreaded it. It caused his stomach to cramp. He had responsibilities to his family. He shouldn't be pursuing what *he* wanted when everyone's hours and wages were being cut.

April 21: *Dearest Helen, Palouse*

I went to your house, but you weren't there. I went to the show and waited outside, in case I would see you, but no luck. I want a date for

Thursday night or I'm afraid you'll find someone else. Well, I couldn't blame you if you did. Lovingly, Joe, Potlatch

In Palouse, the whole town stood together on Main Street to watch the Memorial Day parade. Helen wasn't thinking of her uncles or her grandfather or her great grandfather who had served in the military. Watching the parade and waving her little American flag, she was only aware of the warm spring day and the person holding her hand.

Cheers and applause erupted with the military band, and continued with the high school band, Veterans of Foreign Wars and every group that could organize and march. One patriotic song blended into another until the appearance of the American flag. All stood and the talking stopped. Joe removed his hat; Helen put her hand over her heart. The parade ended with the long-haired boy known about town bringing up the rear on his bicycle, blowing his two-foot-long horn at people on his left and people on his right, back and forth as he pedaled.

They all gathered in front of the platform in city park for speeches, and Joe was distracted by Helen's nearness, her arm brushing his, her peppermint smell, the way she laughed so easily and so often. He felt giddy, couldn't help but smile; being together felt like their own private celebration. A child wearing large red flower petals around her face came to stand in front of the platform.

"A poppy!" Helen giggled, pointing. Other girls joined the first, each with small bouquets of red paper flowers.

A man from the American Legion explained how red poppies

symbolized the blood that was shed in the Great War. They had popped up in Belgium and France after the war, maybe because of the lime in the soil from the rubble left behind. A teenage boy read *In Flander's Field*. "In Flander's fields the poppies blow, between the crosses, row on row..."

As one of the girls passed by, Joe dropped a few coins into her tin can and took a paper poppy, then grinned as he reached inside Helen's neckline to pin it onto her chest.

"Watch it now!" Helen fluttered her eyes.

"You're safe with me." He made sure she saw the pin before he poked it into her blouse.

A trumpet played Taps.

In Helen's yard, Joe helped cut purple and blue iris and big, heavy-headed lilacs and pastel peonies, thankful that she'd insisted he go with her to put them on family graves. She explained what she knew about each relative at Freeze cemetery as they cleaned the gravestones. During the family picnic there, after the honeyed cornbread and cider, she told him about her great great grandfather's huge marble memorial stone as tall as a person that stood at the entrance of Arlington National Cemetery, though she'd never seen it herself.

June 12: *Dearest Helen,*

I received your letter and it sure makes things look different. I'll be down there tomorrow night. I went over to Moscow to the show last night, but it wasn't so good. "Hit the Deck" was the name of it. The hero sure liked himself and the girl sure looked up to him. She was sort of foolish, don't you think? Always yours, Joe

June 27: *Dearest,*

I felt uneasy about you going home with your friends. You didn't have a wreck, did you? I was just over and made a deal for half-case of beer for Ted's special benefit. It's real beer! Tommy went to Spokane today. It seems sorta lonesome without him now. My mother said you were a real nice girl, the best girl I ever had the honor of bringing home. Yours always, Joe

Mariposa Lilies

Palouse, 1930

John borrowed a horse and buggy from work after putting in extra hours for no pay. The family was going to the Kennedy Ford Grange for the big Fourth of July celebration and dance. It was a hectic, bumpy ride, the road torn up by all the automobiles speeding past them. Joe had chosen the calmest horse he knew, predicting the commotion and the horns honking.

From a raised platform, the American flag jitterbugged in the breeze as if it conducted the small band that played patriotic songs. People stood for the Pledge of Allegiance, hands over hearts and sang "God Bless America." Alice wore her dress of little blue flowers with a red bandana poking out of the pocket and a large-brimmed straw hat to protect her from the July sun. Local leaders gave speeches about better times ahead and neighbors helping neighbors.

As families settled down for picnics on blankets, Alice looked for those who had little to eat. She saw a family she knew and took some of her cold fried chicken to them. "I wonder if you'd be willing to try some of my chicken," she said. "I'm wanting to enter it in the county fair, and I'd be much obliged if you'd let me know how I might improve it some."

Joe pined for Helen. He caught himself looking for her among the crowd that day and especially among the scarfs and ruffles at the dance in the grange hall that evening. He knew it was foolish. She'd gone with her friend, Evelyn. It was the first time in his life that he didn't feel like dancing.

Helen wore the bathing suit her mother had made for her, a one-piece dark blue of knitted wool with short pants. As she waded into the water at Silver City resort, Liberty Lake, it began to sag with the weight of the water, and she pulled it up to her chin, hoping it would stay there. Her friend, Evelyn, wore a Jantzen suit. It was emerald with a wrap of skirt over short pants and a skinny white belt at the waist.

The girls had come with Evelyn's family in their Chrysler to stay with friends for the Fourth of July, the drive taking most of the day. It was the only time that Helen had ridden in a rumble seat. They'd talked together over the motor noise about possibilities for marriage, and Joe's name had come up quite a bit. They'd passed an advertisement on separate signs along the road: *If you think/ she likes/ your bristles/ walk bare footed/ through some thistles/ Burma Shave.* When a freak thunderstorm had caused it to rain, a blanket over their heads had kept them from drowning.

As their ride on the Ferris wheel took them higher and higher, they tore off long strips of cotton candy to wrap around their tongues, feeling it melt in their mouths. "My dad calls this fairy floss, you know," Evelyn said. With sticky fingers, she picked pink goo from the tip of her nose and tried to lick it with her tongue, then gave up and wiped it on her arm.

At the highest point, their forward movement abruptly stopped, causing their seat to swing back and forth. Helen gripped the sides, peeked over the edge and swallowed hard. It looked much higher than it had from the ground. A nervous giggle erupted, and she began to laugh, and the more she laughed, the more the seat rocked back and forth. She covered her mouth to try to stop but couldn't stop, and when Evelyn saw a look of panic begin on Helen's face, she yelled to the operator, "Hey! Get us down from here!"

Safely on the ground, they got ready for the dance. Evelyn in her lavender dress and Helen in a periwinkle with a flirty ruffle at the bottom walked to the big pavilion. It was packed with people, and they danced together until a couple of guys came to break them up. Helen's dance partner was clumsy and jerky; and she realized that Joe had ruined her for dancing with anyone else. She sat against the wall and thought about Joe, how wonderful it would be if he were there.

Fireworks exploded over the lake that evening, multi-colored bursts lighting the dark sky. Helen felt the explosions in her chest and forgot to breathe, so consumed by the spectacle. When it was over, she felt numb, yet the world seemed full of possibilities.

July 7: *Hello Honey,*

Gee, it seems we're getting further apart all the time. Let's arrange it so if one goes, we both go and that will be a lot better. We've been

canning and I got Brownie paid for the cigars, so I'm broke again. He
says two can live cheaper than one. Love, Joe

Joe scraped together money for gas and borrowed his brother's
Model T for a drive with Helen to Palouse Falls. It was a long
drive over heavily oiled dirt roads. Stopped at the side of the
road, he held a patch over a leak in an innertube, waiting for it
to dry. Helen sat on a rock, watching.

"This is our second flat, tire boy," she said. "Do you think
we'll make it?"

"I'll be awful sorry if we don't," he said. "Might even be willing
to carry you the rest of the way on my back if I need to. Don't
drink anymore of that water just in case." He grinned at her. She
had never seen the falls and he wanted to be the one to show it
to her, to share the experience together.

Back on the road, the warm day and fields in various stages of
green and harvest seemed encouraging for the future. They got
upstream from where the Palouse and Snake rivers meet, and he
followed the old wagon ruts toward the canyon that had been
worn over the years.

Helen saw white mariposa lilies first as they walked toward
the ridge of the canyon and heard the falls before she saw it. Joe
held out his arm and she held on as she stepped close enough to
peer over the edge of basalt cliffs. He saw her eyes go wide. An
explosive rush of water pounded two hundred feet down to a
bowl carved into the rock below. She gasped and lowered herself
to the ground to feel solid earth beneath her, afraid she'd fall.
Joe sat too, felt her against his arm where she seemed to want to

stay. Her laugh erupted. "I love it!" she shouted over the roar of the falls, and he saw tears in her eyes.

"It comes out of nowhere!" she said as they laid out their picnic: cheese, bread and apples. "Can you imagine how many travelers over the years have been awe-struck when they stumbled onto it?"

Joe poured lemonade and opened the waxed paper holding his mother's icebox cookies. "It's a powerful surprise of nature," he said. "Indian legend says it was created by Beaver who was being hunted by four giant brothers."

They laid on their backs on a blanket, looking up at puffs of cloud traveling the sky. Joe held her hand, smelled her faint scent of lilac. They heard the rumble of the falls and felt the vibration of it through the earth. Helen, who normally had something clever to say or a good story to tell, had no desire to speak. Stunned by the power of the falls, she felt it adhere to her soul. She was thankful for the anchor of Joe's hand and prayed that they would be together forever.

The only consistent part of Joe's life was that he had always helped support his family. The idea of having a family of his own —the enormity of it, the down-right crushing expectation that he might be responsible for his own wife and children someday nearly choked him. It was Helen he wanted, damn it. He wondered how he could even think of asking her to spend her life with him since he hadn't any money. The only thing he could depend on was his family and they could barely keep their own bellies fed.

The future was so uncertain that he couldn't promise her a thing. He was afraid that it might be best to give her a way out, even if he had to suffer for it. If he truly loved her, it was what he should do. She could find a guy with better prospects for a future. Besides, she still had two more years of high school to finish.

Helen was ready to start living. In truth, she wanted a little bit of what she saw in magazines, some glamour and fun; and she was so tired of watching every penny. Like her father, she wasn't afraid of much. After all, what's the worst that could happen? If you could laugh it off, nothing could ever really get you down. And Joe was a handsome, sweet man who said he loved her. She wouldn't need to worry about the way he would treat her. He'd do his best to take care of her . . . as long as he never had to choose between her and his family.

August 13: *Dear Helen,*

I was awfully foolish talking to you about the idea of getting married. You need to go back to school this fall. You need an education that will put you in a class above mill hands like me. So let's just be friends for nothing can be gained by being otherwise. I am Sincerely yours, Joe (Bye-Bye)

Please Be Mine

Palouse and Potlatch, 1930

Helen read the letter for the third time and threw it to the floor. "Oh no you don't!"

Dear Joe,

You might not think you are good enough because you work in a mill but look around! Even if your hours are cut, you have a job! That is success these days! I'm telling you that you are good enough and that I love you, and if you don't ask me to marry you, you will be sorry for the rest of your life! Hard times should be spent with those you love. Helen

With Helen's letter, Joe's heart soared. It nearly hurt to fly so high after it had been dragging on the ground since sending his goodbye letter, even knowing that he couldn't get along without her, that she carried his every thought and dream. He thought he'd be alone.

As with any big decision, he talked with his mother. She was kneading bread as he sat at the kitchen table holding a hot cup of coffee.

"Is there anything wrong with her?" she asked, looking over her shoulder.

"Not that I can tell. A little feisty, I guess." He grinned.

"Does she make you happy, son? Do you love her?" She wiped the itch on her nose with her shoulder.

"Yes, I do," he said more firmly than he expected.

"Then what's the problem, dear? You must know that we want you to be happy. You deserve to be happy. Your father and I will suffer if you're not." She wiped her hands on a towel and squeezed his shoulder before going to get the laundry off the line. "Ask the Lord if you're not sure," she said. "I'll pray for you to know what to do."

September 2: *Dear Helen,*

You be sure to be home tomorrow at noon because I'm coming over and its real important. Tommy is going to school this fall and wants me to lend him money, but I won't. Everyone sure claims that I'm nuts, well maybe so, but I don't care. Don't forget. September 3rd, noon. All my Love, Your Old Man, Joe

Joe held a simple silver band as he got down on one knee on Helen's front porch, surrounded by her mother and siblings, and asked her to marry him. "I love you, Helen. It won't be easy. I promise to do my best, and I figure we could get along okay if we're together. I wonder if you might be willing to be my wife." His heart beat in his ears as he waited, hoping her father wouldn't show up, thinking that he would let nothing interfere with this moment. He'd knock her father out if he needed to, though that probably wouldn't be a good way to fit in with the family.

Helen waited, keeping her face frozen with a blank look. Then she exploded with a laugh, "Finally!" She wrapped her arms around him and knocked him over backwards onto the porch. "Yes!" She planted her mouth right on his kisser, leaving him weak.

"Whew!" Joe breathed, sitting up. "Thought you might say 'No' for a minute there, could've been awkward with an audience and all."

Helen froze. "Wait, you're not doing this cuz I wrote that you'd be a fool if you didn't, are you?"

Now he gave *her* a blank look, and she tensed. "Naw, I wanted to ask you, just didn't want you to have a hard life, that's all."

She pushed him back down again. "When?"

"Now?"

Helen sent her brother to Phillip's store to tell them she wouldn't be coming to work. "Tell them I'm getting married!" she gushed. She hurried to gather her things. By the time she had her best dress on, a light blue remake with some lace across the neckline, her brother was back with a wedding gift from her employer. It was a white satin nightgown. Helen sobbed for a moment, thankful for a store-bought something for her new life.

As Joe was about to drive away in his brother's car with Helen and her mother, he saw her father leaning against the corner of the house.

"Maybe you'd better go see him," he motioned with a lift of his head.

Out of the car, Helen ran up to her father. "I'm getting married Daddy! Are you happy for me?"

His face changed from discouraged and droopy as if gravity were stronger there into a relaxed smile. "Yes, darling, so very happy for you," and he put his heavy arms around her and whispered in her ear. "You go, be happy."

In that moment, Helen realized how distant her father had become and how isolated he must have felt while trying to keep food on the table. Tears flooded her eyes. She wanted him to be happy too. She wanted her confident, boisterous, fun-loving daddy back, but this wasn't the time. This was her time.

Joe noticed her shoulders slumped the tiniest bit as she came back to the car and wondered about it as they drove away to Moscow, Idaho. At city hall, Ida surprised Helen with a nosegay of blue and purple asters from her garden for Helen to hold, and Joe and Helen were married by a justice of the peace, lickety-split, just like that.

There were no bridesmaids, no pictures, no music, no dancing, no cake, no champagne. That night, their honeymoon was spent at Joe's one-bedroom family home in Potlatch. Joe's parents had been asleep when the newlyweds arrived, and they gave up their bed. It was still warm when Helen crawled in.

Making Do

Potlatch, Idaho 1930

"Get up and fix me some breakfast, woman!" Joe called from the kitchen with a steaming cup of coffee in his hand.

"No! Make it yourself! I'm staying in bed!" Their bed was in a corner of the living room with a curtain separating them from the family. She'd been trying to pull her own weight and help out, taking in laundry and doing simple sewing for folks in the neighborhood, making fudge and peanut brittle to sell from a little shelf at the Potlatch Mercantile. Alice was gone for the day, caring for an elderly couple, and the idea of a leisurely morning seemed like a dream.

"This is when you show your husband how much you love him," he smiled, drawing back the curtain and pulling her from the bed.

Helen refused to go, holding onto the bed covers and dragging them with her as he pulled her onto the floor and across to the kitchen. "You brute!" she laughed, sitting among her blankets.

Joe knew better than to try to force her to do anything. She would refuse based on principle. He sat down with her on the kitchen floor and wrapped his arms around her, nestling his face into her neck where he began to nibble.

"Guess I'll need to eat your neck then," he mumbled. "I'm sorely hungry and I know you want me to keep up my strength."

Later, as they stood together in front of the woodstove and she leaned back against him, feeling his warmth and stability, she could only think of one word to say, "Eggs?"

October 3: *Dear Helen, Potlatch*

We miss your noise. It's so hot, everything has burnt up in the garden. Dad has worked better than a week now, and I've been selling two gallons of milk per day, but no one has had a check yet. The new store Penney is opening tonight for inspection. Dad needs new tires so bad for the car now that he drives to work. Love & Kisses to All as they are free anyhow, Mother, Palouse

Scrimping became serious. The new motto, *use it up, wear it out, make it do, or do without,* helped Ida solve the problem of worn-out socks. She sewed the top of the sock closed, cut the bottom open, gave it a finish edge, and her boys wore them upside down.

Clarence's boots were another matter. It took the investment of 20 cents for a pair of rubber soles from the Five and Dime store and the rubber cement glue to attach them to Clarence's boots. His were worn-out, filling with muck every time he tramped out to the barn, which was often.

She wished for enough energy and gumption to take daring steps like some women, like the woman who convinced a landlord to rent a house to her in exchange for her promise. It was a large house across the street from the train station, and she hoped to turn it into a hotel. The landlord gave her two months to try. She scrubbed every inch of the house and borrowed linens and nearly panicked with no business for six weeks. Then a man knocked on her door and asked if he and his crew of ten could stay there. They would be installing the telephone lines in town, and it would take several weeks.

October 26: *Dear Helen, Potlatch*

How I wish we had steady work. Dad hasn't made cider yet. You don't need a coat anyhow. Put a new collar on your old one. Cheer up, laugh, be gay and save your dough for something more needed. It is surprising how much we can get along without. We are going to see harder times. Even stamps get scarce. If we only have love, love and a home and family, we'll be alright. Lots of Love and Kisses, Mother

October 29: *Dear Helen, Potlatch*

Heavens, Helen, don't have a family for a few years if you can help it. Then is when your bills pile up. Got our spuds in the cellar and all my jars full so I won't starve. All we hear is hard times. The work camps are all closed yet. I'm piecing together a girl's quilt. If you have any print pieces you could spare, could you pass them along? Love, Your older Sis, Marie, Hamilton, Washington

November 12: *Dear Helen, Potlatch*

Sorry to hear that your mom is sick. You are young to get married. Always have your meals ready and always have your work done up and don't ask too much of your husband for if he makes ends meet in these times, you have lots to be thankful for. Love, Aunt Minnie

On a Sunday afternoon in December, Joe drove Helen in his brother's car to see her family. She held tins of Christmas cookies and candy on her lap, Christmas presents for her brothers and sister. She was anxious to see them all. After squeals and laughter and hugs and jokes about married life, she noticed that her mother had not gotten off the couch. She looked pale and thin.

"My cough keeps up," Ida said. "I don't want you or anyone else to catch it."

Helen sat beside her. "I'm strong and healthy, Mother. I need to be here to help you more."

"Nonsense. The other children can help me. Maybe having more chores will keep them out of trouble."

Helen wasn't surprised by her mother's tears when she held her hand and told her that she was pregnant. She assumed they were happy tears.

Ida squeezed her daughter's hand, hoping she'd know how happy she was. She secretly wondered if she would be there to hold the baby when it arrived. One thing for sure, she wasn't up to making baby clothes, and that truth was painful.

Helen's birthing pains began in the night. Joe got out of bed and shoved wood into the cookstove, having been told there would be a need for boiling water. John was reluctant to leave his bed, knowing that it would be hours of sleep lost. Alice managed to get him moved to the bed behind the curtain so she could prepare the bedroom with extra linens. Helen decided to make fudge.

"What are you doing?" Joe asked as she clanged a pot onto the stove.

"Making fudge, of course," Helen said, stirring. "Don't want this hot fire to go to waste."

"It's for the birthing," Joe said. "I don't think that's a waste."

Helen rolled her eyes. "Well that's not what I meant. I mean we want to make as much good use of it as we can. It's the perfect heat for fudge and I don't know when I'll be up to making it again. Besides, maybe it will help keep the doctor's bill down if we sweeten him up a little."

Alice came into the kitchen. "Leave her be, son. She needs a distraction for a while if she can find it."

The fudge was nicely cooled and half-eaten when Helen's pains stopped her ability to think. She closed her eyes and knew it was time. "Doctor, Joe, but wrap up that fudge for him first."

During labor, Helen thought about her mother missing her and cried that she didn't want to have a baby, that the child would just grow up and want to get married and move away. Their daughter, Barbara Jo, was born anyway under the supervision of the doctor who happily munched his fudge while Joe and John paced on the little porch outside the window.

Alice placed the tiny bundle into Joe's arms. He could hardly see through his tears as he looked down at her. "My darling, beautiful daughter," he said, kissing the top of her head. *Lord God, protect this child through whatever is ahead for her.*

Thankfully, the family had avoided the Spanish Flu and the Iron Lung—the treatment for polio. It was consumption, also known as tuberculosis, that grabbed hold of Ida. Whenever Helen could leave the baby at home, she rode the train to Palouse to care for her mother. With no money for medical care, Ida slowly wasted away with fever, coughing and spitting up blood while Helen and her sister wiped up the red mess and tried to comfort her the best they could.

Helen grieved deeply. She felt swept down a river. Her older sister was on the other side of the state with husband and children of her own. Her youngest brother was still a child. Who would take care of him now? She saw a page of her life turning; it had been entitled "Possibility," now the page became "Acceptance." She moved back to Palouse with Barbara Jo to care for her younger brothers and sister. The Potlatch mill had failed, and Joe was frantically looking for work.

To Helen, Palouse

Dearest, Nothing's going on in Potlatch. The mill won't start up again unless the dam goes out in Lewiston. Ed and I were offered a thru-ride to Spokane, so we went for fear we'd have to walk otherwise. I need to find something here. Goodbye, Joe, Spokane.

Beyond the Limit

Millwood, Washington 1932

Thank the Lord, Joe's brother James Roy was re-hired part-time back at the Inland Empire Paper Company in Millwood, and the whole family went. There were more possibilities for employment there since it was closer to the big city of Spokane, the busiest freight and passenger train terminal west of Chicago. The population had been growing since advertising had attracted new residents to the city near "76 lakes" including "majestic Long Lake dam with falls higher than Niagara." Mt. Carlton had also had a name change to Mt. Spokane, considered more appropriate for luring people to the area. Helen shook her finger at her family in Palouse before she went, assigning each of them chores, including her father. It was all she could do.

Joe's family moved into a ramshackle three-bedroom house under the railroad viaduct in Trentwood, east of Millwood, an area vulnerable to the homeless who dropped off the train as it passed. John wasn't prepared for the dangers of their new location, and a drunk, senseless intruder got the best of him. Beaten to unconsciousness, he ended up in the hospital. Alice rode the bus to be with him every day while Helen tried to handle the house. Then they nursed him at home; but he carried the shadow of that beating even after his recovery.

Joe and Helen did their best, taking Barbara with them to pick strawberries in season at Tom and Ella Quinn's farm, and becoming good friends with the Quinns. Barbara looked like she'd been in a bloody accident most days by the time they got her home, covered in strawberry juice and mud.

While Joe looked for odd jobs, Helen took in laundry, did ironing and mending. Some days she felt her arms might fall off, hefting buckets and baskets, turning the handle on the wringer washer, hanging it all on the line to dry. When Fels Naptha soap made her hands nearly raw, she switched to gentler Ivory Snow.

She collected S&H Green stamps, gluing them into a collector's book to get free items from the Sperry and Hutchinson's catalog. Betty Crocker coupons piled up in a kitchen drawer, and she stared at the catalogue, hoping for a matching set of flatware in her future.

When sweet Suzanne was born with a serious heart problem, slightly cold and a tinge of blue in her complexion, Helen found a new level of love. Suzanne needed more, she was fragile, and Helen gave her own heart, hoping it would keep her daughter warm and well. Her daily chores were accomplished absent-mindedly then, like an abstract puzzle, as she focused on her delicate daughter.

Joe's clenched gut relaxed a bit when he finally got on at the papermill with James Roy, but the wage was too low to get by. So after putting in the night shift at the mill, he shoveled coal from a gondola for a fuel company during the day. The pay was 35 cents per ton.

He tried to keep their home a happy place. Even though exhausted when he stopped for sleep and a meal, he always put on a smile and sang a song for his girls. It was his way of making up for being gone so much, for life being hard. *"Oh Hel, oh Hel, oh Helen please be mine . . .*

It was before dawn on a misty, cold morning on Joe's first week at the coal bin. The crunch of his shovel into coal was the only disturbance of quiet. He breathed heavily as he worked, mist from his breath blending with the rest as he thought about money, trying to add up the bits of income from two jobs in his mind. His shovel hit something unmoving within the coal, and he lifted the lantern to see, smelling the unmistakable fumes of liquor. A man in an ivy cap with his collar up came out of the shadows.

"Hey, you're not Bill!" the man said.

Joe's head snapped up to see who it was but could only make out the reflection of the lantern in dark eyes. He waited, wondering what was next.

"What happened to Bill?"

"Hell if I know." Joe held onto his shovel, a weapon if he needed it.

"Well look, we had a deal with Bill. Our liquor comes in the coal delivery once a week. If you walk away when you've got enough coal cleared out of the bin that I can get at it, have a cigarette or something, there'll be a few bucks waiting for you when you get back."

Joe pushed the front of his hat up a bit, more space for thinking. Scratching his head, he couldn't get past the words, *a few bucks*. "Do you want me to leave the shovel or take it with me?"

When the papermill needed to cut his hours on the night shift, they apologized for it, explained that they had no choice. Joe shoveled coal, thanking God for what he *did* have and asked for protection for his family, especially for Suzanne who needed it most. The extra cash he found at the coal gondola once a week was not enough. He needed more.

He found it on a house-building crew and told them that he wanted to put in as many hours as possible. That was fine by the crew boss since the big pay-off came at the end of the job, the sooner the better. Now Joe pushed himself for even longer hours. His body became accustomed to constant movement and his mind became numb with exhaustion. The songs and smiles stopped.

Helen's concerns included her husband now. Joe had lost weight, had become pale, was quiet more than before. She stopped telling him about her worries for Suzanne and medical bills, tried to only say positive things like "that rose bush your mother's been tending has bloomed."

On Sunday morning, John and Alice left for church at Millwood Presbyterian, and Joe planned to put in an extra day at the house construction site. Helen was rinsing out a diaper when it got away from her, swirling down into the toilet, plugging it. Eight people in the house and one toilet; it was an emergency.

"I'm so sorry!" she cried to Joe. "There's a diaper plugging the toilet. I'm just so sorry."

Without a word, he removed the toilet and doggedly carried it out to the yard where he poked the diaper through with a stick. Helen had been washing dishes when she noticed that the toilet had been reinstalled and Joe had left without saying goodbye.

She knew he would be at the jobsite alone that day and would probably be there until dark. That afternoon, she made a hot plate of his favorite meal, ground beef patty, mashed potatoes and gravy, cooked carrots and a thick slice of bread with butter to take to him, hoping he'd understand how sorry she was about the diaper.

It was quiet when she got there to deliver it, no hammering, no sawing, nothing. "Joe," she called as she looked around the framed walls. "Joe?"

She found the remainder of his lunch. She didn't find *him*. Panicked, she thought he'd been attacked by a transient, but his wallet and tools were still there on the floor. It didn't make sense. Then she saw a loop of rope hanging in the middle of the construction. Someone had tied a noose. It swayed slightly in the breeze from the ceiling joist as if it were trying to attract a victim. Her hand flew to her mouth as the dinner plate shattered on the floor. Joe was gone.

Irrigating Palouse

Eastern Washington wheat prices had gone from $1.83 per bushel in 1920 to 67 cents in 1930 to 38 cents in 1932, and the value of farms was dropping to less than half their 1920 value. Mills closed or cut back to smaller crews with fewer hours of work. Those who were lucky enough to keep a job would earn only 36% of their previous pay. In 1932 the *daily* wage in mills was $2.60. Folks lost their homes and Hooverville communities developed, people living in shacks made from whatever scraps they could find.

Clarence tried to care for his three children at home after Ida's death, but the truth was, he was in trouble. How could he make ends meet and watch over the children at the same time? Who would keep him and them from falling off the cliff now that Ida wasn't there, and Helen was gone? He commiserated at the still, drowning his sorrows.

He did his cooking at night so no one would see the smoke, but he got sloppy with his leftover sour mash after he'd boiled the alcohol off. There was a lot of it since it took sixty gallons of mash to make six gallons of whiskey, and he was running out of places to bury it. He'd read about the explosion in Butte, Montana, the manhole covers blowing sky-high and coming down with a clang. A moonshiner had dumped so much mash into the drainpipes that it had plugged the sewer and continued to ferment until it had blown. Someone could have been killed. He didn't want to be responsible for something like that, so he'd begun to bury his mash at night on the neighbor's property.

Henry, a neighbor, woke to find his livestock and feathered foul sprawled on the ground, semi-conscious with foamy residue on their beaks and muzzles. "Hey Clarence!" he called, pounding on the door. "You've killed my stock!"

Clarence came to the door red-eyed after a long night and looked up at Henry. He'd forgotten what a big guy Henry was. Then he looked across the yard and rubbed his eyes to look again. "Are ya sure they're dead, Henry? I'm think'n they just found a treat for themselves last night. Maybe I didn't bury my mash deep enough."

"Gawd dammit Clarence! They'd better recover or you're gonna pay for 'em!" He turned to walk away.

"I'm awful sorry," Clarence said, though he thought it might have been a lie. He really had nowhere else to put the mash since he didn't want to get caught hauling it out of town. "I'll keep it on my own property next time," *or bury it a lot deeper.* "Hey, maybe your milk and eggs will be sweeter for a time," he called.

Henry turned to sneer at him. So far, Henry had seemed empathetic with his situation, the death of his wife, but Clarence could see that he was growing tired of his industriousness.

There was a little help available in the community through

the Red Cross and the Salvation Army. The Salvation Army sold enough doughnuts to be able to offer them for free with coffee to the needy along with a place to read, write, shower and shave. Clarence would rather continue with his moonshine activities than be obliging to anyone. Only half the people of this "Great Experiment" thought liquor should be outlawed, and he didn't feel guilty about supplying the needs of the other half. What was the harm? He'd be damned if he would lose his house or have people feel sorry for him.

He *was* lonely, so he enlisted the help of a widow who lived down the block, black-haired Betty. There was also a blonde Betty in town, but she was a hooker. He took a bottle of his brew to black-haired Betty and sweet-talked her like he always could into spending time with him, eventually coming and going from her house as if it were his second home. She helped him feel whole, worthy of a happy life.

He found temporary work on one of the few local farms that was able to operate, and he thought he might slow down his moonshining, spend more time with the children and with Betty too. The children were not as content as he was, however. Perched on the front porch, they took turns peering down the road in the direction that he would come home from work. They were hungry and he would have groceries. At last, they saw him walking toward the house, groceries in hand, and their tummies rumbled. Then he turned down the block and took the groceries to black-haired Betty instead. The children not only cried; they were angry.

Within a week, federal "dry" agents from Spokane arrested him in a sting for trying to sell them two gallons of moonshine.

They found another six gallons at his house but not his still. It was bound to happen, him moonshining so close to home and for so many years. "Stop 'Irrigation' Work in Palouse" was the headline in the Spokane Chronicle that reported his arrest. The Feds turned him over to county officials for prosecution. Although counties tried to give a sentence of a year and a day, just long enough that the state would bear the expense of incarceration rather than the county, Clarence received a sentence of thirty days and a $100 fine. There were children at home to consider.

He might have re-thought his decision-making while doing time, but he was eating pretty well in jail, and his children were eating better than ever. Ages ten to fifteen, they were old enough to take care of themselves and their bill at the local grocery store was paid by the generous Palouse community.

Upon his release from jail, Clarence couldn't wait to get back to black-haired Betty. He let himself into her house as usual and saw a whiskey bottle waiting for him on her kitchen table like a welcome-home gift. Delighted to see it, he grabbed the bottle and tilted it to his mouth for two giant gulps before realizing that it wasn't whiskey. It burned. It choked him. He gasped for air. He vomited and shook. It was DDT.

Betty had mixed her insecticide DDT in that bottle and left it on the table. All the households were using DDT. It was supposed to be safe. The advertisements for it had pictures of babies and read, "No flies on me thanks to DDT." There was concern that flies carried polio, and polio was rampant. Households were encouraged to spray DDT frequently around the outside of the house with the windows open.

Betty must have known that Clarence was getting out of jail.

Didn't she think he would want a drink as soon as he got out? Clarence would die of cancer a few years later, but that was probably just a coincidence.

Queenie

Millwood and Spokane

Helen was in shock. Her life had gone radically wrong. At night, with the girls asleep beside her, when the house was quiet and she had a moment to herself, she bit her lips closed to keep the sobs from erupting, the thin walls providing an echo effect rather than privacy. She muffled them into her pillow until some of the fear and anger and sadness leached away. Bits of fitful sleep presented the noose swinging from the ceiling joist, and when she woke, she knew that he'd had no choice. There was no earthly way that Joe would have left if he could have stayed.

The family searched for him all along the hobo camps and food lines and train tracks and the river. After two days, Tommy contacted the police. The police officer shook his head, saying they would keep an eye out. A lot of the country was on the move, riding freight trains to look for work, and he didn't think they'd be very lucky in their search. "You know how many husbands and fathers are 'missing' these days?" he asked.

John felt pretty sure that if Joe was gone, really gone, he had left on a train. Trains were coming and going in and out of

Spokane constantly in different directions. He couldn't begin to know where to start looking.

It was Alice who kept them steady, pouring coffee, laying her warm, reassuring hand on Helen's shoulder, helping with the little ones. Quietly, she said to her men, "If Joe's hurting, he'll go someplace where he'd feel better. Where was he happiest, do you think?"

"With the horses," they said together.

Tommy asked the police to send notice to officials in Idaho and Montana, and James Roy sent a telegram to the ranch where they had worked in Havre. A telegram came back, saying they hadn't seen him, but would keep their eyes open.

Not knowing if Joe would ever come back grabbed at Helen like a claw. It had been that damn diaper that broke him. If she hadn't let it slip from her fingers, he would still be there. It was her fault.

She knew they were in trouble. She wasn't afraid to get a job, might even look forward to it if she knew her girls were well cared for. Alice agreed to that responsibility, and Helen found a position with Armours on East Trent, a meat-packing company. Her job was part-time on the night shift in the butchering area. With high rubber boots and gloves, she stood with a cold-water hose, cleaning out cow bellies as they came through on hooks. The rubber on her hands and feet did nothing to keep out the cold. At the end of her shift, her feet, hands and joints hurt as much as her back. As she shivered, waiting for the bus to get back to Millwood and walk home, she was thankful for the job, but she doubted she would ever be warm again.

Every day as she traveled to and from Armours, she looked for Joe. Spotting someone the correct height and build, her heart would race, and she'd hurry to get a look, hopeful. Each time she'd sigh and turn away. In her sleep, she continued to search and would sometimes wake in tears, having seen his body along the river in her dreams.

Her mind bounced: thankful for family, angry with Joe; loving him, knowing he was a good man who loved her, then wondering if he'd found someone else, maybe found an easier life without her and the girls. It was exhausting.

Eventually, her job was changed to the day shift, full time. She was to make wieners, which ended her ability to eat them. A preserved meat aroma accompanied her home each night, and when the processing or refrigeration failed, and the stench of rancid meat filled the air for a mile around the factory, she couldn't seem to get the stink washed out of her hair and clothes. At least she was not standing in freezing water any longer.

As she got to know her co-workers, she found friends. They called her Queenie, queen of the wieners; she was one of the four women in her section of twenty men. "How are you to-day, Queenie?" they'd ask. "Tell us another story about Palouse," they'd say. She got them laughing with stories about her child-hood, about Blackie and Laddie, the hired hands, her father's moonshine and her mother's temperance activities. "Tell us about Joe," they'd say, and her throat would close.

One cold, wet night at the bus stop, the frigid wind was blowing rain down her collar no matter how tightly she held it closed. A co-worker stopped in his car to offer her a ride home. She gladly accepted. It was the beginning of a friendship, the first African American she had ever known.

Gone

Joe was confused. He'd been wandering for a while and couldn't get his mind right, as if something had cracked. His brain felt dull, numb. He didn't know what he should be doing, only had a sense that there was something important to do, and he couldn't figure out what. It was as if he walked in darkness, worn out, weights dragging from his legs.

On the other side of Trent Avenue, he saw a train sitting on the track, a boxcar with its door slightly open. It seemed familiar, inviting. It was empty and cool inside and there were a couple other guys there. They told him to "have a seat," and "did he need anything?" Feeling vulnerable, Joe climbed in, pulled his jacket close, put the collar up, and sat against the wall, shaking his head, "No."

As the train started to move traveling east, the *thrunk, thrunk* rhythm of the track began to play, and the boxcar swayed from side to side as it picked up speed. Joe felt the tension in his back and legs and stomach begin to let up and he fell asleep as if he were a babe being rocked in his mother's arms.

He woke with someone toeing his leg. "Hey pal, wake up. You

okay? Train's not going anywhere for a few days. Looks like you oughta get yerself someth'n to eat."

Joe looked around to find himself in a boxcar and realized that he was, in fact, famished. Following the stranger, they walked into town. The sign along the track read "Havre." Joe thought there was something familiar about it.

"What's your name?" the stranger asked as they walked, offering him a piece of jerky.

Joe thought about it and couldn't come up with anything. "Hell if *I* know," he said, nearly choking on his jerky. His mouth went dry.

"You forgot yer name?"

"Guess so." Joe's eyes were big, panic rising.

The stranger patted him on the back. "You'll be okay. Eat some of that jerky and maybe it'll come back to you."

Joe chewed, willing saliva to come into his mouth. The salt was good. It was good to have something to think about. He thought about the salt in his mouth, the chewing action of his jaw as he followed the stranger. He thought about his feet moving one in front of the other. He pushed his panic back. He thought about the stranger.

"Your name?" Joe asked.

"Hap," the stranger said. "Most people call me Hap. I'm usually a pretty happy guy," he smiled, seeing the worry on the nameless man's face. "Say, I got me a short-time job on a ranch here. You wanna tag along? Maybe they'll have work fer you too. Only way I can think of ta help ya right now."

Joe shrugged, feeling the sun's heat on the back of his neck and kept walking, not knowing what else to do. "Thank ya."

At the ranch, Hap told Joe to hold up a while so he could talk to the ranch foreman. Joe wandered over to the horse barn and found himself in a particular horse stall, talking to the beast, examining her leg. She had been injured. *Maybe a snake bite?* he wondered. Joe talked to her and brushed her hide and rubbed her neck. He could see her relax and he relaxed too. Her eyes softened. He was talking to her when the ranch foreman came in with Hap trailing behind.

"I reckon you have a way with horses," the foreman said.

Joe turned with a blank stare. "Seems that way."

"That horse doesn't let anyone in her stall. How about if you come out of there and see what you can do in the corral."

Joe walked to the corral and climbed between the boards of the fence. A dozen horses spooked away from him, into a corner. He wondered if they were wild as they pranced back and forth, agitated. The largest, a palomino stallion, reared up in front of the group, pawing the air over Joe's head. Slowly, he lifted his arms like Moses parting the sea and waited, making quiet talk. The horses stopped and listened, all ears turning toward him. Joe continued slowly, murmuring his sweet talk. The stallion huffed and puffed. Joe was patient. He put his hand on the horse's muzzle and stroked his neck.

"Tell ya what," the manager said. "I'll give ya dinner tonight and a bed in the bunkhouse, and after breakfast, we'll see what you can do around here. What da ya say?"

Joe nodded, stepping forward to shake on it. "Thank ya, sir. Much obliged."

"Ya need a name. What'll we call ya?"

The three men looked at each other. "He got on the train

in Spokane, just off of Trent," Hap said. "How 'bout we call ya 'Trent' for now?"

Joe nodded, "Ok by me, I guess." It didn't seem wrong, but it didn't seem right, either.

Joe was asleep through the noise and racket of the early morning bunkhouse. Hap had to roust him. "Hey Trent," he shook Joe's foot. "You'd better get out there and show the foreman what you can do if you wanna stay on here."

He woke dazed, confused, lying in bed with his clothes on. He thought he'd been talking to Jesus, something about the brokenhearted. Once he remembered Hap and where he was, he ate a little oatmeal and a few swallows of coffee and went out to the corral. He looked out across the valley and to the mountains. His greatest desire was to get on a horse and ride, but he didn't know where he'd go. Hap told him which mount to saddle. There were fences to mend and they'd be working together.

Hap *was* a happy guy. He whistled a tune as they repaired fence on down the line, eventually telling stories that made Joe laugh. It felt like grease to his dried-up brain, softened the pressure in his head, lightened the angst in his stomach. They got back to the bunkhouse as coffee was being poured from the pot.

"You guys wanna cup o' joe?"

Joe's head snapped up. His heart quickened. Breath caught. "Joe," he said. "My name's Joe! I think."

A Holiday

Millwood and Spokane

The days started getting colder and shorter, and Helen decided it was time to see downtown Spokane. At the end of her workday, she stepped up into a streetcar. The conductor with his high collar and cap sat in the middle where she deposited her 5 cents and sat on a bench. As they traveled, it made a click-clack sound. The motorman sat on a small stool in front, driving the car and operating the controls, clanging a loud bell if something got in his way.

She craned her neck to see everything she could out the windows. Spokane had been slow to feel the effects of the Depression, and there had been so many new buildings built the previous few years that it felt like encouragement to see them. The Paulsen Building, City Ramp Garage, Fox Theater, The Chronicle Building, Montgomery Ward, Sears & Roebuck, Kress Dime Store, and Chamber of Commerce building—all had recently been built. The Crescent and J. C. Penney had been downtown for many years.

Co-workers had told her about the inside of The Crescent, a

sea of glass counters reflecting golden light with attractive clerks waiting to help, and all that merchandise. Just to walk down the aisles would be a grand treat, too swanky for her current situation.

The streetcar took her past George's Lunch Counter and Oyster House, Bob's Chili Parlor, the Davenport Hotel, the Clemmer Theater, and the art deco Fox Theater. She'd been to plays and a few picture shows back in Palouse but hadn't had time or money to go since. Fox was a "million-dollar" movie and concert palace with a sixty-foot-wide sunburst decorating the auditorium and a grand stairway that wrapped around up to the second floor, currently showing *The Maltese Falcon* with Humphrey Bogart.

Helen wished she could see something with Humphrey Bogart or Clark Gable or Katherine Hepburn, especially Katherine Hepburn. She'd heard about Miss Hepburn's strong roles, how she was high-spirited and independent, raised by a mother who'd fought for women's rights like her own mother. She loved a good story, had fallen in love with *The Great Gatsby*, reading it in bed as the girls slept beside her, imagining the lavishness, wishing the story would never end.

Other passengers pulled the cord above the windows to stop the car and get off now and then. As they walked away, Helen wondered about their lives, if they lived well or if they struggled like most, wondered if they had families who loved them, like she did.

The city scene was exciting, people rushing about, crossing streets as they dodged cars, streetcars and buses, newsboys hawking papers on street corners. She saw determination among the walkers, a grip around the mouth, eyes looking down and away from others, men's coats turned inside out to look a little cleaner or less worn.

Children stood in line to receive milk from the Salvation Army. She thought about how milk always seemed to be the nourishment even if a meal was only left-over popcorn or bread or some crackers. If you had milk, you'd be okay.

Two women sat together across from her on the streetcar. They had cropped hair fixed with finger waves, a blonde and a brunette. Their clothes were fashionable, even though a bit worn. The blonde smiled at Helen.

Helen smiled back. "I like your skirt," she said. "The Elsa Schiaparelli design."

"Thank you," the blonde replied, looking surprised. She turned her leg with the big, clunky zipper down her skirt to show it off.

Helen wondered if they were dancehall girls. They got off the streetcar together in front of the New Washington Hotel. She thought she saw Joe there and propelled herself off the streetcar, her heart hammering as she pushed through people to touch him on the back. "Joe?"

A man turned around and smiled with nicotine teeth. "Hey, doll," he said, reaching for her. Shocked, she pulled away and was lucky to get back onto the streetcar before it left, her face pinched to avoid tears. She'd gone soft for a moment, thinking it was Joe and that everything would be okay, a fantasy.

Shaking her head as the streetcar continued east on Trent, they passed the old Schade Brewery. It had been vacant for years and she'd heard that the city let vagrants stay there, even set up a soup line. Locals called it Hotel de Gink. Another soup line was at a hotel on east Sprague. She'd read that Albert Commellini, the owner of multiple businesses including the Ambassador Club, had opened a soup kitchen, too. She was thankful that her life hadn't come to standing in line for food.

She and Alice had been inviting a woman and her daughter from their neighborhood to dinner once a week to help them out. Usually, it was stewed tomatoes over macaroni and a little cheese along with bread and tea or coffee. Sometimes they were able to add a bit of baloney "Hoover ham" to the pot. They all enjoyed the visit, a few moments of community.

Helen got home to Millwood a bit later than normal that evening. It felt like she'd been on a tiny holiday, seeing life beyond her own. She knew it was because of Joe's family, his unstoppable father, his positive mother that they were warm and dry and would have a hot, filling dinner. She also knew that she had helped.

On the Road Again

Montana

Joe was getting stronger. Every day he rode the horses, breaking the wild ones, taking care of them. He repaired fence, jawed with the other hands, ate good meals. There were card games and stories and music every night in the bunkhouse and Joe learned that he could play the harmonica and the mouth harp. He found that his toe tapped when music played, and he had to restrain himself from getting up to dance.

A few months went by, and Joe was content, carrying out the rhythm of the day along with the other guys on the ranch. They enjoyed their coffee together. His face weathered and his hands got more callused than normal. He was gaining weight, filling out and was happy to share his dry sense of humor, laughing easily. Often, he would whistle a tune, or a song would come to him. He began to hear himself say "Oh hell." And he wanted to repeat it, "Oh hell," and the angst returned to his stomach.

At a barn dance one evening, the rancher's little daughter asked if he would dance with her. Joe smiled and automatically had her step onto his boots, holding her steady. As they stepped with the rhythm, he looked down at her happy face and was surprised to see a different little-girl's face than he had expected. *I must have . . . or had a daughter,* he thought, and he began to tremble.

In the fall, they branded cattle. Joe found that he could rope pretty well, and when the boys let off a little steam with a home-grown rodeo, he was able to stay on a bull pretty well up until he wasn't. He landed on his head and woke up knowing that something was wrong. He needed to get back, only he didn't know where or why. Hap told him that his brain must have been mending itself.

The morning that Hap told him that he'd be moving on and that their work was done, Joe was quiet. He'd been offered a job to stay if he wanted it. He felt his mind try to tighten around a decision whether to stay or go, but he didn't know where he'd go if he went, and he loved it there. Hap gave his goodbye, and Joe shook his hand, thanking him for all he'd done, for helping him out, for saving him, really.

Hap reminded him where he had caught the train off Trent. "Might wanna go back to that point, see if your memory kicks in. You could check in with the police if you really wanna find your home, your people. Course, it could be you escaped a bad situation. Who knows? You've got a pretty good life here . . . On the other hand, sometimes the thing that causes us strife is also what gives us strength, Joe. The possibility of a family is a pretty powerful thing."

During the next week, Joe questioned himself. The weather was getting colder and if he planned to travel, he should do it. He had a little money in his pocket now, could even buy himself a train ticket. What if he left a family who really needed him? He kept the question close, held it against his heart, tried to think of what kind of man he was.

It was a dream that made the difference—a woman with dark eyes and a dimple in her chin calling him Joe and he started up with "Oh Hell" again. This time it became "Oh Helen." He woke up knowing that he was not where he was supposed to be.

Hat on his knee, he sat at a desk with an officer at the police station in Havre who was flipping through pages of reports.

"What month did you say that was?"

"Sometime in . . . Hell, I don't know. It was hot."

He continued to shuffle paper. "Where were you com'n *from* when you stepped off the train?"

"Don't know. That's why I'm here. Hap said it was off Trent. I was com'n from the west."

The officer stopped shuffling. "Well, I think your name just might *be* 'Joe.' You've got a wife and kids, Joe. Your brother Tommy delivered the report that said you were missing."

Joe gritted his teeth. *What the hell am I doing here?* "Does it tell my wife's name?"

"No, sorry. Say, how about if I send a telegram to your address? Let 'em know you're okay."

"Where's that?"

"Millwood, Spokane Valley."

Joe felt odd riding the passenger train. He didn't want to emerge from a boxcar, make his family think he was a bum. He didn't know how to rectify the fact that he had probably failed them, times were so hard for everyone.

He stepped off the passenger train in Spokane and waited, hoping someone would recognize him. Two men walked toward him: one who looked a lot like him and another who was a bit shorter, stockier, with lighter hair. They grabbed ahold of him like he was falling into an abyss and kept him in their arms for a long time. "You're okay Joe. We're your brothers. You're okay now."

Helen was at Armours, feeding the wiener-making machine on the assembly line. No one had told her that Joe might have been found; they wanted to be sure first. When she saw him looking at her through the glass, she froze, wondering if she were imagining things that weren't there. Then she saw Tommy, and her hand flew to her open mouth, wiener machine running amuck. She ran out the door, cap flying, meat juice dripping, and flung herself at him.

He felt her soft hair in his face, her wet tears, smelled lilac beneath the meat aroma. The corners of his mouth turned up, "Hello Helen . . . miss me?"

In a Melody

Millwood and Loon Lake

Dad loved to dance. He taught us girls by keeping our feet on top of his which eventually led to our dancing on our own feet, a fancy fox-trot with turns and switchbacks.

He was strong, could do push-ups with me on his back and break strings that I tied around his bicep by flexing his arm. He delighted us girls by wiggling his ears and taught me to stand on my head in the corner of the vestibule inside the front door where I couldn't fall too far.

He worked for the Union Pacific Railroad and often lived "on the road" which was usually in the caboose to save money. I'd see him pack his carry bag with his tiny green New Testament and know he was leaving for a week or two. Mom said he wore out a pair of dancing shoes when he was at Kellogg, Idaho. They were second-hand shoes, but still. He'd told her that a girl was trying to go to college, and he'd felt obliged to help her out by buying dance tickets from her on a regular basis at the dancehall where she worked.

We were surrounded by train tracks in Millwood with no lights at the train crossings to slow people down, no safety arms. Plenty of warnings though, in the form of accidents and deaths on the tracks.

Dad taught me the signals for the train using a train lantern: swinging it side to side was the signal to stop. It seemed like an important one to know.

When he became a conductor brakeman, I heard him tell Mom that he'd been given a club and was expected to knock hobos off the freight train with it. He had refused and hoped he wouldn't lose his job. He fell off a freight train himself one night as they were coming into Spokane from Montana, slipped off an icy rung as he was going up to the running board on top of the boxcar and cracked his head when he hit. After a few days off, he was put on the passenger line as conductor for the rest of the winter.

We gathered around to admire him in his uniform, watched him polish his watch and tuck it into the tiny pouch at the bottom of his vest. He looked handsome and important in his conductor hat. He told us that the position didn't pay, but he wouldn't need to wade in the snow and set the breaks like he did on the freight train. It would "ruin" him for switching after a winter off. At the time, I did not know how miserable and dangerous his work could be.

We went horseback riding whenever I asked. We'd ride from the stables on north Argonne along the prairie above Bigelow Gulch toward Hillyard. He sang songs as we rode and would sometimes yodel if I'd ask, songs like "Frankie and Johnny" and "I'm An Old Cowhand." He had a song for Mom and each of us girls and recited poetry: Robert Service's "Cremation of Sam McGee," and Robert Frost's "Stopping by Woods on a Snowy Evening." "I have promises to keep, and miles to go before I sleep."

Dad's comfort around animals surprised me. We went to a farm in Chewelah once, a white house and old barn that used to be red. It was somber in the car as we traveled, and it looked like the place had not received attention in a long time. I assumed that someone was sick or had died. Mom went straight into the house, and I watched Dad care for the few animals that were left, a couple old horses that he let me pet and a few goats. He told me to stay behind a fence while he moved a bull from one corral to another. I was afraid for his safety, but he directed the big brute by twisting his tail and they walked together as if they were old friends. I'd thought that bulls were supposed to be mean. This one looked lonely.

Even then, I felt a catch in my throat as we left that farm in its state of decline, knowing there had probably been a happy family and lots of activity there at one time. I hoped there was someone alive who would keep its memories.

It killed Dad to spend money. Two bits was an investment. We'd ask Mom for our 25-cent lunch money to avoid the pained look he'd get if we asked him. Mom would get after him for wearing his shirts until the cuffs were raggedy and for bringing discarded clothes home that he'd found along the train tracks because they still had "life" in them. "That's what I'm worried about," she'd say.

He was one of many who worked for the railroad and got cancer after more than twenty years, a few months short of being able to collect retirement. Dad was 59 when he was too sick to work. He told me that if he could get up to the lake cabin, everything would be alright. We got him there onto the roll-a-way bed on the deck under the lonely fir tree which had become nearly stately by then.

With a belt tied to the foot of his bed, he pulled himself up into a sitting position and I stuffed a bunch of pillows behind him to keep him up. There were flying squirrels in the woods then. They soared between the trees overhead, turning the sunlight red where it penetrated their stretched skin between arm and leg, like wings.

"Remember that time in early spring," I asked. "You were putting the motor on the boat?"

He shrugged.

"You slipped off the edge of the dock and fell into that ice-cold water but kept the motor up high so it wouldn't get wet."

A smile began to form on his face.

"You acted as if nothing had happened, just stayed in that chest-high freezing water and continued to install the motor. You said it was much easier from there anyway and thought you might use that method from then on."

He chuckled.

We watched the lake change in the fading light from crystal blue to a peaceful purple.

He reached over and took my hand.

The sky darkened to dusky violet. A loon popped up out of the water beside the dock and silently swam away, leaving the ridges of his wake to travel behind.

We listened to the quiet, the water lapping back on itself in perfect rhythm along the shore. The loon's call told us that all was well with the world. Dad's last breath brought undeniable, unfathomable, complete peace.

I see you in a melody
Your smile surrounds the beat
Like arms that hold me up
To meet life's challenges.

PART TWO

The Brick and Lime Club

Loon Lake, Washington

1927-1932

Chasing Bats

Mom enrolled me at a young age in square-dance lessons from the Silver Spurs. Later, I danced with the Dixie Chain Gang out on Sullivan Road. Along with high school dances, I went to whatever public or college-campus dance I could find on a Friday or Saturday night, which was how I met my fiancé, at Sunset West.

Evidently, Mom thought that chasing bats was a good initiation into the family. She sent him up onto the steep roof of the lake cabin with bat repellant. He sprinkled it into an empty space that had opened behind the chimney, and I screamed from the ground, dodging bats that swooped in my direction. That relationship lasted about as long as the bat remedy, and she sent my next serious boyfriend up there, too. He repelled the bats and plugged the hole behind the chimney, ending the bat problem. So I married him.

Dennis was a combat Marine, a slightly angry Vietnam vet with a mustache to cover scars from several helicopter crashes. We were married after college graduation, each of us broke from paying our own way. I sewed my wedding dress on a broken machine by moving the wheel by hand. His temporary dental work that had been completed while deployed in Vietnam gave way two weeks before the wedding, so the bit of money we had for a ring went towards his teeth instead.

After the bat remedy, he built a wood deck at the water over a flat patio of arranged rock that had been created many years before, and another deck on the rock ledge above it. He straightened our little turquoise boat house that leaned to the north and removed the rusty metal track and carriage from inside. Rather than shovel out the outhouse when it was full, he offered to move it, not knowing that the entire hillside was granite; but determination, a jackhammer, and some grinding of new teeth took care of it.

Ten years later, when outhouses were outlawed and a sewer system was installed, we hooked up to it and added a tiny bathroom within the 480 square foot cabin. It contained a flush toilet and shower nook, the water coming in hot and cold waves from the lake as dictated by a pump. It was dubbed "the torture chamber."

Tearing off the center of the roof hurt me. It was a complete violation of the little cabin, making it vulnerable to anything and everything, like King Kong had taken a huge bite from it. And cleaning the corners in what had been the attic was far too intimate with filth for me—thick, black cobwebs were like impenetrable fabric. But Dennis created a bedroom up there to be accessed from a ship's ladder and put a roof back on, and the children had some space.

When we decided to make it our year-round home, I made loo-loo-loon sounds at the Loon Lake post office to announce our arrival. The jackhammer was needed again to break through the granite on the uphill side to enlarge the cabin by twelve feet. We hooked up to water and scrambled to winterize the cabin, knowing the temperature could drop well below zero. It was an elevation of only three hundred feet lower than Snoqualmie Pass.

We constantly shoveled snow, sometimes twice a day, throwing it over our shoulders until our paths looked like tunnels. Unprepared with enough firewood for power outages, we used an axe to pound pieces of the neighbor's wood supply away from their frozen pile for the woodstove. It was an adventure, creating thankfulness for warmth and food and family.

We shopped at Brown's grocery in Deer Park, a town of the nicest people we'd ever met. Our first Christmas tree was gifted to us from a lady who sold them from her front yard on Main Street. The kids went sledding down Lakeshore Homes Road and we played family football on the frozen lake.

The first time I heard loud, echoing moans and screeches, whines and warbles, I didn't know what it was, and envisioned Aliens landing on the ice, but it was only the ice squealing as it warmed up. We started a lottery of guessing what day it would break up, not knowing how the web of cracks would come and go and how it could create changing designs, a gradual process unless there was a big windstorm. When it snowed again in March after having lived with it since October, I gave the children permission to use the word "shit" only at home and only when referring to snow, evidence of my desperation. Amazing the sentences that flowed from their giggling mouths.

In May, after cleaning up yard debris, I added more mortar to the rock foundation, starting on the outside, then moving inside to the cellar. Carefully standing between floor joists to avoid hitting my head, I saw writing on the beam in front of me, "Hail Hail The Gang's All Here 1928." I wondered about that gang who built our cabin way back in '28 and I wondered about their story . . . Could they have ever crossed paths with my parents back then?

Washington Brick and Lime

Loon Lake and Clayton, Washington

At Loon Lake, Hank squinted green eyes against the sun's glare as it bounced off the water. Tall, broad and shirtless, he wiped his neck with a red bandana. "That rock," he said, pointing the bandana between the legs of Willie's bib overalls. "That's the one I need to finish the west wall."

"Why do you get to build the shortest wall in the foundation, and I get the highest? It's not even my house." Willie's freckles, constant grin and shaggy brown hair made him look even younger than he was. It was hard to know if he were being serious or cracking a joke.

"You know we're building the houses together, right? It's neighborly." Hank's toffy colored hair flashed copper in the sunlight.

Willie slid, rolled and fought the rock into a sling. "I guess I'm a little sore my house has to be last." He helped Hank lift it onto his back to haul up the hill.

"You were the third one in on this deal, Willie," Hank huffed. "Feretti's the one who created the big plan, and I'm the builder, so that's how it is."

"Without the booze, you've got noth'n," Willie mumbled.

Just before dinnertime, Al Feretti and his girlfriend Liz arrived with bread and a pot of spaghetti. Feretti patted Hank on the back, "You guys do good work. When you gonna get started on my place?"

"You're a hoot, Feretti. Maybe you should help us on this first one," Hank said. "We'll be in business when it's done. Then we'll have the dough to build the second one."

"I *am* helping. What's that you're eating? That's authentic Italian nourishment right there, my friend. You can keep going 'til midnight on that fuel."

"Hey, if you're in on this deal, then you're in," Hank shouted through his meatball, spewing it on the rocks. "That means you also do the physical work. Those rocks in the sling there, they need to be hauled up to the foundation," he motioned with his head and waved a hunk of bread. "We're going twenty feet by twenty-four feet. Get some rock out of the down-hill side so we can have a smooth, lower basement and room to hide the booze. There's a pick there if you need it."

Willie swallowed a huge mouth of noodles. "Did you bring the mortar mix from Clayton?"

"Have I ever let you down, kid?" Feretti replied. "Brought the wheelbarrow for mixing, too. Who's getting water out of the lake?"

Liz stood, "Guess I could do that." She looked out over the lake. "Such a beautiful spot, so peaceful if you guys weren't throwing rocks around." She was glad that she'd worn sensible flat shoes and her pleated skirt gave her plenty of freedom for managing the hillside.

"You don't even know about this place, right, Liz?" Hank hollered, wiping his plate with the last of the bread.

Liz had put on a hard exterior ever since she'd been kicked out of her family's home when she was fourteen years old. She'd only been trying to help with the family income. Now her tough attitude was a survival tactic. "I promised, didn't I?" she scowled.

The guys had met through their jobs at the Clayton brick-yard, The Washington Brick and Lime Company. Clayton was a company town thirty miles north of Spokane with more than four hundred residents, people who didn't quit. In 1908 when a huge fire took every business in town including the brick plant and train depot, Fred Schonfeld, the plant manager at the brick-yard, was distracted by the birth of his son, George, (whose name would become Bud, his little brother's interpretation of 'George'). The next day after the fire, they had carried on with business under tents and canopies in the muddy street despite the steaming, stinking ash; and when townsfolk were asked how they would recover, they shrugged and said everything would be okay. In fact, they thought the railroad would build them an even better train depot than before.

The brickyard's boardinghouse which housed more than fifty men had survived the fire and had been well-stocked. Anyone in town could get what they needed while they recovered and rebuilt. A half-carload of groceries arrived every day delivered by rail on the Great Northern.

Washington Brick and Lime was the biggest employer in the area. They used clay from a giant pit a few miles north of Clayton which was longer than two football fields, four hundred feet wide and twenty-six feet deep, enough to excavate for sixty years. The clay was mixed with silica sand from Mica Peak to make all kinds of brick, terracotta, and stoneware, the largest producer of fire brick in the West. The clay had no grit, so it could be used to create the finest porcelain.

The plant was an impressive sight, sprawled out in what looked like a mile of warehouses and sheds, seven smokestacks reaching 110 feet into the sky from enormous igloo-shaped kilns, some with the capacity of eighty thousand bricks per firing. There were also eighteen smaller smokestacks from the terracotta kilns used for finishing decorative pieces. It looked like a small city. The company produced more than a million bricks per month in their busiest months.

For bricks, the clay mixture was pressed into molds to sit overnight with "WACo" impressed into the finish bricks. After removing them from the molds, the edges were smoothed, and the bricks sat in the dryer.

Feretti was part of an eight-man setting crew who placed the bricks into the enormous kilns to be baked for several days. The crew made rubber gloves from pieces of old innertube from Carl and Ray's service station, cutting a slot for the index and little fingers to protect their hands from shredding. They threw bricks two at a time from the brick cart to a setter like Feretti who placed them in the kiln just so, to fit the most bricks with good airflow until the mind-numbing monotony of the motion caused some wise guy to goose the man in front of him, crashing their progress.

When the bricks were finished, Willie helped wheel them into the fitting shed to be put into crates for shipping. "Bricks a com'n!" he'd holler to Hank over his carpentry work so Hank would tell him where to wheel them. He was the one who made the crates, each order calling for different shapes and sizes. Then the packed crates sat in a building fifty by a hundred feet along the railroad track to be loaded onto a train.

Originally hired at the brickyard for the never-ending job of splitting wood for the kilns, Willie helped wherever he was needed. He was perfect for it, easy to get along with. He grew up in Metaline Falls, where the Pend Oreille River meets Sullivan Creek. It had been a great gold mining location at one time. Now its biggest employer was the Lehigh Portland Cement Company making use of the area's abundant quartz and limestone. Willie's father was a manager there and had hoped that Willie would join him at the company someday, but he was a car guy, a mechanic by nature.

He loved everything about cars, had even created a working automobile out of spare parts. A bit scruffy, in need of a haircut, he was always in dirty overalls, his hands black and greasy. His greatest desire was to have a car repair shop of his own someday, and he worked at the repair shop in Clayton when they needed him, but it was hit and miss.

Metaline Falls was sixteen miles south of the Canadian border below the crossing at Nelway, British Columbia. Willie knew a lot of people all along the border there, people who knew about smuggling liquor, and some good hiding places, too, like the Gardner Cave. The cave was the third longest limestone cave in the state, full of stalactites and stalagmites. He'd heard about the whiskey trails along the border where guys loaded with ten quarts of whiskey in backpacks walked the trails, and the U.S. Customs patrolled by horseback. He'd heard that they had arrested someone called Black Jack Rowden near the border, fined him $200 and put him in jail for sixty days.

When a customer from one of his car repairs bequeathed him a maroon-colored, 1920 Hudson super-six, one of the big, six-cylinder cars, he believed it was a sign. He loved the look of the car, its long, sleek nose of a hood, its manly grill. He started making modifications right away to haul a heavy load, adding hook-ups for attaching portable, overload springs and a reinforced floor and space under the seats for carrying booze. He saved enough to get special tires that wouldn't blow out over a fast fly down a rough road or across a field. After he loaded the car with a tow rope, cannisters of gas and water, and a tire repair kit, as well as a couple of spare tires, he felt like he was ready for just about anything.

Even though the general trend was that rural voters were *for* Prohibition while city dwellers were against it, Willie found that most of the farmers he knew believed that the government should not tell them what to drink or what they could do with their fruit, or anything else on their own property. He approached them to ask about the possibility of their help in a potential rum-running scheme in exchange for some profit for themselves. Times were hard and they were encouraged to take an income from nearly any means to make ends meet.

He and Hank and Feretti worked at the brickyard when there were orders for brick. When they were laid off between jobs because of the stalled economy, they needed to fill the void.

Morgan Park

Loon Lake, Washington

Hank was from the Chewelah valley, twenty miles north of Clayton, where he'd taken care of himself since he was twelve years old when his parents had died of the Spanish flu. With the family farm going back to the bank, he'd been lucky that neighbors had welcomed him into their home. He had tried to be helpful and had found bits of work in the area to contribute financially. Eventually, he'd been hired for odd jobs by Evan Morgan Sr. on Loon Lake.

Morgan owned nearly two hundred fifty acres of lake property that he had purchased from D. C. Corbin who was a railroad builder and banker among other things. He developed his property at the north end of the lake into "Morgan Park," a public recreation center, advertised as "The Most Beautiful Summer Resort in the State."

Morgan Park included a spacious pavilion for dances, a large dining hall out on a pier that could feed one hundred fifty people, a Ferris wheel and merry-go-round, a huge dock that floated out from shore for swimmers and sunbathers. There were camping sites, picnic areas, a baseball diamond, and an area for track competitions. Although hunting for grouse, pheasant, and ducks "to eat when camping" was good in the hills around the lake, a poster of rules that hung in the park asked guests to not shoot within the resort.

Before long, Loon Lake became known as the summer social center for the Spokane area. Merrymakers traveled to and from the lake on passenger trains. In summer, special flat cars with benches were added to transport people to dances, one hundred forty people in three railcars. They left Spokane at 7:30 on Saturday evenings, and passengers could return on the midnight run or on Monday morning at 6:45 if they couldn't manage the night train.

Hank was sometimes hired by Morgan to help build a dock or repair a cabin or a clinker boat. Some knew the boats as clinch boats because of the soft metal nails that were bent at the end to secure them through layers of cedar planking like clapboards on a house. Hank was expected to use the correct materials: white oak for ribs and keel, yellow pine for seats and flooring, brass or nickel fittings, copper rivets, and finished with oil and varnish or three coats of marine paint.

He also kept the large, steam-powered touring boat, *The Gwendolyn*, in good shape. For most people, *Gwen*, named after Morgan's daughter, was more than a boat. It was a sixty-foot-long majestic lady, twelve feet wide with solid brass trimming over black walnut. A hundred passengers could be entertained at a time under its roof during a cruise while an orchestra played onboard, ten cents per ride.

Marathon Dancing

Spokane, Washington

Feretti wanted to convince Liz that he was worth her time. There was plenty of competition for her attention in Spokane. A lot of booze flowed through there and it wasn't hard to find high rollers. With her blonde cropped hair and skinny, slinky dress with heels, she was everything flapper. Talking sassy and hanging onto the arm of a Mr. Somebody was the obvious way for her to live well. He hoped she'd give up her shenanigans in Spokane if she could see a future with him.

He'd first seen Liz at a dance marathon in Spokane. It was one of those events that looked fun on the surface. Underneath, it was a picture of the misery of the times. She was tougher than she looked. From the moment he saw her, he thought he loved her. He'd paid 25 cents each time he could get to the city to check on her, riding the train from Clayton, and was always surprised to find that she was still dancing. She'd been a favorite, flirting with the crowd, unexpectedly doing a little shimmy or Charleston to make the fringe on her dress bounce. Everyone had loved her.

Dancers had to keep their feet moving 45 minutes out of every hour. Liz had tied her wrists together with a bandana and put them around her partner's neck when she was afraid of falling asleep. She'd kept track of her progress by watching the sign on the wall that counted down the disqualified dancers and the other sign that ticked toward breaktime. Nearly unconscious during the fifteen minutes off, friends had rubbed her feet, worked the cramps from her legs and tended open blisters. Feretti had watched when the buzzer rang after eleven minutes and she didn't wake up. A blast of ice water in her face had brought her up fighting.

Daytime music was often from a phonograph, and the dancing tended to be simple movement; but at night there was a live band and show-stopping dance moves, bringing in a huge audience. Liz had turned it on like a flame hitting fuel and more than once, she and her partner had received a silver shower, the audience tossing coins at them. As exhaustion had set in, they'd begun to hallucinate.

Towards the end, their comatose bodies had been carried out onto the dancefloor on cots so the audience could watch them sleep. Feretti had been embarrassed for Liz. He'd thought it was disgraceful, everyone gawking at her with her mouth open, flies buzzing all around her face and neck. He'd felt protective of her, and he hadn't even met her, had only made eye-contact with her from the sidelines every time he came.

Liz had stayed with it for thirty-two days like a trouper, even holding up her partner at the end, valiantly keeping his knees from touching the floor which would have been immediate disqualification. They had come in fourth place, so hadn't earned any prize money. There was silver shower money, though, and they'd been fed twelve times a day: eggs, apples, milk, oatmeal. Liz had even gained a little weight despite all the dancing and needing to keep on dancing while she ate.

She'd been dancing since she was fourteen years old in San Francisco, had learned about it while waiting tables. A customer at the restaurant had told her that she could make twice her waitress wage by dancing. At that time, she would have been called a taxi dancer, ten cents a dance, half for the house. Her family had disowned her for it, so she had vowed to become a free spirit and had moved to a better place to live, Spokane.

She loved to dance but found that some of her partners were foul and smelled horrid. It helped her take on that hard exterior that could break rock. A hand in the wrong place or sour breath in her face, and she was indignant, "Put that hand back where it belongs, or I'll twist it off." "Turn your face away from me and don't come back unless you clean up." "Don't you have any manners?" "Didn't you have a mamma to teach you anything?" "Step on me one more time and I'll give you one of these heels. Your dancing days will be over." Surprisingly, they loved it. Most of them missed their mammas. Liz knew she was developing a habit of being gruff with men and didn't care. Being on your own as a woman was no easy thing.

Now that taxi dancing was outlawed, she was a dance instructor, one client at a time, working at the New Washington Hotel, the customer paying for each dance. She also cleaned rooms on the upper two floors of the hotel where she lived with roommates. They were all dancers, hoping for careers as actresses, though one was a spiritualist who brought clients to their room for sessions.

When she'd been disqualified from the marathon, Feretti had maneuvered through the crowd and glared at the announcer to get close to her, whispering in her ear that he would help her get home. She'd resisted him at first in her sleep, even lifting her heavy arms to beat limply against his chest. He had nearly carried her to her hotel after she'd said where she lived, although he'd had to yell at her a few times to keep her awake and from picking flowers that weren't there.

At her room, he'd learned that she had roommates, lots of them. It had looked like a cobweb of clotheslines draped from wall to wall inside, hanging with stockings and corsets and other unmentionables. A group had been sitting around a small table, holding hands like a seance, all looking in his direction.

Liz had turned to look at him. "Where'd *you* come from?"

"I'm your knight in shining armor, doll," he'd said. "I've gotten you home, anyway."

He would never forget how she had thanked him so sweetly with a kiss on his cheek, the back of her silky fingers flowing across his face, sending tingles down his spine. Then, with a flutter of her cornflower blue eyes on a bloodshot background, she had shut the door.

The Gang's All Here

Loon Lake

Once the rock for the foundation of the cabin was mortared, Hank and Willie secured the top plate and maneuvered the support beams into place. The floor was one step up into the house on one side and six feet above ground on the other because of the slope of the hill, which gave an elevation for a beautiful view of the lake.

It was drizzly the day they raised the walls, rainwater running up their sleeves as they held the walls in place to be secured by Hank. Hank stick-framed the roof, and Willie helped him lay shingles.

Feretti and Liz installed tongue-and-groove siding together, starting at the bottom and working up the walls. It was fun until it wasn't. Feretti enjoyed holding Liz on a ladder as she pounded nails. To get up high, they put a plank between two ladders for a makeshift scaffolding to walk on.

Liz put her hands on her hips, watching as Feretti stepped from a ladder onto the board and saw it bow in the middle.

"The ladders need to be closer together," she said.

"No!" Feretti was frustrated, stepping back to the ladder. "The span's too wide!"

Isn't that what I just said? "Oh, dry up," she said, walking away.

"Hey, what's eating you?"

With Hank's guidance, they framed a row of windows on the water side for an airy sleeping porch and a small window high on the south wall to let in light. They installed a door on the west side, but on the waterside, they nailed boards across the doorframe, not wanting anyone to go out there until they could afford materials for stairs or a deck.

At sunset, Feretti brought out a few bottles of his mother's homemade red and they sat below the cabin under a skinny fir sapling, passing the bottles between them. "We're done!" Feretti announced to the sky as he lifted a bottle.

"We did the first one," Hank corrected.

Feretti pushed against Hank's shoulder. "Well let's enjoy this first success, shall we?"

"As long as we don't forget about my cabin!" Willie saw a faint light coming from Granite Point across the lake and laid on his back to watch the stars begin to show. Bats tripped through the air after their dinners.

Liz grabbed Feretti's chin and gave him a big smooch. She stretched her tired legs out in front of her and waved a hand toward Willie for the bottle. "Hey Hank. Do you have anything other than flannel shirts? That's all I ever see you wear."

"I've only got two shirts. They're both flannel. What's wrong with flannel?"

Liz rolled her eyes though no one saw it. "Nothing, Hank. They're very nice. Don't you get tired of them though? What are they, a uniform?"

"Why would I ever get tired of them? Quit razzing me about it."

Willie took a few more drinks before passing the bottle to Liz. "What kind of grapes are these?" he asked Feretti. "It's got a bite."

"Alicante bouschet. It's all we can get now—big clumps, tough skins make it easier to ship and the really dark color means we can get two, maybe three pressings if we have to."

With both bottles empty, the group got up to admire the cabin, though the hillside slope seemed steeper in the dark. "It's *amazing* what a group can do together," Willie drawled, bumping against Hank. "I love you guys!" He went to hug Hank but met a hand that kept him at arm's distance.

"Let's mark the occasion!" Liz said. Feretti began to unzip his pants, but she produced a thick construction pencil and asked for a light to go into the cellar. With a kerosene lamp, Hank led their way through the low door space, Feretti in the rear forgetting to duck and nearly knocking himself out on the overhead beam at the entrance. He sat on the ground, waiting for the stars to clear from his head.

"You know that song, 'Hail Hail the Gang's All Here'?" she asked. "How about if we write that on this beam here? We *are* all here, after all."

"Sounds good," Hank said. "Add the date."

She wrote in bold print, "Hail Hail The Gang's All Here 1928."

"Seems like we should drink to that!" Feretti called from the ground.

"We need to buy booze first." Hank held up the lamp to see Willie's reaction. The smile was still on his face, just a little bit crooked.

Z Canyon

Clayton and Metaline Falls, Washington

Al Feretti lived with his parents and two brothers in a clap-board bungalow in Clayton. His older brother had lost an arm to the war, and he had operated the cut-off saw at the Deer Park Lumber Company ever since his return. The whole community was proud of his service, thankful to have him home. He was Al's role model for carrying on, for flowing around an obstacle like water rather than to be stopped by it.

Feretti and Leno Prestini were fast friends. Their fathers, both originally from northern Italy, had worked together in the terracotta plant for years, Feretti's father arriving with a group of Italian artisans who had moved north from San Francisco after the big earthquake in 1906. It had been a 7.9 magnitude, destroyed five hundred city blocks and twenty-eight thousand buildings. Killed three thousand people. Half of the population had been left homeless. So they'd moved north and found work at Washington Brick and Lime.

Like his father Luigi, Leno Prestini was a modeler for the terracotta plant, creating everything from sewer pipes to ornamental tiles, cornices and sculptures for architects. Terra-cotta from Washington Brick and Lime decorated the Spokane Club, the Spokesman Review Building, the Masonic Temple, Spokane City Hall, and the Stevens County Courthouse. Most decorative was the Sherwood Building on west Riverside, its crown adorned with pennants and corner gargoyles. Guests of the Davenport Hotel entered beneath a canopy of gargoyles and rams' heads.

The company still pulsated with pride over the 18 three-quarter life-size sculptures the company created in 1924 for sculptor Allen Clark for the Suzzallo Library at the University of Washington. The library, intended to be the soul of the university, displayed the sculptures each atop its own buttress of exterior walls. They represented some of the chief contributors to learning and culture, people like Ben Franklin, Shakespeare, daVinci, Beethoven.

The terracotta plant was separate from the brick-making plant, four-stories tall, forty-eight thousand square feet and employing fifty people. The process was to dry and powder the clay, mix it with pre-fired clay "grog" to control shrinkage, then leave it to cure in a cool place. Leno created a plaster mold based on a drawing, and the clay was pounded into it with fists, then with wet sacks of clay. The piece was turned out, trimmed and dried, then into a kiln at two thousand degrees for up to five days. Parts of large pieces needed to be fitted together.

Hank created the custom crates for shipping. His most recent crates were for the crown decorations of the penthouse of the new fifteen-story Paulsen Dental and Medical Building, the tallest building in Spokane, the city's first art-deco skyscraper.

Leno was an inventor. He made a scuba outfit with his friend Burton so they could look for gold at the bottom of Loon Lake, or maybe it was to get cash out of a car that had gone through the ice the winter before. They created a helmet from a hot-water heater, decorating it with an octopus. Double glass in the faceplate kept it from fogging, and he made an underwater flashlight from a six-cell battery inside an aluminum cylinder with a Model T radiator cap to seal the end. Burton operated a beer-barrel pressure pump to supply air to him within the helmet through a garden hose.

After Loon Lake, they tried their scuba gear on their gold claim below Z Canyon ten miles north of Metaline Falls where the Pend Oreille River did a switchback. From a rickety bridge, they could see Z Canyon. It squeezed the broad river between granite walls to less than twenty feet where it folded over on itself to make two right-angle bends. The water boiled up as high as twenty feet and they could hear giant boulders bouncing around beneath the water. The sound was deafening as they watched the enormous whirlpool swallow a fifty-foot tree like it was a helpless twig. Their gold claim was further downstream where they had a chance against the current.

Leno Prestini was an artist too. When his search for gold didn't pan out, he painted landscapes on the center of his gold pans. He drew sketches of local scenes, quiet landscapes, and cultural fables that he called "calendar art" and created paintings with enough color "to reach out and hit the viewer" on topics like human and corporate greed, the immorality of power politics, and the marginalization of tribal cultures. The coffee would flow when admirers came to see his art, and his thick, dark hair quivered as he waved his arms, dark eyes sparkling as he talked.

The Brick and Lime Club

Loon Lake

Al Feretti stood on the platform that ran the length of the Loon Lake train station. He knew better than to show up in shabby clothes to meet Liz. Instead, he wore a brown second-hand suit and brown fedora. The train pulled into the station with an exhale of steam, and Liz stepped off in her blue paisley handkerchief skirt, the points floating as she walked, her heels clicking along, obviously from the city. Her flirty grin under a blue bell-shaped cloche bedazzled with a lavender brooch lit him up. He hoped he wasn't dreaming. She locked eyes with him even knowing that all other eyes were on her and walked up to face him toe to toe.

"Hey, hotsy-totsy. You look swell." He grinned and kissed her on the cheek.

"Hi handsome," she smiled, running her hand down his arm. "Don't you look dreamy . . . Where we go'n?"

"I think we'd better check up on the fellas at the cabin."

They motored in Feretti's Tin Lizzy to the south end of the

lake, across the little bridge and up past the farmhouse, then into the trees to the cabin. Hank and Willie were inside, sitting on a bench which was a couple of boards nailed to tree rounds next to a long table. From the look of things, they'd been creating a bar that would run parallel with the wall and were finishing up a pot of Hoover stew from the woodstove, macaroni with sliced hotdogs.

"Swell woodstove!" Liz said, admiring the burgundy enamel. "Where'd you find it?"

Hank swallowed. "Extra from Morgan's cabins. Gave me a deal to take it off his hands."

"Are we set for the weekend?" Feretti asked.

Liz ran her hand over the unfinished bar and examined the fruit jars for glasses and flour sacks for towels stacked in apple-box shelving nailed to the wall. She imagined herself pouring drinks. "Good job on the bar," she said. "It'll help keep bottles away from sticky fingers."

"And maybe some protection for the bartender," Feretti said.

"It's a high-class joint." Hank lifted the coffee pot to them, eyebrows raised. "Want some coffee in a mason jar?"

"I'm going for a run tomorrow night," Willie said, chewing. "We haven't got enough dough for a big load, but that's okay for the first run. I've got my contacts on the route ready to do their part."

Liz's eyes went big. "I heard the Feds were getting frustrated and bullet happy. What if you get shot?"

"Naw, shooting runners got outlawed a couple of years ago. It's gotta be an emergency or self-defense now for them to use a gun. I don't have one, so nothing to get them excited," Willie said. "I did hear that agents planted a gun on a body to justify shooting a guy, though."

"Anyway," Hank breathed after a thoughtful silence, "we figure we need some gin for the hard drinkers. They're probably dying to get the real stuff."

"Yes, that's true," Willie said, bouncing his eyebrows like Groucho Marx. "That bathtub gin is *killing* them." He removed an invisible cigar from the corner of his mouth, "Ta-dah! I've got a million of 'em," he grinned.

Liz scrunched her face. "Have you tried that Peeko flavoring from the grocery? Supposed to put it in grain alcohol. So gross. Speaking of that, what about mixers? People are getting used to putting Coca Cola in their drinks."

"I don't see the point." Willie popped his last bite of bread into his mouth. "They're gradually taking the cocaine out of Coca Cola, so it won't have the kick they expect, and it's not like they need to cover up the taste of moonshine since we're buying the real thing . . . Still, it's easy to get at the store if somebody wants it."

Hank stood up to get another cup of coffee. "I'm hoping we can get Canadian beer. People love it, twelve percent alcohol and hard to get. We could get a great price for it."

"We want to please the people," Feretti said, looking into the pot to see if there were leftovers. "We'll be doing a service for the good people, those folks with money who filled their basements with liquor before Prohibition officially started. They will have run out of their supplies by now."

Liz and Feretti sat scooched together on a bench up against

the wall. Feretti was distracted by Liz's hand on his leg causing heat to travel, well, everywhere. Her legs crossed, top foot bouncing, she was trying to think of other details while blocking from her mind what could go wrong, pretending to not realize the effect she was having on Feretti. "Hey, what about wine?" she asked, turning to him.

It took him a moment to hear the question. Feretti knew that some people didn't trust wine. They thought it was either expensive, imported only for wealthy people, or cheap for homeless winos. In *his* home, wine was a basic source of life. It went with food. His mamma was always pressing grapes in the basement. "Yeah. What about wine?" he echoed, concerned that they weren't planning to stock any.

Both Hank and Willie shrugged as if they hadn't thought of it.

"Wine is part of a civilized life you know," Feretti said. "It's natural, a law of nature that innocent grapes want to be wine."

"It's hard to find," Hank explained, looking helpless. "Not sure there's an interest. Folks think those Vino Sano bricks of dried grapes become wine if they add yeast and sugar for god's sake."

"There's another grape brick from Fruit Industries, Vino-Glo I think it's called," Liz said. "Rossi Brothers out of San Francisco sends a guy with grapes, containers, everything you need to make wine at home. In a couple of months, he comes back with bottles, corks, labels, even tissue to wrap each bottle!" She saw Feretti's jaw grind and looked at the floor, knowing he was sensitive about her dancing. "It's for people with money," she mumbled. "One of my dance clients told me about it."

". . . so you're hoping for some of my family's Dago Red," Feretti looked up, hoping to change the subject.

Willie laughed, glad he didn't have a girlfriend. "Nothing but the best, my friend." He got up and gave Feretti a playful punch on the arm to snap him out of it. "No foot juice, only high class for us."

"Well, we can legally produce two hundred gallons a year for use in our own home since we have four adults," Feretti continued as Liz took his hand. "That would be . . . four gallons a week. We can't go dipping into our own sustenance, might be able to spare maybe seventy gallons over the year. That might get us through the warm months while we'll be in business." He began to compute the extra money he'd make by supplying the wine.

"The booze cruise!" Willie announced, his hand circling his mouth like a loudspeaker. "Ferry on over to the cabin for rejuvenation!"

"You can't call it *the cabin*," Liz scoffed. "It needs a name!"

"Actually," Hank said, "that would be the smart thing, use *the cabin*. No one will know *which* cabin. Maybe it will help keep us out of jail."

Feretti shook his head. "Hey, as head of marketing, I say we name it *The Brick and Lime Club*. We're all from the brickyard after all, except for you of course, Liz. We could start slow with only the guys we trust from Clayton. They could bring their friends, keep it on the down low."

"All this talk is making my gut clench," Willie said as if a confession. He was thinking of actually driving across the border, making the deal, maybe going to jail for a long time. "We need a code word. Something to tell each other it'll be okay. Something reassuring. I could use some reassurance right now."

"Copacetic, Willie. It's copacetic," Feretti said, patting him on the back. "You'll be fine."

"Easy for you to say."

Moose at Loon Lake

A. B. Fosseen was president and superintendent of The Washington Brick and Lime Company and member of the Spokane chapter of the Loyal Order of Moose. He spear-headed the creation of a chapter of Moose in Clayton which would have a large impact on the community. It immediately had fifty members, mostly employees from the brickyard.

Fred Schonfeld, who had come alone to the United States from Switzerland at age 19, had started as a laborer at the brickyard and worked his way up to foreman and plant manager. Department supervisors all reported to Fred, and Fred reported to Neal Fosseen, the superintendent's son who would become "the first modern mayor of Spokane."

The Clayton chapter of Moose declared themselves active in 1927, holding events in the community grange hall while their own building was being built, mostly by volunteers from the brickyard built on property donated by Washington Brick and Lime. A terracotta moose head above the entrance accompanied an engraved stone, "Man's Greatest Good is Found in Service to His Fellow Man." They opened their new building with a "smoker" which included cards, and right away there were a hundred and fifty members. Evan Morgan was one of them.

Hank was thankful to have a good relationship with Evan Morgan who was originally from Wales. Hank knew Morgan as a smart, honest man who had helped build the community for thirty-four years. More importantly, Morgan trusted Hank. He had confided in Hank early on that he was planning to sell ninety acres of Corbin Beach Park on the southwest part of the lake. Each lot would be at least thirty-seven feet wide and up to two hundred feet deep depending on the terrain. Corbin Beach Park would become Lake Shore Homes.

When Morgan had made his official announcement to the lodge, fifty lots had sold quickly. Hank and his buddies had each grabbed a steep lot, side by side, $2 per waterfront foot, about $75 each. It was a place for "cliff dwellers." The flatter lots were more expensive, $3 per foot.

Morgan had wanted to restrict the growth of the area, setting aside another ninety acres above the beachfront properties as a private community park to ensure that lot owners would never have secondary lots developed behind them. He suggested that a community clubhouse be built using wood from an old, haunted house. The sandy beach of Corbin Cove, which he renamed Moose Bay, was to be shared as part of the community park.

It was Feretti always wanting to swing a deal, who had thought of their plan. With several dancehalls on the lake, he'd thought they might fulfill a need and charge a fee for a private place at a cabin to drink their liquor. Then when they'd learned about Willie's understanding of cars and his experience near the border, the plan had become bigger, the cabin would be not only a place to drink, but a place to *get* drinks, too! They hadn't thought about it too much beyond that. It had simply seemed logical.

Willie knew a lot about Canada, had a friend who owned a car garage over the border in British Columbia. Prohibition had not gone well in Canada, and when the U.S. voted to give it a try in 1920, Canadians had seen it as a perfect opportunity to make some needed money. They repealed their own liquor laws to be able to sell to Americans, knowing the demand would be high. Their Liquor Control Board had immediately opened nine government liquor stores to sell only to Canadians and licensed export houses along the border for a hefty fee to sell for export. They were private businesses, ready to accept U.S. dollars.

As expected, the border became more like a sieve than a line and despite it being illegal in the U.S., Canadian liquor exports increased from eight thousand gallons a year to more than a million, generating twenty percent of Canada's revenue. What Canada saw as welcomed relief for their slow economy, much of the U.S. public embraced as an antidote to their misery.

The First Run

Hank rode with Willie to learn the routes and make acquaintances on their first run into Canada. He wore a sage green scarf around his neck, calling it his lucky scarf. Willie laughed as they drove, remembering how Liz had complimented him on his jean jacket and asked him where he was going to hide the booze.

"Don't fret," he'd said, pulling on his farm hat and pushing his hair behind his ears as if in disguise. "If we get into trouble, we'll just outrun 'em." He'd felt like a gangster saying it, adding a big, toothy grin. "Besides, look at this face. I could never be guilty of breaking the law." Liz's eyes had been big as they'd driven away.

From Spokane, they drove west to Wilbur and north fourteen miles to the gorge above the Columbia on their way to Keller. Snaking down the face of the gorge with the river far below caused Hank's whole body to tense. It felt like descending the face of a rock wall without a rope, and he leaned away from empty airspace on each narrow switchback. When they pulled up to the ferry dock where the Columbia and Sanpoil rivers came together to wait for the cable ferry, he finally took a breath.

"So far, so good." Willie's smile had a tightness around it. "You ever hear about a guy named Roy Olmstead in Seattle? He was a cop lieutenant turned rumrunner."

"Really? A cop?"

"Yeah. He knew when and where there would be patrols, see. After they caught him, he did jail time, lost his job. Then he started doing it full time."

"Did he die or something? Why are you telling me this right now?" Hank's teeth were grinding. "Maybe I don't wanna know."

"He had a crew in fast boats and a lot of islands around the San Juans to hide behind and his wife told stories over their own radio station using code that told pilots where the coast was clear. He brought in two hundred cases of Canadian whiskey . . . every day!"

Hank's jaw dropped open. "Until they shot him?"

"Bureau of Prohibition got him with a wiretap. He made massive money, though, for four years."

"Where's he now?"

"McNeil Island Penitentiary."

Hank's gut felt twisted like a pretzel when the ferry finally arrived from across the water, a motorized winch pulling it forward on a cable attached to shore. *The Sanpoil*, named after the Sanpoil tribe, was 116 feet long and could carry twenty cars. This trip, it was empty.

He was still shaking his head after Willie's story. He'd thought they would be small potatoes, nothing that would interest the Feds. Maybe Willie had a different idea. *What have I gotten myself into?*

Willie shook the ferryman's hand and opened the big box on the side of the cabin marked "Tool Box" to get at a ten-gallon keg of moonshine, pouring a healthy shot for himself and Hank. "To smooth out the bumps in the road," he said. "It costs us whatever we can pay. We want to be generous with the ferryman. Give him five dollars instead of the fifty-cent fare. He might help us out in a pinch someday."

By the time they reached the other side, the three of them were old friends, laughing and slapping each other on the back, feeling secure about their plans. They continued to drive north another hour toward Republic.

As he drove and the moonshine wore off, Willie saw Hank staring off into space and tried to bring him back. "I don't think we'll ever be bigtime, do you?"

Hank's shoulders dropped from his ears, and he took a breath.

"Maybe we should talk profit, think about our payoff," Willie said. "We should be able to get a case of whiskey for $36."

Hank put aside his thoughts about Olmstead and federal agents and began to compute number of pours and prices and realized that depending on how much they could carry and how much their co-workers drank, they could make a couple thousand dollars in a weekend. Willie was right; they'd never get so big in business as to end up at McNeil Island. "It might be worth it," he said, "if we stay small."

Wrapping his scarf more tightly around his neck, he thought of Emily, a fragile doll, the daughter of the family who had taken him into their home when his parents had died, his almost sister. She was sweet and kind and looked like an angel with small features, dark curly hair worn up off her slender neck, porcelain skin and the bluest of eyes. She had treated him like he was someone important. She had trusted him and had easily accepted him into the family. Then she'd gotten polio, the greatest fright of his life. He had known how lives could be taken without much warning, how the world could change completely so that the only thing you could feel was absence. He remembered the sharp, empty pain of loss and the worry of it happening again with Emily.

He'd spent as much time at the farm as he could then, chopping wood side by side with Ben, Emily's father. He had hauled water for Meg in the kitchen, mucked out the barn, fed the stock. It had seemed they each felt better by staying busy while Emily, their only child, lay in an iron lung in the hospital.

Hank remembered sitting on the porch with their Irish Setter, Max, under his arm, waiting for Ben and Meg to bring her home. Then Max running down the driveway to greet the car. Hank had held back as Ben had carried her into the house. Emily had not made eye contact with him, and he'd felt it in his heart like a chunk of cold metal.

Emily had survived polio but without the full use of her legs. Hank had continued to come around as often as he could, hoping that she'd ask for him, half expecting her to be in the kitchen when he brought in water. Eventually, he'd given up. In his mind, he placed her in her favorite armchair in the living room near the fire looking as sweet and angelic as ever, having everything she needed.

Willie broke into Hank's memories by pointing out the Kettle River right before they started over the one-lane Curlew bridge. "This'll be our choke point, right here," he said. "Don't want any patrols around before we cross this bridge. Best to always look for alternate routes in case anything goes wrong."

In Curlew, they drove past the Ansorge Hotel, two stories with corner dormers and a central balcony. Hank thought it could be a potential hiding place if needed since the dormers on the second floor allowed them to see outside in several directions.

They drove on to the Danville border crossing. The U.S. border authority there looked at them suspiciously, commented on their "big six" automobile, asked why they were going to Canada. Hank held his breath while Willie smiled. "To get this old beat-up car worked on," he said. "My buddy has a repair shop up here and said he'd do me a favor."

On the other side, the Canadian official in British Columbia greeted them warmly, asked how long they'd be staying. He warned them that the Feds on the U.S. side were new and dedicated and gave them directions to the nearest export house which was in Grand Forks a few miles northeast.

They drove into Sunshine Valley where the Kettle and Granby Rivers met. In Grand Forks with its tree-lined streets, Hank was thankful that Willie knew his way around. They refilled the gas and checked the fluids, then drove up a steep embankment to the export house and around the building to get to the second-story entrance in the rear.

Willie had not installed the portable springs for heavy loads yet, not wanting the car to ride high which could cause border patrol to take notice. Feeling his nerves begin to prick, he got on it right away, make sure it was done during daylight.

As they began the process of making their liquor purchase,

spending all the money they had saved along with investments from friends and trusted co-workers, Hank thought about how everything would change when the deal was done, a change in his life that could be as big as losing his parents or Emily's polio, and maybe just as bad. There would be no going back. They'd need to accept whatever happened afterward. Despite the tightness in his chest, he made the deal.

They bought eight cases of whiskey and gin at $40 a case. Each quart would provide $30 worth of drink with twelve quarts per case or a total of $2,880 less the $320 export house purchase price. They added six barrels of beer, $20 each. Even though the return on beer was less, they knew it would be popular and it was what they could afford. Barrels came in three burlap sacks, twenty-four quarts in each. With the beer costing them $120 and providing a profit of $744, their total haul would make them $3,304 less travel expenses. Unbelievable. Unfathomable. Hank shook his head, grinning like a hunter who had just bagged his trophy.

Gangster Will

In the export house, Hank could hardly focus on his hand of cards at the poker table while they waited for the darkest part of the night to creep back over the border. Willie had told him in advance that he shouldn't win the game. "We want to keep them friendly. Maybe they'll tell us more about avoiding the border patrols."

Hank's first hand was messy, nothing decent he could see. *Maybe this is a sign of how our luck will go on the road tonight,* he thought. *It's not looking good.* "Be gentle with me, fellas. Will knows, this is my life savings here." He laid down a dollar bill.

Willie and the two employees chuckled.

"Don't want to lose it all and not be able to buy gas for getting home." Hank kept the highest card and discarded the rest. The dealer gave him another messy hand, and he folded. *Maybe this is a test of my decision-making skills. Will I know when to throw in the towel?*

The second hand was different, the possibility of four of a kind. He felt heat on the back of his neck as he discarded two cards. *I'm not supposed to win. What if I do win? Hell, they'd know if I wasn't really playing,* he argued with himself. *Maybe it's about practicing my poker face for being a smuggler,* he thought, trying to look nonchalant. The dealer gave him the card he needed. *Luck! The cards have spoken!* His face lit up and he tried to rein it in again.

Hank lost the next two games even though he had to discard some winning cards. During the following game, he felt his body give way to exhaustion, overcoming his stress. He and Willie each fell into cots against the wall for some sleep, the export guys promising to wake them at 2 o'clock in the morning.

Hank felt rummy riding in the car as it sneaked down the road toward Danville and turned west before crossing the border. He heard every crunch of the tires over rock.

"The export guys said that the new border patrol is pretty determined to catch smugglers," Willie said. "We've got just enough moonlight coming from between the clouds that we can maneuver without headlights when we need to. We can stay on the Canada side a bit longer where it's safe."

"I don't know if I want to hang around, Will," Hank said quietly, barely breathing.

"Relax. We're not doing anything illegal on this side. The guys at the export house told me there's an unimproved back road this way to take us across. Border patrol only drives the highways. We don't have the money to bribe anyone, so if someone comes after us, we'll need to outrun 'em . . . just so you know . . ."

"Oh, thanks for that, Will. I can hear the bullets whizzing by now."

Hank remembered Liz's worry about guns and gripped the

seat as the heavy car toddled over the rutted, impossible road. It didn't feel like escape, more like navigating an obstacle course. He expected to see a car waiting for them around every curve and wondered how his parents would feel about him if they were still alive. It was the first illegal thing he'd ever done other than stealing a few vegetables out of someone's garden when he was hungry. *Dependable, hard-working, honest Hank*, that's how folks thought about him. Regret hovered at the edge of his heart.

Reaching Curlew, they pulled off the road and cut the engine where they could watch for activity on the narrow bridge, see if Border Patrol was around. Twenty-minutes was the most they could spare if they wanted to stay ahead of dawn. When they went, it was without headlights. At Keller, the ferryman was asleep, waiting on their side of the river, having thought they might come back in the night, especially since they'd paid him another $5 in advance.

The sky was getting light when they got to Davenport. They parked behind the diner and went in for coffee and eggs, hoping for enough sustenance to get them home. The hot coffee was good, and over the second cup, the waitress told them there had been a robbery in Medical Lake. The Sheriff was out on patrol to find the thieves. With their breakfasts in their throats, they drove another thirteen miles, saying their prayers and rubber necking the view to Reardan. Hank was so consumed by stress that he felt mummified by the time they headed north to Springdale and Loon Lake.

When they finally reached the cabin, Willie turned off the engine and put his head back to take his first full breath. He hadn't realized how much he'd been holding it, so focused on the driving. They unloaded the car, taking it all to the cellar, and opened a bottle of Canada's version of *Old Grand Dad*. It didn't matter that it hadn't been aged as long as the original. Several shots went down easily. They waited for its slow glow, afraid to talk about what they'd done, still afraid they might get caught, wondering if they had actually gotten away with it.

After the third shot, Hank was able to talk. "I gotta say this is good stuff. Nothing like the real thing."

"Sure glad I didn't have ta do that by myself," Willie shook his head and wiped the back of his hand across his mouth. "Now that I done it, I don't wanna ever do it 'gain. I *refuse* to ever do it *alone*." Willie patted his shirt pocket, took out a Lucky, lit it up and had a coughing fit.

"You *looked* like you had everything under control, glad I didn't know otherwise," Hank said. "Hey, I didn't know you smoked."

"I don't, but I'm gonna start," Willie choked. "Guys say it helps them relax."

"Maybe. If you don't choke to death." Hank managed a boozy smile. "A wad of money in your pocket, you'll feel better." He poured another shot for each of them. "Sure hope our luck holds out."

"Here, have a Lucky." Willie held his cigarette pack out toward Hank with a guffaw until he started coughing again.

"Pull it together, man. We've got strategy . . . not just luck. You didn't even ask for your safe word."

"I was too scared to open my mouth," he said. "Copa... copa... I can't remember it anyway. Did ya realize that ya called me 'Will' on the road?"

Hank shook his head as he ran his tongue around inside his mouth, thinking it might be numb.

"I liked it."

"Yeah? You want 'Will' to be your gangster name?"

"Okay," he gave his biggest grin, squeezing his bleary eyes shut, then opened them long enough to turn toward Hank and say, "co-pa-cet-ic," but it wasn't easy.

Opening Night

Nearly every town in the country had at least one local band they could dance to and a place to do it whether it was a grange hall, a barn, a dance hall, or a speakeasy (where you *speak easy* to keep quiet about the liquor there).

The first granges were organized by small groups of farmers who wanted to come together to discuss farming issues, to help each other out, to group together for better deals in buying and selling. It was inevitable that they also affected the economic and political well-being of their areas and provided community services. They provided classes on agriculture, rallies for political and religious groups, and became social centers. They lifted the spirits of neighbors during hard times with card games, athletic activities, picnics, suppers, plays, concerts and most importantly, dances.

Saturday nights were for dancing and everyone who could get to a dance was there. Those were busy evenings for Fred Swanback, supervisor of the setting crew at the brickyard. He played a fiddle, and he had his own dance band. There were dances on Saturday nights in the grange halls all over the area: Springdale, Clayton, Gardenspot, Williams Valley. There were also several dancehalls on Loon Lake: one at Granite Point on the east side of the lake and a large dance pavilion on the north end of the lake at Morgan Park.

Music from Morgan Park Pavilion traveled across Loon Lake as patrons arrived by car, boat and a few by horse and buggy. Some came early to begin their evening with a meal in the dining hall out on the pier. They enjoyed their food as the sun settled, the light fingering through treetops until the sky turned from rose to cinnamon red. The beat of "Toot, Toot, Tootsie" drew them into the pavilion where dancers were beginning the Charleston.

Liz and Feretti danced around the other couples, looking for people they knew, people they could trust, people who might have a little money. Liz ran her fingers under Feretti's collar to pull him down for a kiss, happy with his dancing. He'd gotten much better with her help, had actually become fun to dance with. Her body flirted with the music while her mind looked for patrons, and Feretti struggled to do both at the same time.

After an hour, they had invited friends to join them for an evening cruise around the lake on the lovely steamboat *Gwendolyn*, complete with orchestra playing and a stop to see a "blind pig," which was code for liquor. The boat stopped at the narrow wharf below the cabin, just wide enough for people to walk to shore. Feretti handed the boat captain $5 above the regular fare and saw lanterns traveling in single file up the switchback path, led by Liz.

It was opening night of The Brick and Lime Club, and Hank and Willie were there to greet their guests. Drinkers were surprised that the real thing was being served, including Canadian beer, and they drank with gusto. Feretti filled mason jars with beer and foam while Liz wiped up his mess and collected the money in the soft lantern light of the cabin. She'd been around plenty of drinkers, people making fools of themselves, sozzled women who were pathetic. She liked a party but knew there was a point when it wasn't fun anymore, and she didn't want to be involved in some woman's downfall. Some people didn't know when to quit.

Feretti found himself in the new role of bouncer. With concern, he watched the boozy behavior intensify. Patrons needed to be able to negotiate the trail on their feet rather than slipping and sliding or rolling down the hill when they left. The whole thing would be over before it started if someone upset the boat on the ride back.

"If someone gets too sloshed," Feretti told the gang, "he's getting the bum's rush. He can walk around the lake to get back." Just then, a card player stood up and threw a tin can ashtray against the wall. "Like this," Feretti grimaced, escorting the man out the door, Hank right behind him as back-up.

"Get on your way, buddy," Feretti pointed down the road. "Beat it. You're walk'n home. You're not getting on the boat."

"What about my friends?"

"I don't see any friends. If you had friends, they'd be out here with you."

Inside, he made an announcement to the room, "You get too ossified tonight, you'll be walk'n home. No wise guys allowed on the boat."

He saw a new card game start up in a corner and warned that

they'd all be leaving on *Gwen* when it came, even if they were in the middle of a game.

"So many rules!" a guy hollered. "Dead soldier over here!" he waved his empty glass.

Liz hid the bottles behind the bar and scowled at him.

As they left, Feretti reminded everyone that The Brick and Lime Club was a secret, a private club, only for *invited* guests and warned them to be quiet about the booze. "For all anybody knows," he said, "you brought it in your own flask. If you keep quiet, hopefully you can come back again." He smiled at last. The Brick and Lime Club was in operation.

Dangerous in Daylight

Hank and Willie worked on building the next cabin during breaks from the brickyard and running liquor over the border. Each cabin would have its "hidey hole" for the money they brought in. Hank's was in the cellar behind a rock that he could remove from the foundation wall where he kept a mason jar waiting to be filled.

Their smuggling routes needed to change frequently to different border crossings since border patrol became suspicious when they traveled the same route. On every trip, Hank had his scarf and Willie had his Luckys.

The situation at Greenwood was pretty sweet. There was a wooded hideout near the border where they could watch the movements of border patrol without being seen. The guys at the export house told them that the patrols had increased at night, and they slept during the day. Two o'clock in the afternoon would be a good time to cross even though it seemed foolishly dangerous in daylight. After watching for an hour from the trees and seeing no activity, Hank and Will crawled across as quietly as they could, their hearts thrumming in their throats and Willie, or Will rather, used all his strength to keep his foot from pushing the gas pedal to the floor.

The second time they crossed that border several weeks later and came through Ferry on the U.S. side, they were chased. Will had been secretly wanting to show what his car could do. Even with their heavy load, his Hudson moved like a bat out of hell and was easier to handle than the car used by border patrol. Adrenaline pumping, Will put a few miles between them and rolled into the barn of an amiable farmer to hide, then hurried out to the farmer's front porch to watch the patrol car drive by. Being Will, he couldn't wipe the grin off his face.

It wasn't long before Feretti decided to change the Hudson's license plate to confuse any lawmen who might be looking for them. He procured a new plate at the courthouse in Spokane, giving a fake name, address and serial number as well as the wrong information about the motor and type of car, claiming that he needed a license for a Pierce Arrow. He asked Liz to do the same. She went all out to license a Cadillac, gushing to the court clerk about how it was yellow and a dream to drive. At the courthouse in Colville, Hank licensed a Chrysler while Will went in for a Bentley, claiming he was only the chauffer. The fake plates were tucked in under the driver's seat, ready for use when needed.

The Clayton Moose Lodge held their first annual picnic at Morgan Park on Sunday, June 28, 1928. A large delegation of the Spokane chapter joined them as well as the Spokane Temple's band, creating a merry event for a huge crowd.

Feretti was fishing at the picnic for more patrons for The Brick and Lime Club as he strolled through the crowd with Liz on his arm. By afternoon, they had invited ten couples for a boat ride and a visit to the cabin; and having sworn them to secrecy, they were approaching *Gwen* when a small airplane flew at them from the south. Everyone stopped, wondering why it flew so low. As it got near the picnic area, it buzzed the crowd, papers flying, arms waving. Liz grabbed one of the papers. It was an advertisement from Westby Mercantile in Clayton. They had chartered a plane and were tossing out fliers in every town between Spokane and Loon Lake.

As the plane passed overhead, Fred Schonfeld saw five guys inside. His heart pinched, recognizing one of them as his son, Bud, who was hanging out the plane to wave. Bud was an employee at the mercantile store and had kept quiet about their plan to use an airplane, probably knowing that his father wouldn't want him up there. Fred prayed that there wasn't any liquor involved.

Feretti thought it felt dangerous, drinking in the middle of the day with so many people at the lake, especially on a Sunday. Even so, once drinks were poured at the Brick and Lime Club, he raised his glass to give a toast, "Here's to Prohibition, my friends! Blue Laws be hanged! We couldn't get a drink on a Sunday before now!" They all laughed and raised their glasses, "To Prohibition!" they sang.

The flow of money and therefore drinks slowed, and since *Gwen* hadn't returned, the party milled around outside and went next door to examine the new construction, Feretti's cabin. Hank and Willie had it nearly complete, identical to Hank's except that the ground it sat on was more level at the house site and Feretti had requested a rock fireplace. They'd made him build it himself, though they had piled up the rock for him to use that was excavated from digging the cellar. It *had* taken a lot of time and mortar mix of course, but he was proud of it.

It was the first time that Liz had seen it and he watched her as she reacted, hoping she'd love the promise of it. She went straight to it, feeling the front of the stones, then turning to snuggle up against him. Her mouth at his ear gave him goose-bumps. "When do we light it up?" she asked in a luscious, seductive voice. It nearly melted him.

Once he'd regained his equilibrium, he saw that Willie had been watching.

"I guess she likes it," Willie snickered.

Emily

Chewelah, Washington

Emily sat in her wheelchair in the living room with magazines on her lap, praying for the energy to try and stand up. It seemed unfair that getting better required so much energy when she already felt exhausted.

She couldn't get past what she'd lost. Her mother had told her that her anger was good, it would help her fight back, but it had felt more like rage burning, dissolving her. It wasn't fair. Her mother had agreed. She'd also said that life was never fair. Emily's feeling of being left out had melded into depression, like a thick soggy blanket weighing her down . . . or was it the polio? Either way, it felt like defeat.

The health she still had, her parents and almost brother, Hank, the farm: these were the things she should be thankful for, and she *was* thankful. But what about her future? BP (Before Polio) she'd thought she would have a husband and home of her own and a bunch of kids. Her wedding had been planned in her mind: a field of tall sunflowers planted in the garden near the house, a trellis overhead with wraps of white and yellow scarves. Her dress would have been all lace, white, of course. No veil, only some flowers in her hair and a small nosegay of forget-me-nots.

Forget-me-nots, those tiny blue petals her mother had told her about, how they symbolized true love. She remembered seeing them at a gravesite too, a promised remembrance after death. She shuddered as if a ghost passed through her chest.

Reality was that her condition would keep her dependent on her parents, and they were already working so hard to hang onto the farm. Her medical bills were serious even though her family doctor, the doctor who had known her since she was born, who had set her broken wrist after she'd fallen from her horse, had waved his fee. He'd told her father that he did it to "bolster their courage."

She squinted over the deep ravine of polio to the rest of her life and could see no path to take, no possibilities. Some days, pain radiated down her back and legs and took her breath away. How could she focus on the days ahead when she couldn't get out of bed on her own?

Her friends had come to visit at first, becoming too kind when they had realized that her condition was permanent and acting overly courteous like she wasn't capable anymore, then distancing themselves. They'd spent money on magazines for her, like the ones on her lap with beautiful young women in fashion-able clothes, pictures of them at parties and dancing, showing their legs. There was no one in a wheelchair in those magazines. Emily Pearson had no potential; she didn't matter anymore. She threw the perfect girl magazines across the room.

The next morning, Emily opened her eyes and knew it would be a bad day. Her mother fussed all around the room, wanting it to be spotless, making sure she had everything she needed. It only made her angry. Why did her mother even try? The doctor had said she wouldn't have full use of her legs. The gig called "Emily's Life" would be wasted.

When her father came to sit on the edge of her bed, her mother scooted out the door. "I'm gonna level with ya, Em," he said. "You're old enough to know. We've been having hard times here on the farm, you know?"

Emily pulled herself up against the headboard and wondered if he was there to make her feel worse.

"I've had to make some adjustments soze we could hang onto the place. I had to sell some of the livestock, sold a little slice of land, too. Sold some old equipment I don't need no more. I'm hoping for a better time, an easier life, in the future."

Emily patted his hand.

"And I come to realize, Em, that it's not just about how hard a person works, it's about being able to adapt, a-dap-ta-bility. I'll keep making adjustments the best I can. You need to do the same. Listen to me now." He grabbed her face by her chin.

Her eyes widened and she blinked several times to show she was listening.

"Pearson. It's our name. It's Irish as you know. Did you know it means 'rock or stone'? That means we're hard like stone, darling, and nothing gets to us. I expect you to live up to your first name, too, eager Emily, and face this challenge in life. We all have them and none of us knows what tomorrow will bring.

You have a lot going for you, even with polio, and you need to figure out how to go forward. I'll see you downstairs for supper." He leaned down to kiss her on the cheek and when he left, she found his wet tears on her face.

Emily leaned her head back against the headboard and sobbed. She decided that she would get it all out and cry until she couldn't cry anymore. Then she began to plan for her new life, a different life. Her doctor had given her exercises and fitted her with braces for when her legs got strong enough. That would become her job for now. She would figure out a way to be able to dress herself and to put on her braces by herself, do her best to not be a burden. She'd think about the future later.

The three of them sat at the dinner table that evening, and Emily's mother, Meg, relaxed for the first time since the illness. Ben saw the tension leave his wife's face and squeezed her hand under the table.

While washing the dishes in the kitchen, Meg heard a few keys played on the piano and froze to listen. She'd missed Emily's playing as much as she'd missed her unsinkable energy. The song was beautiful and sweet, from the sheet music they'd given her at Christmas, a Gershwin piece.

Emily's quiet singing floated into the kitchen, *"I'm a little lamb who's lost in a wood. I know I could, always be good . . . Someone to watch over me."*

So thankful to have her Emily back, Meg's tears dropped into her dishwater.

Face to Face

Each week, as the money pot increased, Hank and Will purchased as much liquor as they could afford until the weight was all the car could handle. Fourteen barrels of beer and eight cases of whiskey seemed to be the limit, causing one blowout after another. Stopping along the road to change tires was hazardous for getting caught. With the last blowout of the last spare, they had no choice but to unload the liquor into the bushes and limp the car along on a wheel rim to Ben and Meg's farmhouse nearby.

Starting up the drive to the white, two-story farmhouse, Hank couldn't believe what he was doing, especially not here, bringing his shady problem into the closest thing he had to a home. He could see a few head of cattle still grazing in a field and a bull in his own area. The horse weathervane was still on top of the barn roof. They drove beyond the kitchen door and into the shadow beside the barn, noticing that it needed a new coat of red. He hoped that no one would be home, and they could fix the tire and get out quickly. Angry with himself for getting into such a mess, he walked stiff legged toward the house.

Max came barking around the corner until he knew it was Hank, and he wiggled and hopped and jumped all around Hank's legs. Hank patted his head and ruffled his neck and stepped up the kitchen steps like he always had. He felt his breath shorten, not sure if he wanted to know how Emily was doing. He'd been pretty good at repressing the idea of her being trapped in a wheelchair, dependent. His fist stopped mid-air, realizing how long it had been, six months maybe. He braced himself. *Would they have gotten word to me if she'd had a setback?* He tapped quietly on the kitchen door, his whole body tense.

It was Emily who came to the door. Her face lit up at the sight of him. He couldn't think of what to say, he was so over-whelmed by her standing there on her own two legs. Words were stuck in his throat, nearly choking him.

"Hank! You've come home!" She backed up to open the door further, hanging heavily onto the door with one hand and rely-ing on a crutch with the other, her legs in braces showing below the hem of her dress. "Come in, please."

Hank and Willie wiped their feet, removed hats and stepped inside the kitchen. "It's good to see you, Emily," he finally said. He looked in her eyes and saw the warmth there, refused to look at the crutch. "This is my friend, Willie."

Using her crutch, she was able to serve a plate of sugar cookies and get glasses for Hank to pour lemonade.

"I didn't want to cause you any trouble, Em. We've blown our spare tire and were wondering if Ben might have an extra we could borrow."

He brought the glasses to the table. "How are you feeling?"

"Just missing my Hank." Emily sat with a plunk onto a chair. "I still have some weakness. Doctor says it'll take time." She turned directly toward him, "Why haven't you been around, Hank?"

"I came a few times . . . I wasn't sure if I was wanted here."

Emily reached over and took his hand. "You are wanted, Hank."

Hank and Will each squirmed in their chairs and chewed their cookies. Hank thought that he'd done a favor for Ben and Meg when he'd moved into the boardinghouse at work, one less mouth to feed and it took care of the transportation problem. Most of the crew stayed there, including Willie. Now he wondered if they needed him at home. "So it might be okay if I came to see you now and then?"

"Well it *is* your home, after all. I'm not the only one who misses you."

Hank's spirit dimmed a bit, wondering if she missed him *only* as part of the family. "I'm really glad you're feeling better, Em. Do you think we could take a look in the barn and see if Ben has a spare we could use?"

"Sure, you know he'd say it was okay. Hey, I'm glad you like the scarf I made you."

His face flamed as his hand went to his neck, having forgotten that he wore her scarf. Now he felt like he'd done a dishonorable thing, wearing it on his smuggling trips, like he was bringing her in on his dirty business. He forced a smile and shrugged, "It's my lucky scarf." He hoped she would realize that she was important to him.

Once the tire was on the car and Hank had come out of the house after saying goodbye, Willie had questions to ask, but Hank didn't want to talk about it.

The Feds

Evan Morgan advertised all day events to celebrate Independence Day at his park: dancing, food, ballgames, speakers, Ferris wheel, the lake steamer *Gwen*, and of course, fireworks. To transport everyone who wanted to attend, the Great Northern put on an extra train with thirteen coaches to take passengers from Spokane to Loon Lake and Morgan Park.

It was a busy time for Liz and Feretti and they were beginning to allow their regulars to invite their own trusted guests to come to the cabin. The crowd overflowed to Feretti's cabin, and a path formed between them as drinkers traveled back and forth like a swarm. Feretti realized that once he'd let people outside with their drinks, there was no pulling them back without herd dogs. They wandered, drink in hand.

When folks started showing up by car, looking for The Brick and Lime Club from the road above the cabins, he was pretty sure they had a problem. Visitors told him that it was his own fault. Having the real thing out of Canada . . . well, the word would get out. It was inevitable.

Customers carried their drinks to the water side of the cabin and sat under the fir tree where the world could see them.

They even carried drinks down to the water's edge to greet new customers coming off *Gwen*. When people began arriving in their own boats and in rented boats, Feretti shooed them away, saying it was private property. He traveled up and down the hill between the cabin and shore so many times that his legs felt like they were dragging weights through water. After a while, he stood at the top of the trail and yelled down at people, wishing for a megaphone, "Private Property! Go away!" When *Gwen* approached on her rounds, he shooed everyone "back to the boat" like a preschool teacher while Liz collected their glasses, reminding them that The Brick and Lime Club was *private* and *secret*.

Feretti had had a couple shots of whiskey to fortify his legs into those of a mountain goat when he encountered a group sitting on the rock patio at the water who were waiting for dark and fireworks. He felt his body tighten, his hands making fists. He showed his teeth, which were clenched to keep from yelling and told them that Morgan's fireworks could not be seen from there. They could not set off their own fireworks because it would burn down the woods, and they'd better damn well be on the next boat, or they'd be at the *bottom* of the lake. His smile looked like a sneer.

After everyone was gone and a few calming drinks had been sipped, Hank took the gang out on his clinker boat, a boat he'd rescued from Morgan's burn pile after it had been broken up in a storm. He rowed to the center of the lake where they waited in still water for the fireworks show, explosions on private beaches popping up all around them. Liz leaned against Feretti, dragging one foot in the black water, warm from the heat of the day. They didn't talk much. They assumed trouble was on its way, and they didn't want to think about it. Not yet anyway. They'd already had enough trouble for one day.

In August, the second annual Loon Lake boat regatta co-sponsored by Morgan Park and the Inland Empire Outboard Motor Club was held. Twenty-five hundred people attended from Spokane and the surrounding region, most with boats in the water. The lake was choppy, wakes from boats smashing into each other from all directions and bouncing against the shore. Boats were tied up to the wharf below the cabin, so many boats that boats were tied to boats. It looked like a big party was going on.

A big party *was* going on. The gang was all there, pouring booze as fast as they could and collecting the money. Liz arrived with a short, bomber style leather jacket for Hank. "At least cover the flannel up now and then for a change," she said, helping him put it on.

"It's August!" Hank protested.

"That's right! I got a great deal on it. Just try it on." She tugged the jacket into place across his shoulders. "Now you'll look dashing with your scarf . . . like a pilot."

"Thanks, Liz." He took it off and tossed it behind the bar. "I'll wear it when I fly my plane," he mumbled.

The next day, the Feds showed up. The gang was working on the third house when they arrived and kept working as the agents walked around Hank's cabin, trying to see inside. With small, high windows on the southside and no deck on the water side, it was impossible to see in without a ladder. The Feds walked over to ask if they knew anything about "that" cabin or the owner, and all four of them shook their heads. "Haven't even met them," Feretti said. "We're new here."

After the Feds left, the work stopped. "Rats!" Will said. "The jig's up! We need to hide the hooch."

"What about under this cabin?" Hank suggested. "Will, you don't mind, do you? We could dig a good size hole and cover it up."

Liz had been thinking, running a hand up and down her arm to wipe away the tension she felt. Finally, she spoke up. "What if I sold it? The beer anyway. I know I can sell all the beer right out of the New Washington Hotel."

Clayton Moose Lodge had planned a day of recreation for their members at Morgan Park. Feretti knew they shouldn't sell drinks for a while but couldn't resist. They were getting things ready when alarms rang from Clayton, announcing a fire. The guys arrived at the brickyard along with the rest of the town to see flames shooting fifty feet into the sky, howling in the breeze. A hundred cords of wood were on fire, firewood that had been ready for the kilns.

They joined the fire brigade despite the heat and smoke but couldn't get near it, could only throw water on everything that wasn't burning to keep it from spreading through the buildings and across the street to the town. The wind was with them, and when it finally calmed down, only one building had burned and half a million bricks had been ruined. It could have been worse, much worse.

Waiting at the cabin, Liz was trembling as she thought about selling beer in Spokane. It felt like obstacles were beginning to work against them. *First the Feds, now a fire. Maybe the fire saved us from the Feds.* It had all seemed so simple in the beginning.

When the guys came back from the fire, she had her tough persona back. The glasses were lined up, waiting for them. They walked in, covered in black soot, radiating heat. "Welcome back," she said, pouring. "You're my only customers today and you all stink."

It Had to be You

Liz met Feretti and Will at the back door of her hotel to receive the beer and waved them up the stairs to her room. The fact that she'd lost a few roommates over the months and needed extra money to pay the rent had convinced her that she was brave enough to sell it. And, she had the extra space for storage.

That evening from the window of her hotel, Liz watched the old bootlegger from the second floor being hauled away along with his bottles. He'd been using a funnel to fill pint bottles with clear moonshine from Mica Peak and adding burnt sugar to color it like whiskey. Everyone in the hotel could smell the burnt sugar, including the cops who had busted into his room. Liz shuddered. At least it wasn't creosote or embalming fluid he'd been adding, as far as she knew, anyway. She wanted no part of that scene.

She knew moonshine had been coming into the Spokane hotels from Mica Peak for years. It was known as the "Blue Ridge Mountains" up there or the "Kentucky Mountains of Spokane County," the source of "Mica Moonshine."

Agents' attempts to close down moonshining at Mica Peak had failed so far. The border between Spokane County in

Washington, and Kootenai County in Idaho went right through Mica Peak where it sat on the ridgeline of the southern-most peaks of the Selkirk Mountains. Surveys by each state were a bit off, leaving a 40-foot gap between borders. If Prohibition agents from Spokane County arrived to shut down a still, they were told that they had no jurisdiction there, that the still was in Kootenai County, Idaho; and if agents came from Kootenai County, they were told that their still was in Spokane County. "Bottle men" continued to hike down from the mountains carrying bottles of moonshine in suitcases to deliver to patrons in the hotels.

As she watched the old bootlegger being taken away, Liz realized she'd been an idiot to bring all that beer into her room, especially since the owners of her hotel had already been put in jail for being "jointists," running a joint that sold liquor. Skip, the manager, kept the hotel open and looked the other way as long as he got a kick-back, but now that the Spokane police "dry squad" were frequent visitors, she needed to get rid of it.

There were a couple of her regular dance patrons who were big on beer, especially the twelve percent Canadian beer. They were tired of "near beer" produced by the few breweries that were left. It was less than half of one percent alcohol, so people usually spiked it, which made it especially foul.

Miller produced a near beer called Vivo. Anheuser Busch sold near beer, too, but they made their money by selling supplies to bootleggers. They had become the biggest bootlegging supply house in the U.S. in 1926 by selling more than six million pounds of malt extract as a "useful ingredient for breads and desserts." With the right connection, illegal real beer could be purchased from breweries before they took the alcohol out; it was usually four percent alcohol and came with fake labels marked "12% Canadian."

Liz had had a few dates with Mr. Somebodys that Feretti didn't know about, men who could buy it all. She dressed in her best glad rags, a dress with a lavender sparkly, fringy skirt minus the girdle. Men didn't want to dance with a girl wearing a girdle anymore. She slid her legs into new silk stockings that Willie had brought back from Canada and hooked them up to the black garter belt that hung from her waist. After she strapped on her black Mary Jane heels, she added her favorite silver headband with a wispy lavender feather on one side.

Walking unescorted into the Marie Antoinette Ballroom at the Davenport Hotel as if she owned the place, fringe whipping with her walk, she thought about the thrill of a clean, handsome man holding out his hand to lead her onto the dancefloor. No one would ever question her presence on a dancefloor. It was her home.

The band was hot. She was dancing to "Yes Sir, That's My Baby," thinking the ballroom was lovely and saw a Mr. Somebody on the balcony that she knew. He saw her too, how could he have missed her? She was fantastic the way she moved, flirting when she danced. She gave a little wave, smiled and winked, motioning him down to the dancefloor with a tilt of her head.

He arrived in time for "It Had to be You" and grabbed her around the waist. She remembered what a catch he was, physically anyway, chiseled jaw, dark hair like Feretti, but taller and looking swell in a subtle-striped, expensive gray suit, wide shoulders, narrow waist, full trouser legs. They danced close.

"You're looking swanky, doll," her Shalimar tickled his brain.

"I've got a proposition for you," she whispered in his ear. "If you're as brave as I think you are."

He felt his heart beat double time. "Why Miss Liz, I don't know what to say!" he crooned as if it were a joke.

Her fingernails grabbed the back of his neck. "I'm serious, you high hat!"

"Ouch! Am I bleeding?" He wiped the back of his neck and looked at his hand. "You hurt me and insult me and now you want to make some kind of deal? What gives?"

"Sorry. I really am. Don't be cross." She batted her eyes, trying to show how sorry she was. "I'm just nervous about this sort of thing. I've never done anything like this before."

He grabbed her under the arm and escorted her to a corner where he went in for a kiss. She pushed against him, and when he didn't move away, she slugged him in the stomach with all her might, sending him down onto his knees where he tried to get a breath. She squatted down to talk to him before he could inhale.

"I've got a bunch of Canadian beer for sale," she said to his gasping mouth. "I wonder if you'd like to take it off my hands is all."

It took him a few moments to respond. "Real beer?" he wheezed. "Real from Canada beer? On the level?"

"Yes, Canadian," she repeated, looking for interest in his eyes. All she saw was pain.

After they filled his car with all the beer she had, she went with him to deliver it through the secret entry of the Spokane Club. A few girls were entering there also, girls who were dancers.

The few who knew her only waved since she was with a Mr. Somebody.

"What if I could get my hands on some hard stuff?" she asked.

"From Canada?"

Liz nodded.

He scratched his head. "Would you need to beat me up again?"

"Only if I need to get your attention," she smiled, trying to look innocent.

"Just be gentle with me, and I think we can make a deal."

The Border

Canada made good money off American drinkers during Prohibition. By 1929 their tax for liquor sales from export houses was bringing in twice as much as their income tax. Also, tourism attracted a lot of Americans to Canada for a few drinks or a lot of drinks and a holiday, earning them another $300 million, nearly four times more than in 1920.

Like the U.S. economy, business at the Clayton brickyard was slow, and orders came only intermittently. Hank quit paying for his room at the boardinghouse and bought himself a steel roll-a-way bed with metal springs and a feather mattress for his cabin. The bed could be folded in half and rolled into a corner or closet, if he had one, to be stored. He hoped to save as much as he could to help with Emily's medical bills.

Feretti wanted money to buy a house. There was nothing as attractive as a home when there were so many homeless all around. He wasn't entirely sure that Liz would say "Yes" if he popped the question. He hoped that having a house would provide encouragement.

Willie had gotten cranky, afraid he might get cheated. The construction on his cabin had slowed to a halt since the Feds had shown up. If he could sell a lake cabin someday in the future, it would help him finance a car repair shop.

So, they continued, danger be hanged. They would finish Willie's cabin and move the operation there.

Hank and Will found what would become their favorite export house at Fernie, British Columbia, up from Colville below Crow's Nest Pass, a colorful area known for its rich coal deposits and moonshine. It was a longer drive but more comfortable once they got there. The guys at the export house were great, like brothers. They kept their ears tuned to changes on the border and supplied whatever information they thought might help.

The export house was usually able to find a sympathetic officer who wanted to earn a few bucks on the side. In exchange for $5 per case and $3 per barrel of beer as evidenced on the bill of sale, the border agent would tell the export house what route the rumrunners should use and what time they would send the patrols the other direction so they wouldn't be caught. Not legal, and things could still go wrong, but it was as neat and tidy as they could get, and they had more of an idea of what to expect. Still, Hank couldn't abide by a corrupt official. He refused to pay him through the export house. He made Will do it.

They met other rumrunners at the export house and found camaraderie with them, learned about how they helped each other. A tall driver in a tweed newsboy cap and black vest told how he'd gotten caught and had spent time in jail, his car confiscated. Other runners had lent him a car and pitched in to finance his first run to start over again and were letting him pay them back over time. He had a family to feed and was thankful for the help.

They learned that locally, people called them rumrunners even though the term was usually used for runners transporting liquor illegally across water, and even though they didn't buy much rum. They mostly bought whiskey, some gin, bourbon and rye and of course beer. They'd thought they were simply smugglers or maybe bootleggers. The term "bootlegger," they were told, had come from smugglers hiding liquor against their legs inside their high boots. Bootleggers tended to sell homemade moonshine. Hank and Will were rumrunners, "jumping the line" when they bypassed U.S. border crossings on their way home from Canada.

Sometimes they went to a favorite bar with the other runners for a few drinks while waiting for their designated time to cross. A runner named Fahey, a regular who told them that he was only running for his own line house just over the border, invited them all to visit his place, see his establishment, have a drink.

Hank started to decline, but Will said, "We'll see you there," and headed out to the car.

Hank followed behind, "This is a terrible idea, Will! A parade of big, heavy cars full of booze all crossing the line together and then showing up at a line house together?"

They got into the car. "Just wait, Will. Let the rest go ahead and we'll go on our own a little later."

Will started the engine and got in line with the procession despite Hank's voice getting louder and louder. "Will!" Hank said, grabbing his seat. "Willie! William! *Not* copacetic! What's gotten into you? Are you deaf?"

"I like Fahey," Will finally said. "I trust him, and I want to get to know him better. This is how we show trust."

"This is how we go to jail," Hank tightened his scarf. "He could be from Border Patrol for all we know, leading us to hand-cuffs! I should have made you let me out of the car."

"You're getting paranoid, Hank. Co-pa-ce-tic. Calm down."

Once parked, Hank was the first to get out of the car, distance himself from their liquor.

Inside, they sat together at the bar, and Fahey quietly pointed out a judge and several police officers who were enjoying a drink at a table.

Hank turned to look and there they were, drinking in public view. "Can they arrest us if they're off duty?" he asked.

"Probably," Fahey said, "but they wouldn't want to dry up their drink supply and social hour. They're regulars. Could you stop staring at them, Hank? They might get suspicious of *you* turning *them* in." He shoved a shot of whiskey toward Hank.

Hank downed it to keep himself from running out the door, his heart beating in his ears, and asked for another, keeping his head down and eyes on the bar.

Fahey told them about the Doukhobors on the Canadian side, a group of Russians who believed that Jesus resides in each person. They did not support any government or organized religion, were pacifists, would not bear arms or drink liquor. The important part was that they had no problem supporting others who disregarded the law.

Because of their beliefs, Russian anarchists had financially helped the Doukhobors to escape Russia. They were also aided by pacifists like British and American Quakers, and the Russian novelist Leo Tolstoy who called them "People of the Twenty-fifth Century."

The Doukhobors could be quite helpful for storing liquor or looking the other way if rumrunners were hiding there, for a fee. They owned flat acreage that could serve as an airstrip. More than once they had lit their field at night with headlights from their cars to direct an airplane safely down to deliver car parts for a hasty repair or to pick up a load of booze.

In the early days of Prohibition, local authorities like county sheriffs had been the only patrols. But in 1924, Border Patrol had been formed. Agents had badges and packed revolvers and were expected to travel between entry stations. Recruits needed to have their own horse and saddle for the trails and backroads. Still, the border was referred to as "the dotted line" because of all the unpatrolled spaces available to smugglers. Some agents had vehicles, but they were no match for the speed of rum-runners' cars. It wasn't until officers were allowed to keep and use confiscated cars and boats that they could give a worthwhile chase. They'd finally received uniforms in 1928.

Along with border patrol and federal "dry agents," police and sheriffs continued to enforce the law regarding liquor, at least on the surface. Coming down through one county, Hank and Will were caught in a roadblock by a sheriff that Fahey had told them about. True to form, he let them go, but they had to give up two cases of whiskey as evidence so the sheriff's next report could be about his valiant chase after gangsters with "flying bullets" and his ability to confiscate their alcohol even though they got away. For him, it was all about the glory.

Hank wouldn't look the sheriff in the eye, he thought so little of him. When the sheriff learned of Will's access to beat up cars, he said he would expect a car to "capture" next time they got caught. He'd be watching for them.

"Maybe we should go through him next time," Will said when they were on their way.

Hank raised his eyebrows. "You mean give him a broken car?"

"Yeah. You know, good relations. At least we'd know what to expect."

"Unless there's a witness or he changes his mind. Then we'd go to jail, and he'd get a good name for himself. Will, you can't trust guys like that. He's a liar and a thief and cheats at his livelihood for god's sake!" Hank's voice was getting loud over the car engine. "That man disgusts me. We give him nothing. I'd rather go to jail." He turned to look out the window.

Hank felt a new tension build. *"I'd rather go to jail"* rumbled inside the car with the engine noise as they drove. He wished he hadn't said it.

"Take it back," Will said, feeling his chest tighten.

"I take it back," Hank agreed. "I didn't mean it." Though he wasn't religious, he crossed himself, hoping he'd done it right. "Let's change the license plate when we get back. That sheriff probably wrote this one down."

Trains, Chains and Coal

Ever since the beginning of U.S. Prohibition in 1920 and the end of it in Canada the same year, Canada had shipped liquor south, over the border. It was legal if used for medicinal purposes. Also, suppliers from Canada shipped it illegally in railroad coal cars, hidden in the coal.

Early on, Will and Hank had arranged with the export house to hide small orders in coal to be delivered with regular weekly shipments to a fuel company in Spokane Valley. Small shipments meant no great loss if confiscated and not a lot of interest from dry agents should they find it.

Then, feeling that the risk of losing product was better than the risk of getting caught, instead of running booze over the border themselves, they arranged for a full order to be shipped by train with a load of coal to Montana. They followed it as it went to make sure it didn't get lost.

Once the train stopped in Montana, Hank paid the conductor and crew while Will got started digging coal to find their hidden load. Hank nearly ran back to Will when the conductor told him that the train would leave again in fifteen minutes. He grabbed the second shovel and ground it hard into the coal, imagining Will running alongside the train as he tried to pass cases of whiskey to him, impossible. They unloaded the last case as the train began to roll.

They were covered in coal dust and sweat, which created a lovely black grease that made them look like ghosts with white eyes. Will walked stiff legged around the loaded Hudson.

"I'm completely black!"

"Your mechanic hands look the same." Hank chuckled. "If you keep your eyes shut, I wouldn't see you at all, but anyone can see the car and booze. Let's go!"

Will put his arm out to protect his car. "You're not getting into my car like that!"

"Wanna drive naked then?"

"Naw." Will threw Hank a towel and had a coughing fit, sneezing black snot onto the ground. "Pretty sure I've got black lung now, though."

"Sure, it's the coal that did it. For god's sake, Will! You wanna have black lung in jail? Let's move!"

As Will drove, they both agreed that this was not the easiest or cheapest way to transport liquor.

Coming out of Paterson after a trip to Rossland in British Columbia, Will and Hank had a problem. The dry squad was waiting for them in a Buick that had been seized from a rumrunner. As they drove in the dark, the road was suddenly interrupted with bright lights in their eyes and bullets hitting the radiator and gas tank as they passed. Will gunned it, knowing that the car would stop when it overheated, or when the gas had leaked away. He was surprised that the Buick could keep up with him. "Aw nuts! We might be in trouble," he hollered. "That Buick's gotta be a straight-eight."

Instead of fear, Hank got angry. He was incensed about the bullets flying and leaned out the car window, throwing out chains, oil, large tacks, everything he could find to get the Buick to pull over. Will turned onto a bumpy field and drove into the woods until it was thick enough to hide them. They covered the car with brush and walked to the nearest farm, hoping to borrow a car for a fee.

There wasn't much talking as they walked, both stunned by the gunfire. After storing the load in a barn, it took a week for Will to repair the Hudson. He added armor plating in front of the radiator and to protect the gas tank. He also added a rear-view mirror so he could see what was coming up on him from behind since agents were driving faster cars.

Hank continued to fume, even had a nightmare about having a bullseye on his chest *and* on his back. He couldn't hide, no matter which way he turned. They needed to find a route that was a lot more relaxed.

The Bare Necessities

The popularity of gambling in the 20's spilled over to rapid investment in the stock market enabled by easy credit, which caused the market to have unprecedented growth. The Federal Reserve tried to slow it down by raising interest rates in August 1929, the final straw before the crash in October. Still, the effects of the failed economy were not felt immediately throughout the country.

Loon Lake was able to build a new school that year, moving students from their previous log cabin into a new split-level brick schoolhouse. The Moose Lodge still held dances every other Saturday night. One was attended by more than two hundred couples, and proceeds were used to finish the inside of their lodge. The following summer, they continued with their annual picnic at Morgan Park in June and the boat regatta in July, and The Brick and Lime Club continued to offer their hospitality services.

When hard times could no longer be ignored, the Moose Lodge held a card party to collect money for an emergency relief fund for the community.

Wheat sold for twelve cents a bushel in 1930, and cattle for

$9 a head. It was pitiful. Even the Spokane County Fair went bankrupt after being active for twenty-nine years. The die-hard farmers of Deer Park took up the slack, deciding to support their community with a fair of their own for the first time. With volunteers and donations, it would be free. Mrs. Feretti donated her son, and the committee decided he would be perfect to introduce speakers and judges at events.

On August 28, several big farms in Deer Park set up exhibits. There was a motion picture and informational speakers at the high school on Crawford Street. At the Old Red Livery Barn there was livestock to see as well as all kinds of impressive produce, homemade jellies, and such to be judged, including Mrs. Feretti's traditional Italian giardiniera relish. In true rural community spirit, volunteers were many, and donations were generous.

Within a few months, the unemployment rate reached sixteen percent, and the American Legion helped the Clayton Moose Relief Committee collect food to distribute to those in greatest need, along with clothing and bedding collected by the home economics class at school. Necessities of life had become the focus for everyone, including Feretti whose mother volunteered him to deliver the donations with his car.

Feretti spent his days with Liz when he had time, hoping to keep her away from his competition in Spokane. He looked good in his new suit, dark gray tweed with a burgundy tie and matching pocket square. The hatband on his black hat shined like his slicked back hair from a dab of Brylcreem as they strolled through Manito Park on Spokane's South Hill. Liz was his most powerful adornment, hanging onto his arm. There were blooms of every color all around. Sunshine warmed their shoulders, and Liz stopped to smell most of the roses as they walked, despite the bees.

Manito Park Zoo had been popular over the years. Lots of regional animals were there including various birds, elk, buffalo, coyote, cougar, even skunks and beaver as well as kangaroo and monkeys from other countries, up to 165 animals at one time. The most popular were the bears. There was a black bear, a brown, polar bears and a grizzly bear.

Liz couldn't stop watching the little black bear, thinking he was so cute. She worried about the polar bear. He looked uncomfortable, out of place. "Shouldn't they give him some cold water at least or some ice?" she asked Feretti.

He shrugged, not wanting to have an opinion. He didn't tell her that bears were not a necessity, that the zoo itself was not a necessity and was closing for lack of funds. He didn't tell her about the little girl who'd lost her arm to the polar bear. The little girl had been feeding the female polar bear who had accidently drawn blood, which had caused the male to lung at her, biting her arm. The staff had pulled her away after the bear had ripped off her arm at the shoulder. The family had said that it was not the bear's fault, not to punish the bear.

"He might be lonely," Feretti said. "I read that he jumped on his mate from the top of the cage and broker her back. He deserves to be lonely."

Maintenance had been a challenge financially since the zoo opened in 1905, and with the Depression, it was impossible. The animals that could be safely released or go to private homes would go; the rest would be shot. Several bears would survive in a fashion, thanks to taxidermists, and they would grace lobbies of establishments around the Spokane area.

Hank's mentor, Evan Morgan, also died late that fall. He collapsed in the street in Loon Lake town from heart failure. In his mid-sixties, he had been on his way home at the time, worried about Halloween pranks that had occurred two nights before in the community. The funeral was held by a somber group at the Moose Temple in Clayton.

It was the first time that Hank had attended a funeral since his parents had died. He had thought he would never choose to attend a funeral again, but this one was important. He wished he had Emily with him. She would give him the right amount of empathy, not sympathy. He wanted someone to know how much Mr. Morgan had meant to him, how he had given him a leg up, had trusted him; and Emily was the only person he knew who would understand.

Saved by Grace

As a child, my favorite outing from the cabin was to the old soda fountain in Loon Lake town. It must have been a tavern at one time, the lovely, long polished wood bar that could tell a million stories, the wonky floor. Our children's favorite was to Clayton Burger for a tall, soft ice cream, though Dennis and I remembered its original building across the street before it had burned.

Summers were nonstop swimming and fishing, the slamming screen door announcing our comings and goings. The only time our daughter held still was to catch a fish—it was a miracle. Our son had a little toy boat he pulled along the beach and dock, and a tree fort where he could be king.

We enlarged the cabin again, building out onto what had been the deck, right up to the lonely tree. Dennis created a fireplace in the addition and dormers upstairs for actual bedrooms and an upstairs bathroom.

Books saved us when the weather fouled. I'd visit one of my favorite spots in the cabin, the little nook of bookshelves built into the stairs. I'd stay there to read inside the small-pane window if the sun was shining on the step or sometimes cozy up to the fireplace.

Relatives came and entire days were spent splashing in the water and lying on the dock in the sun, hoping for a rosy glow. We helped the children hunt snipe at night and thought we heard them, but didn't see them, laughing until it hurt. We trekked through the woods to Moose Bay for a sandy beach swim and to the old rock foundation that had been prepared many years before for a community center someday. Each year our young ones buried their treasures along the foundation and made maps to retrieve them the following year until too many bushes grew inside the space, and beehives and ant nests moved in.

If thunder and lightning came, we turned up the music on the radio and danced barefoot on the hardwood floor with the doors open, stomping in the water as the rain came in. Outdoor night fires began with s'mores and ended with stories passed from one person to the next according to our imaginations. Card games carried on into the late night, playing for matchsticks.

In winter, when the snow was piled high, we kept a path cleared from the cabin to the road. It went up a slate walkway and a series of steps. My desk looked out the window at the base of that path, the view providing on-going entertainment. Tiny birds and bauble-headed quail searched for food along the shoveled path, pecking as they went. Two quail inevitably kept watch from a fence post while the others ate. A moose came through our wrought-iron fence along the path without much bother, breaking it in half. Wild turkeys strutted about in their chaotic fashion, leaving messes behind, then roosted in the neighbor's mountain ash tree. They ate the fermented berries until they began to sway, eventually falling out of the tree in a drunken, fluttering heap in the snow. Remaining berries were gobbled by robins in early spring, with the same result.

The cleared winter path was also used by family coming for holiday meals, actually filling the tiny cabin with hugs and laughter and bright colors, the stair banister trimmed in red and green. Cooking was hip to hip along the kitchen counter as the fire snapped in the fireplace, and the long row of end-to-end tables stretched a festive scene from wall to wall.

Returning from a movie in the city one night, Dennis and I drove down the narrow, wooded road toward the cabin through lightly falling snow. The trees were draped in heavy white blankets the deeper we went into the woods. It looked like we traveled in a tunnel of frosting. Like a gatekeeper, a long-legged moose stepped out from the darkness between trees to look down at us through the windshield, lowering her head as if to fight. We stopped, backed up, and waited.

Twin youngsters came out of the woods to join her, evidently unconcerned since their mother was there. They looked like they should have some snow pants on those long spindly legs of theirs. We waited . . . and waited. It seemed that moose are very patient in standoffs. It was late, and I thought we should all be getting home, but there was no alternative route.

Grace had known we were there, our neighbor's dog, an elderly black lab with a white mussel, arthritis, and cancer. She worked herself up from her cozy doghouse to come out in the wet snow for us. It was one of her last days. She was such a good dog, always greeting us when we were outside and then going on her merry way, wagging her tail as she went.

Stepping from between the trees, she faced the moose and barked once. The moose stepped toward her, head down as if to charge, and Grace took a step back. Grace stepped forward two steps and barked twice. Mother moose looked at her for a long while, and I worried for

Grace. Slowly, Mrs. Moose turned around and taking her time, walked back into the woods from where she'd come, her offspring following behind. I wondered if she'd seen Grace as our reinforcement or if she'd sensed Grace's age and illness and had left out of respect. Either way, we were saved by Grace that night.

PART THREE

The Gang's All Here

Loon Lake and Spokane

1932-1933

Summer Cabin

Lying in the sun, I remember my mother's voice calling down from the cabin "Time to turn." It came about every thirty minutes. The dock rocked gently as ripples lapped the shore or bucked hard when a huge wake from a boat hit, sending water over the dock or up through the boards, dousing us. No matter, we'd be swimming again in no time anyway. The water was especially cold off the end of our dock where a spring flowed in, the same cold clear water that we had in our well.

On summer weekends before kids, Dennis and I got a glimpse of times gone by. We bought the newspaper from a boat that delivered to the docks in the mornings and rowed or motored across the lake for breakfast at Granite Point. Occasionally there was a Saturday night dance there, and a small steamboat toured the lake at dusk with a three-person orchestra on board to serenade people at their cabins.

July was the best month. The big celebration on Independence Day, loads of food, family, friends. Watermelon from Hermiston. Everyone came to their cabins, even the very elderly couple about six lots to the north who used a track and trolley to get up and down the hill between their cabin and their dock. Boats paraded single file around the lake, American flags flying, celebrators waving. Fireworks were shot off the docks like a competition between neighbors. Visitors were stupid, sending flames to float through the air under paper lanterns while the locals gasped and followed them into the dried trees, praying against fire. The lonely fir tree saw it all.

The fourth week of July was the most predictable for good weather. The wakes from ski boats, and later, jet skis, traveled from all directions making the water bounce like it was being shaken in a jar. At dusk, waning visibility caused the boats to slow down, restoring the calm, and fishing resumed. Late at night there might be some skinny-dipping if no one was in a boat with a spotlight.

Wind typically started up on the lake in August. It would stop at dinnertime, and everything seemed to rest. The water would flatten out like a pool of ink and beckon to me, the warmest water of the year. I submerged myself while wearing jeans and a t-shirt once without making a ripple of disturbance like the vampire scene in the Twilight movie. It felt like a baptism, sinking into that silky warmth, the experience only slightly marred by the thought of some neighbor calling the paddy wagon to take me away and the weight of my wet jeans pulling me down.

It made me remember the day as a child that I found out I could swim. It was at Morgan Park before we owned the cabin: Dad pulling me up onto the floating dock with the big people to warm up in the sun, taking off my lifejacket to lie down; then me jumping in, swimming to shore and walking back to our tent. When Dad found my life jacket, but he didn't find me, he thought I'd drowned. It hurt to imagine his panic, my uncle swimming under the dock to look for my body. Dad had missed out on lunch that day.

On Labor Day, visitors had their final hoorah. Year-rounders waved *happy goodbyes to summer-only neighbors as they pulled away, trailing their boats behind them, taking their noise back to the city.*

Later in autumn, when bushes dried crisp and dead leaves and bits of broken seaweed and even a few dead fish littered the water, the lake was turning over. Our neighbor, Bud Schonfeld, told me about it. It would happen again in spring after the thaw when the temperature at the bottom of the lake matched the temperature at the top and its turning would bring oxygen to the fish at the bottom. It was the lake renewing itself just like it renewed its fish, just like it renewed its people.

Whiskey for Water

Loon Lake

In exchange for a pint of Canadian whiskey, Hank hired a water witch for his recommendation on a spot to dig his well. Luckily, it was only ten steps outside the door. He started with a shovel and a pick and a lot of grit. It wasn't long before he was using a steel-rod rock buster and a five-pound hammer and sweat poured from his face and neck. He cussed at the rock, thinking that he might as well be using a teaspoon for the slow progress he was making.

He called on Willie to help him with the big rocks. At sixteen feet down, he hit solid granite and knew he needed dynamite. Willie lowered him down into the hole with a rope and winch so he could set the powder, cap and fuse and then pulled him back up once the fuse had been lit. The blast gave him three more feet.

"Wow! That was slick!" Hank said. "You think I could get another three feet?"

"Why not? What have you got to lose except some dynamite?"

"Ok, let's try. Bring me up quick since you've got another three feet to get me out of the hole before it blows."

Willie lowered him back down the hole and waited.

"It's lit!" Hank called.

Willie tugged on the winch handle, cranking it as fast as he could, pulling him up, and then it jammed. He tried again with all his might, but it wouldn't move. "It's jammed!" he yelled.

Frantic, Hank tried to reach back down into the hole to pull the fuse out of the dynamite, but he couldn't reach it.

"Get out of there!" Willie yelled.

Panic and adrenaline sent Hank hand over hand up the rope out of the hole right before it blew. He laid on the ground panting until he stopped shaking enough to sit up and see the damage. Water trickled in as they cleaned out bits of rock. He had a 22-foot well of the cleanest drinking water that ever existed.

Hank went up to Chewelah to visit Emily and her parents now and then. He showed up once in a Dodge rather than hitching a ride or walking from the train. Ben was impressed.

"Swell car, Hank! You must be doing pretty well!" Ben gave him a congratulatory slap on the back with his handshake. "How's work go'n?"

"The car's a loaner," Hank lied. "It's good. Make'n good money. In fact, I've got a little here to help with Emily's medical bills. I hope you'll take it." He held out an envelope.

"I can't take your money, Hank. You're like a son to me, I hope you know that. You're the son I never had. *I'm* supposed to be taking care of *you*."

"You did that, remember?" Hank laughed. "Now it's time for me to pitch in. I'm an adult now with a good job. If you take it, I'll muck out the barn for ya."

Ben laughed.

After the barn, Hank took Emily for a ride in his Dodge. It took her a while to get outside and into the car. She made it clear that she wanted to do it by herself. With blue skies above, he drove about twenty miles to Gifford and onto the ferry for a boat ride across the Columbia River. The ferryman greeted Hank warmly with a handshake, asked how he was doing, said hello to Emily, asked if they wanted anything. Emily thought it was odd.

In Inchelium, he parked where they could watch the water. It flowed and swirled and flowed some more.

"The river looks high today," Hank said, disrupting the silence.

"This is nice. I'm glad you're doing well for yourself, Hank. I thought the brickyard was slowing down."

"It is. I usually create the crates for shipping, so I get to work for most jobs. The brickmakers are down to one crew, though. It's been hard on everyone."

"I need to get better with these stupid braces so I can help at the farm." She picked up a leg and let it fall. "You're handy, Hank. I doubt you'll ever be out of work."

He reached over and tugged on a lock of her hair. "It's okay, Em. You make the world better just by being here." He smiled and felt heat in his face.

The river flowed and the silence grew.

"I feel like a heel, not coming around for so long. The first guy who hired me, Evan Morgan, died a while ago, and at the funeral, I wished you'd been with me. You're important, Em. You make my life better."

Emily took his hand and kissed his knuckles. "My sweet Hank."

Trapped

Up at Creston in Canada above Bonners Ferry, Idaho, Hank and Will got stuck with four other cars waiting with their loads to go back over the border through Kingsgate. The U.S. Border Patrol had been changed there and the new guys were determined to stop the smuggling over their piece of the border. The export house said the new agents acted like rats going after their cheese; there was nothing the export house could do.

Hank felt like one of too many chickens in the chicken coop waiting for the wolf to open the door. He paced back and forth in the export house. There were too many of them. No way they would all get through.

He and Will drove seventy miles west on the Canadian side to Montrose to separate themselves from the crowd. The problem there was that two Canadian customs offices converged to one U.S. customs station a few miles below the border. It was too much traffic for maneuvering. Worse, two cars had followed them. They found a small, neighborhood tavern and a table at the window where they could keep an eye on the Hudson and hopefully learn about local conditions for getting over the border.

The tavern owner told them that it was harder than ever to get through, smugglers were being caught, no deals were being made.

"This is why we need to keep crossing the border regularly," Hank told Will, "or stop altogether. Gotta keep up with the changes, so we know what's what."

"The U.S. patrol's been pick'n off runners," the owner continued, "like skeet at a gun range."

Hank did not appreciate the analogy. "They're not shooting at us, are they?"

A stiff-looking, straight-backed man at the bar in a tweed jacket and driver's cap turned to face them. He licked the beer foam from his mustache, "That would be illegal, wouldn't it?"

Hank felt pinned. He'd been too loud. For all he knew, the guy at the bar was communicating with U.S. border patrol, might even make some money for letting them know when cars were waiting to cross. He looked at the tavern owner and tried to read his face, wondering if the bit about skeet shooting was meant as a warning.

"For all we know," he whispered to Will, "that guy is with U.S. border patrol. Hell, he could follow us across the border, nail us the minute we get on the other side."

"I say we go for it." Will glanced out the window, trying to look nonchalant. "I'm gonna change the plates, check the car. Let's camp for a few hours as close to the crossing as we can and run it when we get a chance. I've got the radiator and gas tank protected. How are they gonna stop us?"

Hank shrugged, "I don't know. A roadblock, maybe?" He

tugged on his scarf. "I'm not sure we've thought of everything that could go wrong."

Will lit one of his Lucky's and got a coffee. Another driver came over to their table. He seemed a little shaky, a young man, thin, behind a dark mustache. He wore an old suit vest that had seen better days. "Hey," he whispered, "I'd like to make you an offer."

Hank nodded, motioned for him to sit.

"My name's Jeb. Hell of a deal we got go'n here."

Hank nodded again.

"If one of you'll drive my car across, you can have half the load on the other side. I don't want to go to jail. I've got a wife and new baby at home."

"Listen Jeb, you could leave it at the export house here for a fee," Will said. "Wait for a better time, get it later. We could give you a ride home, if *we* make it. Seems like they're really get'n tough everywhere."

"I wanna be done," Jeb said, "but I don't know where I'd get the money without this. It's not like there are any jobs to get, at least none that pay anything."

"Don't know what to tell ya, Jeb. It's risky, that's all." Hank downed his coffee, feeling like he needed to go. "If you go to jail, we could ask other runners we know to help out with some money for your wife, if that makes you feel easier."

That night, Will crouched behind an outbuilding to watch the U.S. border crossing. They couldn't get the car close enough without being seen, so he'd come on foot and squatted until his knees froze. He and Hank had talked about which was better or maybe which was worse. If the border patrol cars were at the station, they would likely be followed when they went through. If the cars were away, they could be waiting in a trap.

Will hoped to see a routine or route that border patrol used. Unfortunately, one car was out, and one car was parked at the station. After about thirty minutes of nothing moving, Will stood up, said, "Oh hell," out loud and walked back to the car. "Let's go," he said. "Noth'ns mov'n."

Without lights, their car quietly rolled through the station. "Nice and easy," Hank whispered. "Maybe they're sleeping."

In the rearview mirror, Will saw Jeb come out of nowhere and pull up tight behind them in an old LaSalle.

"Shit!" Will ground his teeth. He stomped on the gas and tore down the road, turning on his lights. Jeb's lights came on right behind him, nearly blinding him because of the rearview mirror and then border patrol's lights showed further behind. Will pushed it hard, taking the curves along the river with squealing tires. Jeb kept up the pace; so did the patrol.

Will took a left onto Aladdin Road and Jeb went too. It was a mistake. Border patrol was waiting, and the bullets came in rapid succession as they passed. One hit the steel plate against the radiator, one shattered the back window, and the one aimed at the gas tank came through Jeb's window. Will saw him take it in the head and careen off the road.

Will kept driving, though the steering seemed stiff and jerky as if the wheel had frozen and his foot kept slipping off the gas pedal. There was nothing they could have done.

Further down the road, after a long silence, Will spoke first. "It was Jeb who saved us, you know." The smile had slid off his face.

Hank had trouble working his throat. "I know." He lit a cigarette for Will and put it between Will's lips. The car carried them toward home, the seriousness of their business having punched them in the face.

The next day, they found an account of Jeb's death in the newspaper. The article reported that he had hung a gun out the window as he'd passed border patrol and they had shot in self-defense. "Hell, that ain't even true!" Hank fumed. "It might have been an accident, they were maybe aiming for the car, but I doubt that Jeb ever had a gun."

"Now we know who Jeb is, we can deliver some money to his wife," Will said. "We told him we'd help. We can tell her he was worried for her and that he wanted to quit."

"And that he didn't have any damn gun!" Hank spit.

There had been a dancehall on the east side of Loon Lake at Granite Point since 1921. People who had been coming to the lake on the train to fish for mackinaw and rainbow trout, kokanee, black bass, yellow-striped perch and bullheads had also been coming on Saturday nights for music and dance, some with hipflasks and some with an invitation to take a secret cruise if Liz or Feretti got to them.

Plus, there were places to stay on the lake. Both Morgan Park and Granite Point had rental cabins, ten of them having been built at Granite Point between 1925 and 1929, encouraging visitors to spend the weekend. And there were camping spots.

Feretti and Liz had become a good team on the dancefloor. They found a new group of potential drinkers at Granite Point as they danced through the crowd, looking for the bulge that indicated a flask on a hip or in a jacket or the scent of liquor on someone's breath. As the band took a break, they had six interested couples and a few singles interested in a booze cruise to The Brick and Lime Club.

They had planned to leave for the cabin when a stranger began to play the piano. All talking stopped and everyone listened, stunned by the power of his playing. Liz was smitten. As she listened, it was like the rest of the world fell away. She'd never heard anything like his playing. Strong, passionate, free yet controlled.

He wasn't with the band. People said he was "the wood-cutter," a loner who showed up at dancehalls sometimes and played classical music on the piano when the band took a break. When he quit, they asked him for more, the band told him he could stay. He walked out the door.

Liz couldn't quit talking about it and about him during their booze cruise. A woman told her that he was mysterious, had a wealthy family back east that he was hiding from, wanted nothing to do with them. "Who knows," the woman said. "He could be hiding from the law for all we know. He shows up out of nowhere, any place there's a piano."

That evening at The Brick and Lime Club, Liz flirted with Feretti and batted her eyes at him and asked if he thought they might be able to afford a piano.

Horse Packers

After years of the U.S. pleading with Canadian Parliament to stop selling liquor for export to the states, they finally did it in 1930 with the passage of their Export Act. The export houses along the border were closed. It was a noble act on Canada's part since they lost that source of income that they'd enjoyed during the previous ten years. Even so, they continued to make money from tourism, and no one could stop liquor from slipping across the border illegally.

The gang's importing business needed to sashay around the changes, and before closing, the export houses helped them connect with individuals willing to offer liquor through a black market. In the U.S., the number of smuggling violations doubled, whether from more smuggling or from agents removing their blinders and deciding to do their jobs. With greater risk, the gang's costs increased; they needed to pay higher bribes and compensations.

Joe and Hank had fifteen pack horses strung between them with empty packsaddles, winding their way in the dark from a ranch on the U.S. side of the border through the mountains to a farm in Canada. This was the horses' trial for being sure-footed and sensible as far as Joe was concerned and a chance for him and Hank to get more familiar with the trail before they had a load with them. He'd already ridden it once up to Canada and back to make sure he could find it in the dark and to learn which places the horses might have trouble.

Normally, a slow walk on a horse down a wooded trail would slow life right down, give a guy a chance to contemplate his situation, but he worried all the way, wondering if he was doing the right thing. He hoped he wouldn't be leaving Helen alone again to pay the price if he got caught. The horses were the only thing he felt sure about. The weather was perfect, no wind or rain, just enough moonlight to see the trail.

He had to stop himself from whistling or singing like he usually did on a horse. He would have found it helpful to calm himself and the horses, except not now, not when they were trying to be invisible. Instead, he did math in his head: *Each case weighs 34 lbs. Five cases per horse . . . they'll be fine carrying 170 lbs. each if we strap it carefully. 75 cases all together. I'll make $5 per case. $375 for a night's work . . . a little better than my $2.60 a day!* he guffawed. Shushing himself, he remembered people saying that you could tell when someone started selling liquor because they ate better.

Joe shook his head as he thought about Helen and his girls. He'd do whatever was needed for them. He'd tried to do it the hard way before, and it hadn't gone well. Now he would accept more profitable ways to make money and not kill himself doing it. It was no good how his family had suffered with him gone, all that worrying and scurrying for every dime.

He had remembered his family once he'd seen them, especially his parents, his mother's sob and long, tearful hug. She'd served him a bowl of crumbled graham crackers in milk, and he'd remembered it was his favorite. He'd been expecting to see them at the farmhouse in Midvale somehow, and the house had looked foreign to him; but when they'd all held hands around the dinner table that night and he heard his father's voice giving the prayer, he knew he was home. He felt like he was riding some kind of wave, surprised that he'd been offered both his jobs back, night shift at the papermill in Millwood and shoveling coal at the fuel company. This time, he wouldn't be building a house at the same time.

It seemed like his bosses had felt sorry for his trouble. They had an odd kind of concerned look in their eyes as they'd shaken his hand. Feretti had been so happy to see him when he came by for his whiskey hidden under the coal that he'd hugged him, saying that the other guy had been a dishonest goon and a drunk. Then he'd asked Joe if he happened to know anything about horses.

Hank brought up the rear of the horse train, knowing that this was the biggest, most dangerous haul they'd ever done, but he didn't want Joe to know that and back out of the deal. Hank needed to act like everything would be fine, and he whispered *copacetic* under his breath now and then to keep himself calm. They had chosen a route north of Kettle Falls and Northport, knowing to stay away from the area above Metaline Falls where border agents patrolled on horseback. He'd gone with Joe to rent the packhorses and had been impressed with Joe's knowledge about horses.

Will had gone alone to Canada to buy seventy-five cases of liquor, transporting it in multiple carloads to stockpile at a farm there. When the horses arrived at the farm, they were fed and watered and five cases were diamond-hitched to each pack saddle, two cases on each side, one on the top. Joe checked each horse to make sure the padding was sufficient, removing his hat now and then to wipe his brow with his sleeve, realizing what a huge load of illegal liquor he was transporting, wondering if he would ever see his family again.

When the pack horses were ready to go and set off on their journey, Will hightailed it through Customs and drove to the ranch on the American side, nothing to worry about, nothing illegal in his car. Then when they all met at the farm below the border, they unloaded the cases from the horses into Will's Hudson until it couldn't take any more weight and hid the rest in the barn until they could move it all.

Hank drove his Dodge to scout the route to a different farm where their new inventory would be stored. His Dodge was considered a pilot car, essential as rumrunning was getting more hazardous all the time. He drove ahead to scout for a roadblock or border patrol or a sheriff while Will waited out of sight for his signal that the coast was clear, and they stayed on the back roads which weren't patrolled as often.

Joe remained with the horses. He brushed them down and told them what a nice job they'd done, thankful that the trip was finished. All the while, he thought about Helen. He was sorry that she needed to work outside of home. She'd made it easy for him, though, telling him that it was the new trend, lots of wives were working. She'd said that both of them making money was the only way to get out of poverty, the only way to move up in the world, have a comfortable life, take care of their girls. He had to admit that things were changing for everyone, and what she said made sense.

He quivered, remembering their quiet time together when he'd first gotten back from Montana, how she had held him and told him that she loved him. Then she'd slapped his face and tried to shake him, telling him that if he ever did anything like that again, she would . . . well, she'd broken into tears. He had shed a tear too, thanking Jesus that he'd found her again. It had been awful, feeling so alone, not knowing his own name.

"I guess I let you down," he'd said.

"It came close," Helen had replied. "I saw my father separate himself from the family, try to handle things on his own. Don't you dare do that to me. We're in this together, remember? We need to talk things over. Make decisions together."

He knew she could be courageous but had seen the fear in her face and had comforted her while she'd sobbed into his chest. He didn't want to do anything illegal but didn't see any way around it, especially with other family members coming around for meals. They needed to be fed somehow. They were family.

He had taken the horses back to their own barns and was having coffee after breakfast with the family at the ranch when Feretti arrived for him.

"I'm glad you're back, Joe," Feretti said as they walked to the car. "You're a stand-up guy." Feretti shook his hand and paid him an even $400. "Thanks for helping us out."

"Might as well drop me off at the fuel company," Joe said, folding it into his pocket. "I need to get the day's coal shoveled. Course the 35 cents a ton doesn't seem so important at the moment, but the weekly bonus is nice." He grinned at Feretti.

It had been a lucky, expensive trip. With many pockets to fill, only their largest load made the trip worthwhile. Money had been paid to the farmer on the Canadian side and to the rancher in the U.S. and it could have been worse. If either had been caught, they would have gone to jail, and the horses would have been sold. Being stand-up guys and empathetic with the fact that everyone was experiencing the same hard times together, the gang would have felt the need to post bail, re-purchase the horses, and take care of their property during their absence.

Their new cache was near the town of Valley where they had a deal with a farmer for the private use of one of his barns for $100 a month. Will and Hank drove into the barn to uncover the hole they had previously dug, first removing hay from the area and shoveling nearly a foot of dirt away until they reached the planks used to cover the hole. Hank got a case of whiskey out of the car and carried it over to the hole.

Will climbed down a few rungs on the ladder to receive the first case, "Well, now that we got it, where do we sell it?"

Hank shrugged as he carried the next case over. "That's Feretti's deal."

Bubble Gum and Speakeasies

Feretti drove Will's Hudson and wore his new three-piece suit, black with the tiniest white stripes. His shoes shined like midnight in a full moon. Liz was at her best, hair and makeup perfect, a new beige slinky number that reflected the light. They arrived at the Davenport Hotel to discuss business with Liz's friend, Del, a Mr. Somebody.

Feretti felt like a long-tailed cat at a square dance in such a swanky place. Liz squeezed his arm and smiled at him like he was the most important man there, hoping he'd feel better. They met Del in the lobby and moved to a private room where they ordered soda water, and ice. Feretti would have loved to have offered all seventy-five cases for a quick sale, but two dozen cases seemed safer.

"Twenty-four cases, huh? Haul it yourself? How do I know it's authentic from Canada?" Del wanted to know.

Feretti produced his flask of *Old Hermitage* and poured Del a shot. Del smelled it, held it up to the light, took a tiny sip, and savored it as his whole face relaxed, like he was having the best moment of his life. Feretti and Liz were a bit embarrassed by his reaction.

"Wow, it's been a while since I've had the good stuff," he said with a greedy grin.

Feretti waited a few beats before asking, "Have we got a deal?"

"Deliver it to the little parlor across the street Tuesday night between 2 and 3 in the morning. The door will be unlocked. Take it downstairs. We'll make sure the police are not in that part of the city at that time. If you see a red bow on the door, keep on driving. It'll mean that something's gone wrong."

"How do I know you aren't gonna double cross us?" Feretti asked.

Del withdrew five bills from his wallet, $100 each. "You'll get the rest when you deliver. You don't deliver, you'll be hearing from us."

There were pockets of underground tunnels in parts of Spokane where business owners had built on top of old basements after fires in 1889 and 1910. Liz had heard that one of them connected to the Davenport Hotel. She wondered if their liquor would be consumed at the parlor where they were to deliver or end up at the Davenport. As they drove away, Feretti asked Liz, "Who was that guy?"

"Just a guy with some money. I thought he could afford to buy it himself. I never thought he might be part of some group. I've no idea who he means by 'us.'"

"I hope we haven't gotten into something we'll be sorry about."

Liz felt a chill as if a ghost passed by.

On delivery night, the whole gang was there, dressed in drab garb, even Liz, her favorite gray cloche pulled low over her eyes. They parked the Hudson right outside the door and began unloading the cases, carrying them inside and down the stairs like they were fire fighters, in a hurry, focused.

Slightly panicked, Liz was the lookout on the street. She chewed her bubble gum and popped it without realizing she was doing it, trying to look casual, like she was waiting for a bus in the middle of the night. It wasn't long before a big black Cadillac crawled by, taking a close look. She felt her spine turn to ice yet walked right up to his window to ask if he had some kind of problem, and he drove away. She thought she'd seen him before at the Ambassador Club.

Then a gray Packard drove up and parked behind their Hudson. Her gum popped, exploding all over her face and she scooted inside, slamming the door. "Somebody's coming! Hide!"

Will dropped the case he was carrying. It crashed, whiskey leaking out into a liquor lake. He swiveled to find a towel and his foot went out from under him, landing him on his butt in the booze, and he scooted across the spill into a dark corner where he hoped he could hide. The others watched through the glass as a man examined the Hudson, looking in all the car windows, then tried to open the door of the shop, his face pressed into the glass of the door.

"It's Del," Liz said, opening the door. "You come to check on us?"

"Thought you'd want the rest of your dough." He looked around. "Hey, what's going on in here? I'm not paying for that," he said, pointing at the mess on the floor, "and what's with the guy hiding in the corner? and Liz . . . doll . . . what's happened to your face?"

There were plenty of speakeasies, sometimes called 'juice joints' or 'blind tigers,' in and around Spokane. Some were in apartments and homes, wherever you could put together a bottle and two chairs. There was a speakeasy in the basement of the Hutton building on Washington off Sprague. It looked like a restaurant with a little kitchen. One was off Browne between Trent and Main. It looked civilized and took on much of the dinner trade. The drinking went on upstairs there, and everyone came, even the socialites. Liz had been there once with a different Mr. Somebody. She thought about it now as she considered ways to move the gang's liquor. Liz was a city girl. It was Feretti who said, "What about roadhouses?"

Roadhouses were like speakeasies but outside city limits and in rural areas along highways. If they were near the Canadian border, they were called line houses. During Prohibition they became soft-drink parlors. They sold "set ups," ginger ale or soda with ice to customers who brought their own flasks of liquor. Many of them served food and booze in a back room or on a different floor. Some places held card games, gambling, even cockfighting; or they could be ritzy nightclubs with bands and shows which appealed to businessmen, bankers, public officials and off-duty lawmen.

Feretti and Liz visited as many roadhouses as they could find, looking for outlets for their liquor. There were several north on Division as well as east on Sprague and Trent all the way to

Idaho. They found an interest in Canadian beer, and although they also sold some cases of liquor, most places did not want to pay for the real thing. They were satisfied to serve moonshine. It was cheaper, and people had gotten used to it, and they could make modifications in flavor to make it taste somewhat like gin or bourbon or whatever the customer ordered.

The only way the gang could sell a good load of the expensive stuff from Canada would be at private parties on the South Hill or in Browne's Addition or to groups with money at places like the Spokane Club or at the Davenport.

With all their poking around, the whole gang became paranoid, thought maybe they were being watched. Will put the Hudson into hiding except to haul booze and they used Feretti's Tin Lizzy or Hank's Dodge to get around. Hank had a new desire to not get caught, Emily. She was also the reason he wanted to keep going. Even if Hank were able to find a handyman job, he'd likely be paid in eggs or milk or a chicken. It wouldn't be enough. He had plans.

Tracks

The beach below all three cabins was a rubble of rock, flat-sided fractured granite the size of a loaf of bread but thinner. At the water's edge on Hank's property, the gang had stacked it to create a walkway to the dirt trail that led up the hill to the cabin, hoping visitors wouldn't twist an ankle or break their necks. They'd used large stones for steps at turning points in the switchback trail.

Hank imagined Emily with him at the lake cabin, and Ben and Meg too, for that matter. It motivated him to make improvements. He spent the first half of the day arranging rock like a jigsaw puzzle to create a flat patio above the water's edge. Then he terraced above that, forming a wall with a flat ledge on top. He was sitting on the ledge to take a break when Feretti glided up to the dock in a rowboat and stopped on the other side from Hank's rescued clinker boat.

"What's with the boat?" Hank asked as he grabbed the side. "Haven't seen you in your work clothes in a while."

Feretti stepped out. "The train was com'n through Clayton, so I hopped on. Rented a boat across at Granite Point. Makes me feel like I'm on vacation," he grinned.

The sun was behind them where they sat on the warm ledge of rock. "I thought maybe we should talk things over now that all three houses are finished. Thanks for the nifty cabin, by the way."

Hank nodded.

"I'm wondering about the business," Feretti continued. "Level with me. Where do you think we should go from here?"

"Beats me," Hank tossed a small, chunky rock from his feet into the water. "We've got our cabins and that's swell. If we quit the business, money will get tight pretty fast. The brickyard is bound to close completely unless something big changes."

Feretti wiped his face with his handkerchief. "Do you think we should try to keep going? I'll need some kind of income if I'm gonna ask Liz to marry me. At least she knows the risk. How does Willie feel?"

"I think he's in. Needs more for his car repair shop, and he's been looking for one of those super 8's ever since one chased us. They *are* fast; I had to throw everything we had at it to get away."

Feretti admired Hank's rock work. "Maybe I'll do the same at my place," he said and got up to go to his own cabin. "It'll give me an excuse to get Liz up here, you know, for help."

Hank arranged rock, continuing the ledge about eight feet deep for a patio. He imagined Emily and her parents enjoying the lake. Maybe they would swim and want to fish. He could bring them in the boat.

As he walked up the trail to the cabin, he realized that Emily would never be able to get up there in her leg braces and she refused to be carried. Even if he drove her to the cabin using the road above, the path from there down to the cabin would be difficult too. It was a problem.

In March 1932, the unemployment rate was twenty-four percent and Clayton Moose Lodge was on the verge of closing. Their last hurrah was generous, fixing up their basement as a gymnasium with a punching bag, exercise equipment and a boxing ring where the high school boys and community could learn to box and maybe even settle their differences. It was a gift, and Washington Brick and Lime was magnanimous too, maintaining the facility as long as they could.

Five banks had failed in Spokane County before the crash in 1929. Many farmers hadn't had money to put into the bank or hide or bury anyway. Despite assurances, three more Spokane banks closed their doors April 1932: American State Bank, Spokane State Bank, and Wall Street State Bank. The others hung on by their toenails. Washington Trust Bank in Spokane had a short run, but it was over before noon. Tensions in the state continued, and a year later, still hoping to calm things down, Washington State Governor Martin called a three-day "bank holiday."

At Washington Brick and Lime, orders for bricks pretty much stopped by July 1933 and the plant was sold to Eric Johnston to do whatever he could with what was left. He began selling anything extra while trying to keep the plant intact as long as he could. He received a few orders; it was not enough.

Bud Schonfeld, son of Fred, the plant manager at the brickyard, worked at Westby Mercantile in Clayton. He saw the town begin to die and kept on filling ten-pound sacks of grain, beans, macaroni, split peas from hundred-pound sacks for 20 cents an hour, paid in scrip. Eventually, his hours were cut to two hours a day even though he had to walk five miles to get there. He cut firewood on his father's property to use as payment for places that wouldn't take his scrip wage. Mr. Westby at the Mercantile shook his head and said, "If my scrip's no good, it means my name's no good too, and that would mean the world is going to hell anyway."

Mr. Westby accepted about anything for payment at his store when people were hurting: cord wood, home canned food, a goat; and he let folks buy on credit if they couldn't pay, until he went out of business. He must have known that people wouldn't be able to pay him back, but what else could he do? Watch people starve? Bud said, "Good people went under, and the rest survived." When Westby Mercantile closed, Bud and his wife, Freda, moved to Spokane to look for work and found a home in Millwood.

With the brickyard closing, Hank made them an offer to buy eighty feet of their track and one of their trolley cars. Emily's situation created an engineering problem that he thought he could solve, and he was excited to go after it. He hired Willie to help him lay track straight up the hillside from the beach to the cabin above. Spikes were extra-long, pounded into the ground between rocks and cemented into little pillars on each side of the track with metal bars across as support.

He created a seat inside the trolley car and built rock plat-forms as stations, one at the top and one at the bottom of the track. Then he found a small, gas-powered tractor motor and a cable long enough to bring the trolley up the hill and control its descent on the way down. He kept the leftover track to run his boat into a future boathouse.

On his way to the Pearson farm, Hank was hoping to convince Emily and her parents to visit the cabin. He was proud and excited to share his track and trolley system and hoped Emily would be willing to use it.

As he drove, he remembered his beginnings with the Pearsons, how they'd welcomed him into the family. Emily had made his favorite gingersnaps to make him feel at home soon after he had moved there, and she'd gone with him to visit his parents' graves and had held his hand. He'd pushed her into the pond when he'd been feeling sorry for himself, and she'd told him he didn't know from nothing. The mud had ruined her dress and made her cry. He was still sorry about that. She'd made his neck scarf for his birthday, his lucky scarf, cream and sage green to match his eyes.

At the farm, he was expecting to see happy-face greetings, but no one came to the door. Max was there wagging his tail and licking his hand with a little whine as if he needed something. "At least someone's glad to see me," he said.

The car was gone. He opened the kitchen door to see if Emily was there. She sat at the kitchen table, her hands covering her face. Two chairs were on their sides and the coffee pot had bounced off the wall from the look of things.

Hank's heart knotted. "What's going on, Em?"

She stared at him, red-eyed, as if he were guilty of something. "Tell me, please!"

"They went to the hospital."

"Is someone sick?"

"Two goons came. They beat up father out in the barn. Mother tried to stop them with the shotgun. They took it away from her and pushed her back into the kitchen. They wanted to know where you were keeping the booze. Father didn't know what they were talking about."

Air sucked from the room. Hank sank into the only chair that was upright. *Am I going to lie to her?* "Are *you* okay?" Ashamed, he could hardly look at her. "Do you know who it was?"

Emily shook her head.

"I'm so, so sorry," he said, putting the chairs upright. Slowly, he picked up the coffee pot without making a sound and carefully put it on the stove. "Is there anything I can do?"

She stared at him with dead eyes.

He dragged himself out the kitchen door.

After a sleepless night, Hank went to see Ben and found him in the barn. The right side of his face and around his eye were purple-blue and puffy. It was swollen along his jaw.

Hank froze when he saw it. "I'm really sorry," he said from a distance.

Ben didn't move.

"I got into a deal to make money. I had no idea that anyone could get hurt except for maybe me. If I'd known this could happen, I never would have done it."

Ben was quiet. He moved his mouth gingerly, "Stay away from Emily, Hank."

They stared at each other until Hank turned and walked out the barn. He wasn't welcome in the only place he could call home.

They're better off without me.

Bacon Grease

Hank brought a sawed-off shotgun to meet the gang at the cabin and knew he had their full attention when no one sat down. Liz refused to come out from behind Feretti as he told them about what had happened at his home in Chewelah, about Ben getting beat up by two guys looking for their booze.

"We've got to find out who it was, stop it from ever happening again." Hank was dead serious. He wanted revenge.

Feretti hoped he could calm Hank down, avoid trouble. "Maybe it *is* done, since they didn't find anything."

"Yeah, maybe it's done there, maybe not. Maybe they'll be looking at *your* house next. You want *your* father beat up? What about your mother?"

Feretti swallowed. He hadn't thought of that. "Of course not."

Hank was adamant. "We better find out who it was and do something about it. Someone's been talking. It may not even be someone we know."

"You've got to have some information, Hank," Liz said. "You've got to ask Meg if she saw something from the kitchen or remembers anything, even what kind of hat they wore, anything at all to go by."

Willie spoke up. "If she saw what car they were driving, we'd be able to look for them that way."

Early, wet snow had dumped and mostly melted off the roads the day they saw the cream-colored Studebaker. It was parked outside a mansard-roofed roadhouse on north Division Street. Willie waited outside to keep an eye on the Studebaker while Feretti and Hank went inside. It took a moment for their eyes to adjust as they sat at the dark, gloomy bar. They ordered glasses and ice.

Feretti recognized the bartender and noticed that he looked nervous when he saw them. Over their glasses and ice, Feretti asked him if he wanted a shot from his flask. "The real thing my man," he said, stopping mid-pour, keeping his flask in the air above the glass for anyone to see.

The bartender looked around, hoping there weren't any kind of lawmen in the house to see it.

"Do you happen to know who owns that Studebaker out in the parking lot?" Hank asked.

"It's mine. What's it to ya?"

"Man, your car is a disaster!" Feretti said. "Someone's run into it! There's pieces all over the parking lot!"

The bartender ran out the door, Hank and Feretti right behind him. He got to his Studebaker and stopped, becoming confused. It looked untouched. Hank shoved him into the back of Willie's Hudson and tried to restrain him as they drove north. When the struggling didn't let up, Hank sunk his knuckles into

272 - VICTORIA VENTRIS SHEA

the bartender's nose. Then the only irritation was Willie warning him about getting blood in his car.

As they passed the new golf course at Wandermere, Hank tied a kerchief over the villain's eyes.

"What should we do with him now that we have him?" Feretti asked.

"I don't know. Let's pop him off." Hank winked at Feretti, but Willie didn't see it.

"Hey! I'm not going along with that!" he said.

Arriving at the lake cabin, they lead him blindfolded with his hands tied behind him, through the snowy woods and over the hill as they talked about the wild animals in the area, a bear, lots of skunks, a really mean badger, a huge pack of coyotes, even a few wolves. They tied him to a tree, saying that he would be food for the critters and if he ever got out of there alive, he'd better not be looking for booze that wasn't his. If he wanted to tell them who his partner was, they might let him go.

They walked away far enough to see him from a distance as dusk set in. Willie lit a Lucky. Feretti walked down to the cabin to make a pot of coffee. When the bartender began to struggle and whimper, Hank walked closer to remind him that he should give them the name of his partner before it was too late.

They were shocked when an animal *did* come their way. A young deer wove between the bushes and trees like she was about to fall over, completely unafraid. She moved on down to the road and beyond towards the water. They'd heard that there was a moonshine outfit further up in the woods and wondered if she'd gotten into some sour mash.

Feretti came back with cups and the hot pot of coffee. He also brought Hank's cruet of bacon grease. Smearing it on the man's hair, neck and clothes, he explained that the bears and wolves would not be able to resist his smell now. They'd be able to smell him for miles. He would surely be some animal's dinner within a few hours.

Willie complained that the bacon smell made him hungry.

Hank approached once more to say they were leaving for good, so if he wanted to tell them the name of his partner, it would be a good idea.

The bartender heard him walk away and panicked. "Steve!" he said.

They drank their coffee as they watched him struggle and listened to him talking to himself.

"Steve what?" Feretti called.

"Steve Miller."

"Not good enough!" Hank lost patience, stomped over to him against the tree and slugged him in the stomach. "That's too common a name, idiot. How do we find him?"

The reply took a moment. "He works at the same roadhouse."

Hank put his hand around the bartender's throat and squeezed. "If you get back in one piece, you tell him that we are coming after him when he least expects it. Stay away from anyone and anything connected with us, or I will cause the end of you and your roadhouse too. You beat someone up, it's gonna come down on you a lot harder than this."

They kept him blindfolded on the way back to town, Willie

whining about getting bacon grease in his car. At Wandermere, Hank grabbed the blindfold off and kicked him out of the car. "Better get your nose fixed," he said. "Probably shouldn't let it heal that way."

It was quiet in the car on the way north until they reached Deer Park. "Seems like we've reached a new level of bad guys," Willie said. "Not sure I like it."

"I don't like it," Feretti said.

"The problem is that if you do illegal stuff, you have no protection, and sometimes other guys doing illegal stuff are actually criminals," Hank said. "We've got to find a way to make an honest living."

They drove in silence, each trying to think of a way to make money. Hank broke into their thoughts, "In case you need it, the gun is under the bar."

What they hadn't known was that earlier that day, while they'd been up in the snow, Spokane deputy sheriff Easlick had been up there too, about a mile away to investigate a moonshine operation. He'd received a report of forty gallons of moonshine having been delivered to local lumber camps during the previous two months. A man named John had ordered nine-hundred pounds of cornmeal. On a tip, the sheriff and a couple of deputies had searched in several abandoned cabins. In the fourth cabin, they'd found a large still and seventy-five gallons of sour mash left behind. They'd dumped it, of course, and the forest critters had enjoyed it, some more than others. If the sheriff hadn't found that still, he had planned to check the cabins on the lake next.

On Moonlight Bay

Joe thought that he and Helen had earned a night out, something special. She'd found him a used wool suit and had become a seamstress after all, modifying a navy dress with a peach-colored sash at the hips. As she squeezed her slightly swollen feet into her old dress shoes, she hoped for a store-bought dress in her future, something classic. She had no interest in short-lived trends. Classic was best.

It was a warm summer evening with the sky still bright as they drove north through Pleasant Prairie in his brother's car, the dirt roads heavily oiled. They turned west at the Peone Grange to Mead and continued north on Highway 395. It smelled like home. It looked like home. The *kerthunk, kerthunk* of the tires over seams of highway concrete was relaxing, the sun shooting streaks of light between clusters of trees.

Facing the sun, Helen closed her eyes and the movie screen in her mind played pictures with each flash of light like she'd seen in the movie shows in Palouse: The hanging noose, Joe looking out-of-place with his brothers, Joe being hugged by his tearful mother, Barbara jumping onto his lap, Suzanne teething on his shoulder. He was home. She reached over and squeezed his arm.

She still worried for him sometimes, found herself listening for him to sing or whistle. Those were the signs that he was happy and content.

The highway took them through Deer Park and Clayton, and they turned left down into Granite Point on Loon Lake as the sun was beginning to sink below the hill west of the lake. Nearly every spot between the trees was filled with parked cars and Joe maneuvered the small Model T between two trees where the larger cars would not fit.

Music carried from the dancehall across the parking yard. Joe didn't mind waiting while Helen checked her hose one more time. In fact, he didn't mind watching one bit. She'd had to mend a run clear up near her garter by creating stitches to fill in the gap. "There's nothing automatic about that 'silk chiffon automatic run mender,'" she said, "just thread, needle and directions. I barely had the time or patience for it!"

"Looks like it paid off to me. Let me see." Joe bent to get a better look.

She pushed him away and stepped out of the car, long legs first. All Joe's struggles and worries fell away, and he remembered their first dates, Kamiak Butte, Palouse Falls, her father's broken moonshine jugs.

"You look swell," he smiled, extending his arm. "Remember when you said hard times should be spent with someone you love? You were right."

"You didn't tell me you were taking me dancing, you devil," her hand went up to cup his jaw, "especially way out here."

"You liked the drive, though, didn't you? All the wheat fields up here."

"I felt like I could breathe deeper the further we got from town." She squeezed his arm as they walked. "Oh Joe! Just smell the lake, so fresh and sweet!"

Inside, Fred Swanback was playing the fiddle with his dance band. Joe was reminded of his earlier years, his brother playing fiddle in the barn, what it was to know all your neighbors as family. . . His throat gripped, remembering. There had always been music.

Full of melancholy, he grabbed Helen and swirled her around. She hung on, feeling his grief, remembering her own younger, carefree days.

"It's been such a long time," she whispered.

"We're still getting along," he spoke in her ear. "Doing better than some *because* we're together." He spun them in a tight one-step twirl. "Let's have fun tonight, Helen. We deserve it, don't you think?"

Helen's smile was her answer. She was desperate to have a fun night, determined to seal off any worries that might interfere.

They danced together as they always had. Their one-step became their two-step became their fox-trot until they needed to take a break. Helen was rubbing her feet when a man in a black leather bomber jacket came up to them. "Joe," he said, extending his hand.

Joe looked around to see Hank and shook his hand, happy to see him.

"What are you doing way up here, Joe?"

"Having a night out with my wife Helen here. This is Hank," he said, turning to Helen. "He's the guy who hired me to work with some horses. How are you doing, Hank?"

"I've had a bit of a setback, actually. Kind of got my legs knocked out from under me. Say, how would you two like to come to my place. It'd be a quick row straight across the lake. I've got my own boat. You could come back whenever you want."

Hank was glad that the Brick and Lime Club had moved to Will's cabin even though they'd reduced it to a smaller, more intimate group since the Feds had shown up. He enjoyed having his own cabin to himself. He offered beer to Joe and Helen while they admired the cabin in lantern light.

"You build this yourself?" Joe asked. "I bet it's got a hell of a view of the lake in daylight."

"Yeah, I had some friends to help."

Joe saw the framed doorway on the waterside, the space nailed shut. "What's the problem there? No door?"

"Let's just say it's a big step, a safety precaution." He led them to a table to sit.

"What's new with you and Emily?" Joe asked. "You talked about her quite a bit when we were with the horses."

"I think I've lost her, Joe. That's my setback. Her father told me to stay away from her."

Joe laughed. "Helen's father told me the same thing. We got married anyway."

"But Emily needs someone who can take care of her. I'm not sure I'm the one."

"Do you love her?" Helen asked.

"I do." He *did* love her. He just realized it himself! His heart beat faster. Hearing himself say it sounded like a commitment of some kind.

"Why not give *her* a chance to decide?" She gave an accusing look at Joe. "Why do you men think you need to decide *for* us? Ask her for goodness sake. What have you got to lose?"

"What if she says 'No'?"

"Well, you might regret her answer," Helen said, "but at least you'll never regret not asking her. If you love her, you need to try."

But could she love me as more than a brother? "If I could get her on a horse with her leg braces, do you think you could come and be there to help me with the horse, Joe? I know she'd love to ride, if she could."

Joe swallowed his beer. "I don't see me ever turning down a chance to ride if I'm not working. Do you think we might all four ride together?"

Hank grinned and looked at Helen, saw her eyes light up.

He invited them to Will's cabin to say hello, and they walked single file on a path that had formed between cabins. Inside, a few drinks were being poured while a patron crooned, and a dice game was in progress.

Feretti gave Joe a handshake and a pat on the back like old friends and lifted the back of Helen's hand to his lips, dark eyes meeting dark eyes. He introduced Liz who turned to see Helen. Both women stopped. "I've seen you before . . ." they both said and laughed. They moved to a corner to talk about how they might have crossed paths, Liz needing a break anyway.

Will abandoned his post where he stood to watch for trouble and brought his smile over to the guys at the bar. A rendition of "Frankie and Johnny" started up, a guy singing in the corner, and Joe needed to join in. He couldn't help himself. As the song ended, he turned to see a man leaning over Helen as if to put hands on her and moved without thought, grabbing the guy by the back of the collar and jerking him upright. When the guy put up a fight, Joe gave him a left to the stomach and a right to the face for a knockout. It sobered the room for a moment, then glasses were lifted. "Yay!" the crowd hollered. "Someone finally shut up that son-of-a-bitch."

Together, Will, Joe and Hank carried him outside and set him up against a tree. "He really is a wise guy," Will said. "Always drinks too much. We won't let him in again. Thanks Joe."

"Sorry for the ruckus," Joe said when he came back in. He sat with Helen and Liz, his arm around Helen's shoulders. "You both okay?"

Feretti came over with drinks.

"I'm fine," Helen said. "Liz was about to rip his face off before you came over."

"He was pretty dodgy," Liz said. "Glad you sent him pack'n."

"We saw each other on a streetcar in Spokane," Helen said, smiling at Liz. "Liz wore a design I recognized, Elsa Schiaparelli."

Joe shrugged. "Sounds like a foreign language to me."

"Helen said she would look through my closet to give me ideas since she learned about fashion from her mother." Liz fluttered her eyelashes and laid her hand on Joe's arm. "I sure hope you can help her find the time, Joe."

He felt heat bead up on his forehead and thought they should return to the dance.

A few fish jumped near the bow as he rowed Helen back

across the lake in lantern light. It was the first time that he sang "On Moonlight Bay" to her. "You have stolen my heart . . ." The pulling of his oars made ripples in the water and matched the tempo of his song. She felt loved and safe with every pull.

The Desert Hotel

Prosecutions regarding liquor seemed to be more common in small towns than in cities, maybe because rural folks had voted *for* Prohibition while cities were against it; or it might have had something to do with money. Spokane had voted against Prohibition, and there were rich, powerful people in Spokane. It was ripe for business.

Now that Liz had some money, she wanted to move further down First Street to the corner of Post to the Desert Hotel, a more respectable place to live. She and Feretti had agreed that she should move. Living at the Washington Hotel made her nervous and they needed to locate a clientele willing and able to buy Canadian liquor.

Wearing her most conservative dress, she shimmied into her Miss Somebody persona and spit out her gum before walking into the hotel on Feretti's arm. She'd been around enough hoity toity people to do it, chin held a little higher, a little too nice with a demanding tone in her voice, as if people should *know* she was important.

She saw the manager sitting behind his big mahogany desk and was glad that she'd brought Feretti. It was too much to expect a hotel manager to deal with a woman alone. Women needed fathers, or husbands, or brothers, or uncles or at least chaperones with them to be respectable. She found it to be quite irksome. The manager asked Feretti if he would guarantee payment, and Feretti knew they were in trouble. Immediately, he slapped six months' rent onto the manager's desk and asked indignantly, "Is that enough to ease your concern?" hoping his irritated response might appease Liz's wrath.

Liz turned to Feretti and mauled him, kissing him ferociously open-mouthed, running her hand up his shirt and said, "Oh Uncle, I *do* hope you'll let me show you my *immense* gratitude!"

The manager was torn between lust and horror, and he couldn't let go of the six months' rent money. He looked to the floor instead, hoping to hide his brilliant red face. Standing up, he said, "Thank you, Mr. Feretti. I'm sure your girl will be happy here."

As they stood to go, Liz accidentally knocked the ashtray off the manager's desk, and Feretti squeezed her bottom as they turned for the door, hoping she would appreciate his contribution to the performance.

The Oasis Restaurant was on the ground level of the hotel. Its sign read "Coffee Shop with Fountain Service." To Feretti and Liz, "fountain *service*" was code for speakeasy.

Inside the restaurant was far more impressive than inside the hotel: a huge space, three giant columns down the middle decorated with Egyptian hieroglyphs. Four large, open brass and glass sconces glowed around each column to light sculptured faces at the top. Long, art deco chandeliers hung from what looked like marble ceiling panels high above. A bar ran half-way down one wall as a soda fountain. Glasses were stacked there, ready for service, sparkling in the light. Behind the fountain bar was a wall of private booths with several more private booths in the front corner where patrons might look through a sheer, loosely woven curtain to see outside without themselves being seen. Clearly, the booths were for secret drinking.

The floor was large granite tiles, alternates of dark and light, laid in a checkered pattern. The opposite wall was a long lunch counter and in the middle were more than thirty tables with rounded back chairs, set for parties of two or four with linen tablecloths. Only a few tables had patrons at the time.

The bartender, Marty, was obviously a good judge of people. He asked if they would like a booth. Feretti ordered two cokes, ice and glasses. When Marty brought it over, he pulled out his flask and said, "You don't mind, do you?"

Marty said, "I don't see a thing."

Feretti introduced Liz and himself. "Liz is a guest here now," he said. "I wonder if we might be of some service to you."

A week later, the gang sat together in one of the booths. Feretti wanted Marty to meet Hank and Will, so he'd know who they were when they made a delivery. Marty had been hesitant to carry booze himself, preferring that people brought their own, but he couldn't pass up the chance to get high-class Canadian liquor and make some extra money. He wanted to keep it small, only interested in one case at a time, for his special customers who could afford it.

They were all surprised how quickly business picked up in

the fountain section of the restaurant. The well-to-do became regular customers, asking for his "new drink" which he poured from a syrup carafe. Marty, and therefore the gang, were happy for the business but also nervous that the word had gotten out so quickly, drawing attention to them.

Marty froze in his spot the day a judge walked in with two police officers and sat in a booth. He hoped they wouldn't see the tension creasing his forehead when he went to take their order. They asked for his "new drink," and he looked carefully in the police officer's face, the sweat breaking out on the back of his neck. The judge patted Marty's arm. "It's okay my man. We're only here to get a drink, nothing else."

Marty served water, glasses, ice and a syrup carafe, assuming they didn't want any mixer. It seemed safer to let them pour for themselves. "I'm only a server here," he said, turning away.

As they stood to leave, Marty told them it was "on the house," thinking he couldn't be convicted of selling it that way. He released a heavy breath after they went out the door, wondering what would happen next. How many law enforcers would come? Would they all expect to get a free drink? Would he be expected to pay a bribe? He didn't like the unknowns.

Right before Marty closed the door for the night, a big black Cadillac drove up and Albert Commellini came in. The place was nearly empty.

"Mr. Commellini," Marty said, surprised to see him. "It's good to see you, sir."

"Hey Marty. I hear you have a new drink. I'd like to try one, if you don't mind."

"Sure thing, Mr. Commellini. You'll have it in a jiffy."

Commellini had been noticing activities of a group who seemed to be bringing booze into the country from Canada, thought he saw them unloading across from the Davenport one night. It was beginning to cut into the demand for moonshine. He didn't make the moonshine, only supplied the ingredients for others to make it at Mica Peak. He might have facilitated deliveries and encouraged certain law enforcement to be in certain areas of the city at certain times. He'd been arrested a few times, but it had only resulted in a fine or a very short sentence.

He owned an Italian import company in Trent Alley, between Washington and Stevens streets. It was an area of speakeasies and underground tunnels originally created for pedestrians to avoid streetcar traffic in downtown Spokane. Now it was used to smuggle liquor. Trent Alley might have held the first take-out service. Story was that a thirsty walker strolling through the alley could drop money down a hole and a drink would come up in exchange.

Albert Commellini also owned several hotels and the Ambassador Club on East Sprague which had a dance hall, a movie theater and a dining hall with fifteen private dining rooms. He was known to drive a Cadillac around town at night to check on his establishments.

Liz found that her Mr. Somebodys were more relaxed about picking her up at the Desert Hotel than they'd been from the New Washington Hotel. Evidently, she'd moved up the social ladder.

She tried to make friends wherever she went. At private parties, she paid attention to what people were drinking. There was more moonshine being served than Canadian liquor, and she didn't hear many complaints. *Had people gotten used to it? Or found a stable source for good moonshine?* People were even drinking near beer, making her wonder if there was a lack of money for Canadian beer or a lack of supply. She could help with a supply problem, if only her anxiety would stop twisting her gut every time she thought about it.

Happiness on a Horse

A load of pre-cut lumber bounced in the back of a borrowed truck with every bump in the road. Hank was tense, gripping the wheel on his way to the farm. He walked straight into the barn and found Ben cleaning out a stall.

"Ben, please hear me out." His throat was constricted.

Ben turned towards him with a tight face, leaning the pitchfork against the wall.

"I'm hoping you'll give me permission to see Emily, Ben. I'll do right by her, I swear."

"Are you done with the liquor business?"

"I guarantee you that if anything ever happens like that in the future, it will have nothing to do with me. I think I can get her on a horse, Ben. I brought stuff to build steps and a platform so she can get into a saddle, and . . ." Seeing tears in Ben's eyes, he stopped talking.

Ben nodded. "Emily has missed you. She's got enough to deal with. Her legs . . . I was hoping you could help."

Hank grabbed Ben's hand with both of his own. "If I finish cleaning out the barn, would you let me build her a platform for getting on her horse?"

Ben laughed and nodded.

Emily was having her daily nap, dreaming about being in the iron lung. It breathed for her, changing the pressure inside to pull her diaphragm in and then pushing it out again. Her body had been laid on a padded tray and inserted into the metal-tube lung with her arms at her side. Only her head and neck stayed outside. She dreamt that there was a terrible itch on her nose and no one to scratch it, her hands imprisoned at her sides. In her sleep, she practiced eating, being careful to only swallow while breathing out so she wouldn't choke while trapped on her back. She heard the lung's rhythmic sound, *breathing, bump; breathing, bump.* When the rhythm changed to *bump bump bump bump,* she woke up. Someone was hammering outside.

Once she got on her braces, she sat on the edge of her bed to rest, remembering when she never needed to rest at all, when she had all her strength and complete control of her legs. She threw the memory away with a toss of her hand to focus on "now" and grabbed her crutch. When she got outside, she was surprised to find Hank packing up to leave.

Seeing her struggle, Hank carried a bench over so they could sit together. He held her hand gently; it was cool and light. "Ben said I could see you . . . if you're willing. I don't know what I'd do if anything happened to you, Emily."

Emily stared into his eyes, confused. "Something bad has already happened, Hank. Don't you see this?" She lifted a braced leg and let it fall.

"It doesn't matter to me. I'm sorry but I've realized that I love you. I think I always have." He hadn't planned to say it, but now it was out.

Emily's mouth dropped open. "You're sorry? That you love me? Like a sister, right?"

"No, Em. Like I never-want-to-be-without-you love. It's kind of scary."

She sucked a mouthful of air. "Well, that's a fine kettle of fish." She'd always known that Hank would push boundaries. "But you're my Hank."

"Problem is, I want to be your *only* Hank."

"I'm incapacitated, a cripple. You don't want me." Tears began to form.

He kissed her knuckles. "Let's just spend a little time together, see how it goes?"

On Sunday afternoon, Hank drove Joe and Helen north beyond Loon Lake. The highway stretched through forested mountains and then crested to the view of a flat, green valley, Chewelah at its north end. It was part of the Colville River Valley that began in Springdale.

"Looks like you've got some industry going on here," Joe said, seeing a big plant left of the road towards town.

"Yeah, poor farmer downwind lost his crops because of the dust, even killed his livestock, but they paid him $11,000 damages and have cleaned it up now. It's magnesite. This guy Talbot was looking for dolomite for your papermill in Millwood and found magnesite instead. Found out the government wanted it for the war, so Talbot quit the papermill. Now it's the largest producer of magnesite in the world."

"Well, it's still a beautiful valley," Helen said, "even with that monster at the entrance of town."

"Chewelah means 'snake,'" Hank said, "for the creek that winds through it." He turned the car right to a farm up against the hills. "The old timers call this valley 'Fools Prairie' cuz only fools would try to farm it. It's full of clay."

Ben had the horses saddled. He was pacing back and forth in the barn, worried about how Emily would do. Meg fussed in the kitchen. The coffee was ready and warm peanut butter cookies sat on the kitchen table. Emily was unsure, especially when she saw two people she didn't know get out of Hank's car. As they came toward the house with Ben, she sat down at the table. She'd been standing too long at the kitchen window, dressed in some baggy pants that Meg had created for riding.

Helen's was the first face that Emily saw, warm and kind, a fun-loving face. She wore wool riding trousers and handed Meg a wrapped package, thanking them for a chance to ride. "It's fudge," Helen said. "I haven't gone riding in over a year. I miss it an awful lot."

They sat at the table while Joe wondered about Emily. *How much has she suffered? How strong is her spirit? Do her braces hurt her?* He wondered if anyone had talked with her about those things. He asked Ben to show him Emily's horse.

In the barn, Joe met Molly. She was a healthy chestnut quarter horse, and Joe liked her right off, very sweet and personable. There was also a feisty black and white paint, a gray appaloosa and a cream quarter horse. Joe spent some attention on the paint, thinking he might be perfect for Helen. She would appreciate his spirit.

Emily came from the house, walking slowly toward him with the others. She wore her braces over the top of her pants under a skirt. Assuming that the fabric against her skin padded the braces, he watched how she walked with her crutch, how her braces moved.

Hank walked beside her. He had explained to Joe how he wanted Emily to know some normalcy in her life. Hank looked as tense as Emily did.

Molly was lined up to the platform and as Emily approached her muzzle, the horse perked up, pumping her head up and down. "Did you miss me, Molly?" She scratched Molly's forehead and rubbed her neck.

The platform was wide enough for two people to stand side by side. "Hank or Ben," Joe said, "if one of you would help Emily onto the saddle, I'll hold the horse."

Emily looked to her father, so Hank stepped back. From the high platform, she sat onto the saddle and with her father's help, swung her leg over the top of Molly's neck.

Immediately, Joe saw that the braces were uncomfortable for Emily and probably for the horse. "How would you feel about taking the braces off, Emily? The horse doesn't need them," he grinned.

With her braces off, Emily relaxed and bent forward to hug Molly's neck, wanting to hide her tears of relief. Joe led Molly around the corral to see how well Emily stayed on the horse. When he saw her grip the horn with both hands, looking tense, he ran a soft leather strap under the cantle of the saddle and over her hips and strapped each leg to the fender above the stirrup. The next trip around the corral was much better, and she took the reins for the third trip.

With all four of them mounted, they rode at a slow walk down the access road that edged the property. Oh, how Helen wanted to flick her reins and run her paint down the lane, feel the wind blow in her hair, remember riding Blackie in Palouse. The paint wanted to go, too. She kept reining him in, wanting him to walk beside Molly so she could visit with Emily.

"Molly seems like a sweet horse, Emily."

"She is. I've missed this so much, and the fact that I can do it without my braces makes me feel, well, free I guess. This gives me something to look forward to."

Joe was happy to be on a horse, and he broke out in song, couldn't help it. "I'm an old cowhand, from the Rio Grande . . ."

"You shouldn't go out alone until you're stronger," Helen said. "I could come and ride with you sometimes, if you want."

"Yes, Helen, I would love that."

Emily smiled at Hank who'd been watching her every move, and he rode up next to her. "Thank you for all of this, Hank. I love it, and now I'm really tired."

"Let's turn around then," he said, "let Joe and Helen ride for a while?"

Joe and Helen took off, letting their horses run, and Helen got her wish. It was a wonderful holiday to be on a farm in a beautiful valley on a horse. Emily reminded Helen of her mother-in-law, Alice: quiet, kind, determined. Emily had liked Helen, too, not overly obliging, just practical. Being practical was a good fit for Emily.

Thunderbird Wine

I grew up in a tiny red house on a corner in Millwood, a four-way stop where students grabbed hold of car bumpers in winter to ski the icy road in their shoes. Our double lot had a substantial vegetable garden tended by Dad with his hoe to keep the rows of ditches clear when irrigation water bubbled up from the back corner of the lot on summer weekends. When I complained about the sulfur stink in the air, Dad told me that the papermill smelled like money, and I should be grateful for it.

My parents were frugal. We were required to eat the brown trout from the tiny icebox in the fridge no matter how long it had been in there or how desperate I was to escape outside from the smell of it cooking. I remember going out for a meal four times—when Grandma died and we met relatives at a restaurant, when the kitchen burned and we went to the A&W drive-in, when Ron's drive-in opened on east Sprague with fish 'n chips, and when my sister Cathie saved money for us to go to the Ridpath Roof for our parents' wedding anniversary. She forgot to bring her money, but it was lovely to see our parents gliding across the dancefloor in their fanciest clothes.

In addition to the Dairy man, the Watkins man, and the Fuller Brush man, a beggar sometimes came to our door. Since Dad was usually gone on the railroad, Mom would visit with him outside on the porch, a quiet, private conversation. He'd sit on a step to wait while our dog Rusty got all the petting and attention he could want, and Mom made up a bundle of food. Then he was on his way, Rusty following him if he got the chance.

One time, Rusty didn't come back. I thought I was joining Dad's search party but was surprised that he seemed to know where to drive. We found Rusty two miles away in an alley behind a business on the south side of Dishman. He was tied to a clothesline outside a shack. I thought Dad would be angry with the man for stealing Rusty. Instead, he shook the man's hand and thanked him for taking care of our dog.

The last time I saw that man, he came to our house for a bath and Dad gave him some of his old clothes. When they drove away, Mom said that Dad was taking him to live at the old farmhouse in Chewelah. It felt right, knowing that someone who needed a home would have one and a farm that needed care would get that too.

Family said that my paternal grandfather worked hard to an older age than most people and wouldn't take any money that he didn't earn, wouldn't even accept a tip for a job well done, felt it turned his work into a type of servitude. They told me that his only peace before he came to his reward was when a nurse tied "reins" to his hospital bed so in his mind, he could work his team of matched mules that he had loved on the farm.

Dad's mother moved into my bedroom once when she needed care, sending me down to the basement with my sister. Her oak rocking chair and bookshelf filled my small bedroom, and her blue and yellow sun bonnet quilt brightened the foot of my bed. She sat in her chair, the

Bible in her lap and one hand on a magnifying glass. Even at my young age, I could see a lifetime of perseverance around her kind smile.

I didn't realize then that she was missing an eye until I saw it the next morning looking at me from a glass of water on the kitchen table. I shied away from it at first, then came back for a better look. It was a glass eye. Once I became brave enough to look more closely at her face behind her glasses, I saw the sunken eyelid where her eye should have been and the other eye magnified, making me think I must look huge like under a microscope to her.

Her quietness created mystery for me, and I wondered about the invisible scars she might be carrying, like war veterans who only speak of their experiences with other vets. She was treated gently and with respect. It was clear that she would always be cared for by the family, whatever that took.

At a doctor's recommendation, she measured whiskey as medicine by the tablespoon, even while riding in the back of our Nash on our way to Bryce Canyon. She refused to swallow it from the bottle because she did NOT drink. It was medicine, and it spilled down her chest like wicked, pungent perfume.

My parents didn't drink except for an Irish whiskey at Freda and Bud's house at Christmastime or a beer on the 4th of July or to console a friend who'd lost a job or a loved one. The medicinal bottle of whiskey was kept in the cupboard above the broom closet just in case a need arose.

The bottle of Thunderbird wine that Dad bought for me when I was eleven years old was medicinal too. It was supposed to cure my pneumonia. Mom had given up on the mustard plasters on my chest which had blistered my skin. She'd switched to lard and turpentine but didn't think it was as effective. Still, it took six weeks and a nurse *coming several times with a big needle to stick in my backside before I could get out of bed.*

Boat and Trolley

Hank drove to Granite Point and down to the boat launch and docks. Emily got out of the car, her crutch slipping in soft sand. It was the first time she'd been out in the world other than her earlier ferry ride with Hank. She was glad to have her straw sunhat and a sweater since it looked like they would be going in a boat. Hank had been very secretive about it all. From the dock, he got into his rowboat first and held the dock to steady the boat with one hand while holding her hand with his other, hoping she was willing to step in.

Emily stalled. She didn't know if her leg brace would bend enough for the big step. Those green eyes looked up at her, and when he said, "You can do it, Em," she stepped and fell on him, her nose smashing against his shoulder.

"Sorry!" she struggled, trying to right herself, her legs not helping much.

"Now I've got you where I want you," Hank grinned, not letting her go. Some of her hair had come down, the curls tickling his nose. She smelled of vanilla. "You're not hurt, are you?"

Put upright, she looked around to see if she'd had an audience for her fall although she couldn't see inside the windows of the dancehall above them.

He handed her a Mae West life preserver, insisting that she put it on. "It's new, holds air. Much better than the big cork vests that can actually drown you by trapping your arms."

"You've thought of everything, haven't you." Emily grudgingly pulled it over her head which took the rest of her hair down.

Hank stopped. He hadn't seen her hair down for years; they were practically kids then. It looked right, like it *should* be down since they were out on the boat. He put his knees outside hers and began to row as he looked at her face. The sunlight reflecting off the water bore deeply into the bluest eyes he'd ever seen. Her skin was pale, translucent with a bit of flush. Halfway across the lake, he pointed behind him. "See that flat area above the water?"

Emily nodded, hanging on. The water was choppy because of a breeze.

"That's where we're going. Keep me pointed in the right direction, would you?"

Emily used her finger to direct him as she watched him row. His shoulders seemed to grow as he pulled the oars. Auburn fuzz covered his forearms, lighter than his skin. She focused on his mouth and jaw, clean shaven, a few freckles beginning to show on his nose. *Hank, my Hank. He thinks he can save me*, she thought, eyeing his lips again. She thought about kissing those lips, and her mind intervened. *Don't fall for him. It wouldn't be fair.*

She couldn't imagine what was in store for her. She trusted Hank but wondered if he realized her limitations. "You're making me feel pretty vulnerable, Hank. One hundred percent dependent on you right now." The wind gusted, taking her hat, and he maneuvered the boat to retrieve it.

"I saved your hat, didn't I?" He held it over the water to drip as the boat drifted. "You know you're safe with me, right?"

"Yes." She threw the hat behind her into the bottom of the boat. "Keep rowing if you're going to save me too!" A wave splashed up the side of the boat, wetting her face.

Swells applauded against the shore as he pulled up to the narrow dock. He held the boat steady with the dock the best he could against the waves. She sat on the dock with her legs in the boat, then Hank got onto the dock to help her swing her legs around and pull her up to stand. He held her there awhile with his arms around her, feeling how fragile she seemed.

"Do you feel steady enough for me to get your stick?" he asked.

With her crutch, they walked together up the ramp to the stone patio. "Whose place is this, Hank?"

"It's mine. Ours someday if you want it to be," he blushed.

"Where'd you get the money? Is that your cabin up the hill that I see?"

"Yeah. I built you a trolley so you can visit, if you'd like."

Emily's jaw dropped when she saw the trolley car waiting for her, her eyes following the track where it led up the hill to the cabin. "I can't believe you did that, Hank! I can't believe that you did all that for me!"

"I only care about the place if I can share it with you, Em. Not to put any pressure on you or anything."

"Right," she laughed.

"I only want to make you happy. It's all I want."

One step up to the trolley platform, he opened the little door that he had cut in the side of the car and showed her the bench seat. "If you would like to sit here, ma'am," he motioned downward with a sweeping arm, "I would be happy to start the motor that will escort you to your cabin."

With Emily in her seat, he skittered to the top of the trail with his heart in his throat and started up the motor. It was loud, echoing off the hillside. The trolley started with a jerk and continued nice and slow, almost too slow.

She thought about covering her ears and looked around to see if anyone was watching. Presenting herself to the world as a disabled person was hard and having to wait while she was loudly and slowly "escorted" up the hill seemed to emphasize her crippled legs. "Hey look everyone!" the motor said, "I can't walk!" She remembered Helen's practical voice when they'd ridden together. Emily had started to feel sorry for herself. "That's right, Emily," Helen had said. "You need braces. You've got to accept it and move on." Helen had helped her feel whole, like she had some power over her own life.

At the platform on top, Hank opened the door to help her step out. His heart pounding, he hoped she would see that life would be easier with a handyman like him.

Emily held onto Hank and leaned over to kiss him on the cheek. "This really is a big surprise, Hank. It must have taken a lot of work." They walked slowly, carefully up the slight incline to the door of the cabin. "How did you afford all of this?"

"Well, I did all the construction myself. The brickyard is slowing down and they're selling off what they don't need so that is where I got the trolley and tracks. Now that they're closing, though, I need to find a new job."

Inside, he helped her sit on the roll-a-way bed which was up against the wall like a daybed. "This is taller, probably easier to sit on than a low bench," he said. He sat next to her and held her hand.

"What do you think?" he asked, looking around.

"Well, it's lovely, especially the view." The only thing between them and the expansive water view was a single fir tree near the cabin slightly to the right of center. "Very cozy in here."

"I'll build a deck out there one day when I get a little more money," he nodded toward the water side. "You could sit out there and watch the lake and the critters in the trees, your own private part of nature."

She leaned back, putting her head against the wall. "You seem to be able to do just about anything, Hank."

"I'm hoping I can persuade you to marry me someday. I won't ask, though, until I have a steady job."

Married, she thought. Sunflowers and forget-me-nots flashed in her mind. Her breath quickened. Could she really have a happy life? "Oh Hank! I won't hold you to it. What would I do without you?" She turned to hug him.

"You'd suffer of course." He put his fingers into her hair and kissed her on the mouth, tenderly, until he felt her go limp.

She put her head against his shoulder, enjoying the manly smell of him. "I don't know if I can allow you to waste your life on me," she whispered.

Hank sat straight upright. "The world, my world, is better, so much better, with you in it. It's because of you that I want to *be* someone, to accomplish things. There's no point to anything without you."

She felt heavy, like a burden had been added to the weight on her legs. "I'm so tired, Hank. Could I lie here for a little while do you think?"

"Sure. Do you mind if I stay?"

"Will you help me take my braces off?" She pulled the hem of her skirt up to the top of the braces about half-way between her knees and hips.

Hank shuddered. "Yes ma'am. I'll help," he grinned.

She fluttered her eyelashes. "I don't suppose my parents would approve."

A metal rod ran the length of each leg, one on the inside and another on the outside with a hinge at the knee. He untied the wide leather band around her upper leg and the narrower straps above and below her knee. Then he untied the ankle strap where the metal rod ended and carefully pulled the braces off. He covered her with his only blanket and laid down beside her, providing his arm for a pillow.

"It's the only pillow I've got," he said, "unless you'd rather have a stack of old newspapers."

With her head nestled into the hollow below his shoulder, she listened to his heartbeat and had never felt so safe. He felt the softness of her hair against his neck. Within a few minutes, her breathing changed as she slept, and Hank prayed his thanks to God for that moment. He felt complete.

She woke at the beginning of dusk. He spread peanut butter on bread and gave her water fresh from the well "on the house."

"Oh good!" she smiled. "I had a hankering for peanut butter!"

Hank knew she was only being nice. He helped her back into her braces for her trip home, careful to tie the straps so they

304 ~ VICTORIA VENTRIS SHEA

would be as comfortable as possible without getting too fresh, but his hand traveled the inside of her thigh. He couldn't help it. Evidently, his hand had a mind of its own. Her skin felt like silk there. He had known that it would.

Her body responded, sending shivers down her legs and into her backbone and stomach and everywhere like electricity. She tried to cover it up, but it was impossible, her lips parting, her eyes softening . . .

Their boat ride by lamplight was quiet. At home in Chewelah, she put an arm around his waist and kissed him goodbye. Because of him, her future felt hopeful.

Tractor Trouble

Hank and Feretti drove up to the lake and found several cars at Willie's cabin. Inside, six guys were drinking and playing cards. Feretti picked up an empty bottle off the floor and asked Will to step outside.

"Who's collecting the money, Will?"

"I keep forgetting," smiled Willie. "We're having a friendly card game, that's all. I was concentrating on that."

"We're not risking our necks so you can have fun with your friends. Tell 'em they have to pay for their drinks and see how many of them stick around," Feretti said. "You'll need to pay for the ones who won't. It's a business, Will. Not free. Free comes out of your own pocket."

Hank grabbed Will's arm to make sure he was listening. "Will, you've got booze hidden in your cellar," he whispered. "Don't have parties during daytime. What are you thinking?"

Will's smile turned down. "Sorry Hank."

"So let's get rid of them, get the money you can, you owe us for the rest, and then lock it up and come over to Feretti's cabin to talk business."

"Next buying trip," Hank began. "I think we should pick it up for a few weeks. Really go for it, and then quit. We've been lucky so far, but the longer we go, the more likely we'll get caught. Get what we can, then find a regular job."

"Good luck with that," Feretti said. "You know everything is closed or closing."

"Yeah," Willie pulled on a Lucky. "There's nothing to repair. People let their cars sit up on blocks if they break down. They can't afford the gas anyway."

"Hey, I heard about another supplier if we want to try him," Willie said. "He's in Montana, Havre I think, right on the border. From what I hear, he's got a big place, hotel, dancefloor, everything. The guy's name is Shorty Young, he owns Honky-Tonk Tavern. He's the biggest beer supplier around, makes his own Canadian beer, well, he calls it Canadian. He has underground stills and tunnels. He makes hard stuff too, uses a lot of Gordon labels. The Feds have been trying to shut him down for years, but he's too shifty for them."

"I heard about him." Feretti shook his head. "That place got shut down in '29. He burned it down himself. Hell, we can get moonshine from Crow's Nest Pass or Mica Peak or from a local farmer if that's what we want, but they don't call it 'coffin varnish' or 'horse liniment' for nothing. I don't think that's what we want to sell, is it? Let's stick with the real stuff, sell to people with money who are willing to pay for it. Keep it high class. It feels more respectable, and I don't want to poison anybody."

Willie shrugged, "It's just that they're making arrests near the border like mad now that the export houses are closed."

"If we could get some through our friends in Creston," Hank said, "there's so many rivers and creeks and lakes all along the border, maybe we could bring some by boat . . ."

"What about Joe and horses again?" Feretti asked.

"Hey!" Willie spouted. "We could use the train again, have the crates marked "varnish" or "floor paint.""

"It's been done," Feretti said. "And it's been confiscated."

Hank and Will had not planned to buy anything. It was supposed to have been a scouting trip to check out the connections they'd made through the export house before it closed, but since they'd found booze for sale at each stop, they'd made purchases. It had seemed like the right thing to do. Now the car was full, and they needed a quick plan for getting it over the border. They drove west across Canada from Creston and were hiding north of the border above Metaline Falls in the garage of Will's friend who owned the car repair shop.

"I feel like we're hanging out here on our own this time without the export house." Will lit a cigarette. "And in my old neighborhood."

"That's because we *are* on our own." Hank thought about the increases in arrests, double what it had been. Moonshine was getting more popular because the real stuff was too hard to get. "We should be able to get a high price for it . . . if we can get it home."

Hank had been thinking about getting electricity to the farm. A modified electric sewing machine might be a way for Emily to make an income.

"How's your luck today, Will?"

Will lit another cigarette. He thought about the Gardner Cave below the border. "I'm thinking if they are so busy patrolling by horseback and watching the trails in this area, why not drive right through? I pretty much know the backroads here."

They rolled into Nelway and went west from the main road to a narrow backroad to cross the border, hoping it wasn't deep mud since there had been some rain. Hank remembered the first run, how he couldn't take a breath, he was so afraid. This run felt the same except that he had a more important reason than money for getting through. Emily. A big maroon Hudson loaded down and traveling the backroads would surely cause notice. He knotted his lucky scarf around his neck and gripped the seat.

Will was on such extreme alert that he could feel the ends of every nerve vibrate. He hoped the Hudson would be able to do what was needed if he had to push it to the limit. It was such a narrow road, he wished they had a pilot car to investigate the route, make sure it was open. As if his thoughts were a premonition, around the next bend a tractor sat in the middle of the road.

"Farmer must've gotten tired of smugglers going this way," he said with a shiver, stopping the car. "Now what?"

"Can't back up. Gotta go forward somehow," Hank said. "Can we push it out of the way?" He climbed up into the tractor and took it out of gear, then turned the wheel as far as he could to the left where the bank was low. The Hudson coughed a little as Will slipped the clutch, pushing against the tractor. It didn't move. They unloaded some of the crates and tried again, pushing it off the road just enough to get through. Having reloaded the car, Will was lighting a cigarette and heard a motor coming up from behind.

He jumped into the car and put the gas pedal to the floor. The tires dug into mud and sprayed, finally gaining traction. Picking up speed, Will prayed for the car to hold together and they bounced and jostled forward. Hank held onto the seat and door to keep his head from banging the ceiling. Will saw a log laying across the road up ahead, and he turned into a farmer's pasture, breaking through a fence line. Through his rearview mirror, he saw a man running. Then he saw a bull chasing behind the man, and the runner got to a tree just in time.

"Ha! Even the bulls want us to get through!" Will laughed.

Hank was still hanging on. He'd closed his eyes a long time ago.

They were unloading into the hole inside their rented barn when Feretti showed up. He handed a note to Hank. "This came to you at the brickyard. One of the guys brought it to me. It's from Emily's dad, says the Feds have been going from farm to farm looking for you. They probably know you're the one who owns the cabin now, too."

All the blood drained from Hank's face, not because he was being chased, but because Ben was involved again, and he had promised that would never happen. He dropped to the hay, squeezing his head to keep from thinking. They would never trust him now.

Feretti kept looking out the door and around the corner to the road, expecting agents to drive up. For once, it was Will who calmed them down. "Do you know how many farms are all around here? I'd say the odds are with us, not against us, and everyone we've dealt with are good guys. They wouldn't turn us in. I'd say our mistake was letting so many people come to the cabin. Too many found out about it."

"We either need to close it down and sit on this load until things calm down or get rid of it immediately." Feretti paced back and forth with cases from the car to the hole while Will stayed in the hole to stack the crates.

Hank managed to lift his head. "I say we get rid of it. I don't want the owner of this barn to find trouble. Let's move it and be done."

Feretti nodded. "Let's make one more run."

Hank looked at him like he was nuts. "Easy for *you* to say!"

"Is this load going to put you where you want to be money-wise?"

In his mind, Hank saw Emily and the farm. "Fine," he said. "This time, you're driving a pilot car, and we're doing it in the dark and traveling the main roads."

Hank and Will went back to their same connections in Canada to load up. Feretti waited in Hank's Dodge on the U.S. side of the border, facing the border with the headlights off. He'd been there an hour, watching the comings and goings of the Border Patrol. When Will drove the Hudson to the line, he flashed the headlights once to let Feretti know they were there, his lit cigarette reflecting in the windshield. Feretti flashed back twice, signaling that it was clear to cross, so they drove across with headlights on, and Feretti pulled in tight behind them, keeping his lights off, making it look like one car rather than two in the dark.

They drove that way about five miles, thinking they were nearly into a safe area when lights flashed behind Feretti. Will saw it in his rearview mirror and told Hank to hold on. At the next turn, which thankfully was wooded, Will cut his lights and turned hard off the main road. At the same time, Feretti turned his headlights on and drove about a mile before he finally pulled over. The sheriff had him get out of the car and open the trunk, searching everything and finding nothing.

In the meantime, Will and Hank had gotten far enough away to turn on their headlights and continue driving.

"I've been wanting to try that maneuver ever since Fahey told us about it at his line house that time," Will said. "Actually, I didn't know if it would work, and I always would have wondered, but it was slick, wasn't it?"

"Slick," Hank said. "Thrilling, actually, and it's a good time to be done."

Stillwater Fish'n

Sitting in the boat, Willie sucked on a Lucky. "All I know is, when you want to think things over, the best thing to do is go fish'n. Stillwater fishing's perfect for it. Of course, it's okay to fish when there's stuff to do, too. I'm just saying it's a great way to get away, think things over. Nobody's gonna come bother you when you're out on the lake."

"What if the guy pestering you is in the boat with you?" Hank dropped his weighted line into the water, the worm wiggling on his hook. "Stop flapping your jaw, Willie. You'll scare away the fish." He unscrewed the lid from a mason jar and took a long swig from cool Canadian beer before passing it to Feretti.

Willie shrugged, "Scaring the fish . . . I thought that was just something your daddy told you to get some peace and quiet, keep kids from yakking all the time."

"Well, it makes sense, doesn't it? To not scare the fish?"

"I guess . . . about as much sense as telling kids to rest after eating before they swim. It was probably our parents who wanted to rest."

Feretti let the cool liquid flow down his throat and relaxed. "Glad we're doing this. Been a lot of tension lately, and we're almost done. One more night for The Brick and Lime Club and one more delivery to Spokane."

Hank and Will looked at each other and Will lit a second Lucky. "Maybe you ought a knock on wood, Feretti," Hank said. "Let's not dwell on it being the last night and the last delivery. Feels like you're tempting fate."

Feretti knocked on his seat and said, "I take it back," hoping he hadn't jinxed them.

"We've already got tension," Willie said. "Wasn't it your girl-friend who said if we didn't get some fish, we wouldn't get any lunch?" His stomach growled, and he raised his line a little to get some action on the lure. That's all it took. There was a tug, and he began to reel in a fish until his reel froze, refusing to turn. He grabbed the closest jar of beer and began wrapping his line around it, trying to not spill the beer, bringing in a nice little rainbow trout. "Don't need to worry about *my* lunch," he grinned.

"Forget about lunch," Feretti complained. "What about the beer!"

Willie held his rod and jar up to his face and took a long drink, then set it between his feet to unhook his fish.

Liz was trying Hank's roll-a-way for a lovely nap, luxuriating on the feather mattress and enjoying the absence of people. Listening to the quiet, she heard movement in the cellar and sat straight up. The guys hadn't been out fishing very long and she doubted they would be back yet. Quietly, she stepped off the roll-a-way and tiptoed to the windows to see if Hank's boat was back. It wasn't. She didn't think there was liquor in the cellar any longer, but Hank might still have his money stash down there behind a rock in the foundation.

She wasn't sure *what* to do but went to the bar to get Hank's sawed-off shotgun. The stranger's steps echoed through underground spaces between rock in the hillside as he came up step after step alongside the cabin to the door. Having no idea how to hold the gun, she quickly tried it up by her face and then down at her waist and nothing felt right. She had no idea if it was loaded or how to check. Somehow, she needed to bluff, make it look like she knew what she was doing, hopefully scare the intruder away.

Putting on her toughest dance instructor persona, she readied herself, shotgun at her hip. The doorknob turned, the door opening a few inches. Standing her ground about ten feet inside, she waited, holding her breath. The door swung wider, and she took one step forward, shotgun in front and said in her toughest voice, "Hey creep! You'd better get out of here!" lifting the gun as if to shoot.

The creep's eyes became big dollar coins, jaw dropped, palms pushed at the air in front of him as he backed out the door. She followed, stopping at the doorway, shotgun still pointed, and saw him scramble up the hill. She'd never felt power like that before, a new sensation. It felt good for a second, until her legs began to shake.

Wobbling to the roll-a-way, she dropped, keeping the shotgun across her knees and was still there when the guys came up the hill from fishing.

Willie was saying how they really needed to fish at dawn or

dusk if they wanted to catch fish when he walked in the door with his one fish dangling from his finger to show Liz and suddenly stopped, Hank and Feretti crashing into the back of him.

Feretti pushed through, "What is it!" He saw Liz sitting on the bed, holding the shotgun across her knees, staring at the floor. "Liz?" he said gently. "You okay?" He took a few steps toward her.

She thrust the gun at him, and he jumped back, then realized she was handing it to him.

"What's going on?"

"Whiskey," she said.

The first swallow loosened the tendons of her throat as it traveled to her middle, helping her relax, and she told them about the intruder. Hank went to the cellar, and Will and Feretti went to check on their own cabins, and Liz poured another shot.

Browne's Addition

The gang held back two cases of whiskey and some beer for themselves, storing it in the hole in Will's cellar. Liz's Mr. Somebody at the Spokane Club took half their cache, all they could get into the Hudson; but there was another load to sell as well.

A new Mr. Somebody, Teddy, danced with Liz at the Ambassador Club on East Sprague. Feretti sat at a table against the wall, his eyes attached to her baby blue chemise dress, not wanting to lose track of her. It shimmered as she moved, and a cluster of beads on one hip reflected light. They knew the club was owned by Albert Commellini; they didn't know that he had been watching them for weeks.

Feretti felt especially protective after Liz's fright with the gun. What a flirt she was on the dancefloor! A sparkly blue headband lit up her eyes. One shoulder lifted and she arched her back with only a tiny strap as thin as a spaghetti noodle to keep her dress up. Teddy was hooked, practically drooling. It made the hairs on the back of Feretti's neck stand up.

They left the dance, and he followed them to Browne's Addition, a big white house with front columns. It was clear that a party was in progress. Luxury cars were parked outside, and a butler stood at the door. Feretti knew he was out of his league as he followed them to the porch. The butler grabbed his arm to keep him from entering through the door.

"Hey!" Feretti said. "Hands off, buddy."

The butler, who was dressed in a black suit much nicer than Feretti's, let go of his arm. "Excuse me, sir. I don't think we know you, Mr. . . .? This is a private party."

"I'm her bodyguard," he said, pointing at Liz's back.

"The madam with Mr. Theodore?"

"Yeah, him," he nodded.

Inside, he grabbed a drink from a makeshift bar and found it was the real thing, good whiskey. Most of the wealthy houses had exhausted their supplies from their basements. He hadn't been in many homes like this one. The ceilings were high, and the hardwood floors were covered with imported rugs except for the dancefloor in the middle of the room.

Looking around, Feretti realized that he had lost Liz. She wasn't on the dancefloor. He poked his head into several rooms on the first floor and began up the stairs when the same butler grabbed him again.

"I'm sorry, sir. No one is admitted upstairs."

"Look, buddy. I've lost my girl. You've got to help me find her." Feretti felt panic rising.

"Now now, sir," the butler condescended. "I'm sure she's alright."

Feretti was ready to push the butler down the stairs when he saw the blue dress on the dancefloor. He patted the butler on the shoulder and went to stand against the wall. Liz made eye contact and nodded her head toward a hallway ever so slightly. Feretti walked that direction and waited until she arrived.

She was breathless. "I'm on my way to the powder room. We've got a deal. Deliver the whole thing to this house tomorrow night. They have a cellar entrance. I can't disappear now, though." She saw the worried expression on his face. "You musn't worry. I'll be fine. I took care of myself for years before I met you, ya know." She started to close the bathroom door in his face, but stopped and opened it enough to say, "copacetic" with a big grin.

Feretti couldn't go home. He parked in view of Theodore Somebody's car and waited in the cold, his imagination going wild. *She probably wanted to stay and dance,* he told himself. *In a big, fancy house with lots of rich people.* He ground his jaw.

The big house began to empty. He stood shivering by his car to be able to see better. They must have been the last couple when they finally came out, and he followed them to Liz's hotel. He saw her get out of the car and stop to talk through the window.

"Hey Tootz," Teddy said, "did you know that someone is following you? Either that or they're following me. See that car behind us?"

Liz stood to look. "Oh, don't worry Teddy," she shrugged and gave her most beguiling smile. "That's just my brother. He's harmless."

The next evening, the Hudson arrived at the big white house with front columns in Brown's Addition. They followed the driveway which went to the back of the house and backed up to an open cellar door. All four were there to unload, collect the money and get out as fast as they could.

Liz was the look-out, watching the street, chewing gum like she always did when nervous. Walkers strode by, a few people on bicycles, and Commellini in his Cadillac, though he didn't stop this time. A few minutes later, a police car drove in front of the house and her jaw stopped mid-chew. She hoped it would go on by, but it slowed and turned onto the driveway. Panicked, she ran around the corner of the house yelling, "The cops! The cops!" and inhaled her gum, choking her.

Most of the booze was already in the cellar with Feretti and Will. Hank slammed the cellar doors shut with them inside and locked the padlock that hung on the outside. He told Liz to hide, and she ran between bushes and beyond, gagging to dislodge her gum and get a breath, causing neighborhood dogs to bark.

Hank drove the Hudson around the other side of the house and through their rose garden to get onto the street, then on through Browne's Addition. Police cars were blocking his access to the only road out of the neighborhood, and he turned to find another route. He tried one road after another and each one stopped in a dead-end at the edge of a steep bluff, Hangman Creek meeting the Spokane River far below.

His mind slowed, and he thought about the words "dead end," even chuckled at the irony. *Only a fool would try to smuggle booze into a neighborhood with only one exit,* he thought. He tried to drive through a park but got into a spot where the trees were too close to drive between them. Finally, he stopped and got out of the car with his hands up.

The Devilish Delfoes

Police came to Liz's door at her hotel and searched her room. She only had a few bottles of beer and two bottles of whiskey, and they arrested her for it, saying she was planning to sell it. She was fined $200 and sentenced to one month in the Spokane City Jail.

Deep down, Feretti supposed it was inevitable that someone would end up paying the price for their shenanigans, but he never thought it would be Liz. He came to the jail as often as he could to visit her in the women's section, always waiting on a bench up against a cement wall, simmering in guilt. Ever since his first visit when he saw down-hearted children waiting to see their mothers, he'd come with candy in his pockets. When he handed it out, their faces lit up. It made him feel like he was doing *something* good.

He'd brought candy for Liz, too, hoping it would brighten her day. She walked toward him with her swag and feisty attitude, a better tonic to his weary spirit than a stiff drink. "There's my fella," she said, and he knew that she was okay.

Sitting across a table from him, she told him that the worst part was the boredom. "Been scratching the wall to count the days until I get out," she said. "Gives me something to do. Twenty-three days left."

Feretti tightened his smile. He knew she was tired of hearing him say he was sorry.

"I'm teaching the other girls to dance," she said, "even though we have to sing our own songs."

"I don't suppose this is a good time to ask you to marry me," he said. He hadn't meant to say it. It hadn't even crossed his mind to ask her now, but he'd let it out. "We got the money from the sales, you know," he whispered.

She scowled at him. "Well this is every girl's dream, to be proposed to in jail, and to have it be something about money. Why don't you hold on to that question for twenty-four days, and I'll pretend this never happened." She waved her hand back and forth between the two of them.

Feretti looked sheepish. "It'd make a good story to tell later on, though, don't you think?"

She stared at the ceiling, bouncing her foot with her legs crossed as she often did while waiting.

"We could have a really good party," he said, passing the cigarettes and matches to her under the table that she'd asked him to bring. "Are you safe in here?"

"Yes, Albert. Quit worrying about me, will you? Thanks for these. I can trade 'em for stuff."

Feretti chuckled. "I guess you're never gonna need me, are you."

Liz's face softened. She leaned forward and stroked his face, hearing a shout from the guard. "I need you in the worst way, you big, gullible oaf."

She never told him about Del coming to visit. He had called her "doll," said that he was sorry, that he'd wished it hadn't happened to her. She'd given him the cold shoulder and told him to get lost. He had confessed, hoping it would make himself feel better, telling her that the Feds had tried to nab *him*, that he came from a good family he had to protect, and the only way he could get off was to turn someone else in.

"What the hell does *that* mean?" she'd screamed. "A 'good' family? Oh, you mean rich. We poor folk need to protect the rich people, huh? Well, you're all wet you s.o.b.! What kind of a guy are you, Del?"

He said that he had known she wouldn't get much of a sentence. They didn't lock up women very often. He'd told her that the Feds had been watching her and her friends for a couple of weeks.

The rich get drunk, and the poor go to jail. Liz had heard that statement many times and now she knew it was true. It was illegal to make, transport or sell liquor. Why wasn't it illegal to buy it, or own or drink it? It seemed like the law protected the rich. She realized that they shouldn't have done business in the city without paying the big bribes to the cops, but she'd thought the buyers were taking care of that. The four of them had been in over their heads.

She also knew that if she'd told Feretti, he'd do something about Del, and Feretti would end up in jail too, and for a much longer sentence. She needed to protect Feretti; he was the only person in her life that she could count on.

Del would get what was due him. She had nothing better to do with her twenty roommates than to tell them all about Del and plot ways to make his life hell when they got out. They named themselves "The Devilish Delfoes." There were a lot of ways that a girl could make a guy sorry.

Honor Farm

Will didn't see his Hudson again after Hank's capture but was thankful he'd been willing to take the heat by driving it away with some booze in it. Losing the car didn't bother him too much. He'd already been repairing a Buick with a straight-eight engine for himself, something he had wanted since he'd been chased by one. As soon as he had it running, he drove across the state to visit Hank at McNeil Island.

Hank got two years and a $2,000 fine. He figured somebody needed to go to jail, and it might as well have been him. The only thing he truly regretted was Emily. He let Emily down, and Ben, and Meg, his family. He couldn't contact her from the penitentiary, not with the shame of being a convict. He wondered if he could have done things differently, maybe he could have survived up there at the cabin without money, chucking wood in the stove all winter and trying to not starve to death. Maybe that would have been better than prison.

McNeil Island wasn't that bad. Hank was put into the Honor Farm right away with two hundred other men. The prison authorities felt he could be trusted once they realized that he had skills. He became part of the instructional staff in two areas of their work program: boatbuilding and the brickyard. There was comradery among the inmates, and it kept him busy, which he appreciated since it helped him not be completely consumed with worry and regret about Emily.

He wanted more for her than to have a suitor who was a criminal locked up in a penitentiary. Instead, he wrote to Willie, asking him to check on her. He told Willie to take his share of the money from his mason jars at the cabin and his cut from the last sale to get electricity out to her farmhouse and to pay the electric bill as long as the money held out. Months later, he asked Willie to sell his cabin and to buy Emily a radio and an electric sewing machine and electric kitchen appliances. The least he could do was give her an easier life; it reduced his regret to the pain of a toothache.

Emily knew he wouldn't contact her. Having made a promise to her father that he'd broken, he would be embarrassed and ashamed. He was brave as far as she was concerned, willing to put himself at risk to make a better life for them.

She remembered putting him in his place for trying to help her too much. "Let me have whatever independence I can find for myself, won't you?" She was sorry for it now. His face had shown that she'd hurt him; it was the last expression she'd seen, the one that lingered when she thought of him.

At McNeil Island, they had vanilla pudding after dinner one night. It put Hank right back with Emily. She'd always smelled of vanilla. He dreamed of her all night—the time she fell on top of him in the boat, when they'd ridden horses together, how she'd lain in his arms. She laughed in his dream as she rode her horse, as if they were having a race. It fed his soul to feel that she was happy, and he was at peace for days afterward.

A few months before he was to be released from prison, he had sketched out a plan to enlarge the farmhouse to build a bedroom for Emily on the ground floor so she wouldn't need to manage the stairs. He was anxious to get started, counting the days. A letter came from Willie telling him that he was so sorry, that Emily had caught a cold which had become pneumonia and she wasn't able to fight it. A letter from Emily was enclosed.

Hank inhaled, struggling to reconcile the words he read. His hand closed around Emily's letter, clutching it to his chest, causing tiny dry blue petals to fall out of the edges of the seal, and then he exploded. The pain of her loss WHILE HE WAS IN PRISON turned him inside out, completely unhinged. He screamed, saliva spewing from his mouth. He wasn't there when she'd needed him. He beat his head against the wall. She had been dying and he hadn't even known it. Prison guards tried to restrain him; he hit and kicked, bit and spit on them. Everything he'd ever loved was ripped away. It was *always* ripped away.

Hank got extra prison time, was removed from the Honor Farm and put into solitary confinement. He *wanted* to be punished after letting Emily down. He hadn't been with her, and she'd needed him.

He was allowed to keep her wrinkled letter since it was the only thing that calmed him down, but he did not open it. There was something precious inside that he never wanted to let out.

Recovery on a Rabbit

The U.S. economy suffered from lack of revenue, and on December 5, 1933, Prohibition, also known as "the great experiment," was repealed by the 21st Amendment. President Roosevelt called it "a return to individual freedom." It was the only amendment to the U.S. Constitution to have ever been repealed.

Economic help for families began with Roosevelt's New Deal in 1933, partially funded through liquor taxes. Laws were created to reform banking; programs were created for emergency relief and agriculture. People found work through the federal WPA Works Progress Administration (highways, cleaning up slums, improving rural areas) which included the Civilian Conservation Corps (roads, trails, cabins, campgrounds), the Civil Works Administration (small public works), and the Public Works Administration (bridges, roads, tunnels, Coulee Dam).

The New Deal insured individual bank deposits for the first time, up to $10,000. Roosevelt told folks who had money to take it out of their mattresses and coffee cans and from under the floor and put it in the bank. Even more helpful to farmers, the government bought surplus corn, beans, and flour and gave it to the needy. The Agricultural Adjustment Administration paid farmers to limit production in an attempt to correct the balance between supply and demand. Over six million pigs were slaughtered and given to relief organizations. Even so, trains coming into Spokane arrived with boxcars full of homeless families looking for work. Many ended up joining the hobo jungles and shacks along each side of the river downtown.

Joe worked with his father for the Public Works Administration digging ditches that were part of the canals for the gravity-fed Corbin Ditch that ran from the Spokane River in Post Falls to irrigate the Spokane Valley. They walked six miles to the site; and in the winter, it was through mud and snow, leaving before dawn and returning after dark. It was cold and miserable, but good for him to be outside with his father. They encouraged each other day by day. During down times, they cut cord wood together, one dollar per cord.

Each state handled the end of Prohibition differently. In Washington State, hard liquor could only be sold through state-owned and controlled liquor stores as directed by Liquor Control Boards, which also controlled hours of operation.

The following year, a second New Deal included union protection programs, the Social Security Act, and programs to aid tenant farmers and migrant workers. The National Industrial Recovery Act also provided for collective bargaining. Unfortunately, the economy did not improve until we entered World War II in 1941.

Helen screamed as the Jack Rabbit roller coaster at Natatorium Park hurled her down its first and most severe drop at 70 miles an hour. She screamed so violently that no sound came out of her mouth. At the bottom, the train took a hard left so fast that her fingers went numb, gripping the bar to stay in her seat. Then two fast hills, up down up down and another hard turn to the left, the Spokane River coursing far below on the right, the depth of the view sucking all her remaining breath. More downs and ups and fast turns to the left and a final turn to the right and up to the passenger platform.

In shock, she sat, still gripping the bar across her lap until Joe pried her fingers away and pulled her up from the car. Numbly, she went with him, letting him lead her down the steps, back to the ground.

As soon as she recovered, she slugged him in the shoulder with all her might.

"You *looked* like you were having fun," he laughed.

She stared at him, her eyes round. "I've never gone so fast in all my life and in an open car? So high above the ground? We could have died!"

"Nobody's died so far, at least not that I know of." He looked up at the roller coaster. "It's made out of a whole lot of wood. Even if something broke, I think it would still stay together." They sat and watched from the ground as the cars flew around the track, passengers screaming. After several trips, he felt her grip relax and saw her breathing slow.

Her eyes had softened. "The carousel is plenty exciting for me, close to the ground."

"I think you're ready to go again," he said, grabbing her elbow.

"The carousel?"

"The Jack Rabbit. I'm not taking you home 'til you can ride it without screaming. Have fun, not be scared to death."

She gripped his arm again, determined to keep her mouth shut, and as the car on the track carried her through the dark, wooden tunnel and started chugging up up up the track to the top, she knew she'd be screaming within seconds.

Joe was patient.

It took six times.

And she laughed from beginning to end.

The Favor of our Love

Everything changes. It began when a large summer cabin was built on our north side so close to the property line that the owners stepped from their porch onto our yard. It shook my father's faith in what it meant to be a neighbor.

It was Karl, our neighbor two doors south, who told us how a group of friends had built our three cabins in a row during Prohibition as private drinking cabins. He was fun to visit, always offering to pour a drink from his gallon jug of Pisano Chianti. After he finished a complete remodel of his cabin, it burnt to the ground because of a forgotten electric blanket. Karl was broken-hearted and the property sat vacant for years, a house-size hole left behind where the rock foundation had been. Then a new owner built a two-story log cabin in its place, dwarfing the other cabins.

My "Aunt" Freda and "Uncle" Bud Schonfeld, who had the cabin between us and Karl, sold it when maintenance became a chore. Their cabin had been where we'd first danced barefooted to Bing Crosby's "S'posin." "S'posin I should fall in love with you . . ." The scratchy tones came through the horn on their tall wood-cabinet Victrola after a few cranks, Freda reminding us that she'd danced with Bing at Laeida's Dance Pavilion in Dishman when he was with the Musicaladers.

The family who bought it enjoyed it until their family grew. They enlarged the ground floor and went up another level, blocking our light. We didn't blame them, but what had been sky and trees and sunlight out our south windows became a wall that could have been the view from any tenement building in the city. Of course, we'd done a similar remodel at our place. Still, winters, when the sun only partially showed above the treetops, became depressing. I perched myself in front of the east windows to catch the morning sun each day as it came up, its light and warmth as important as breathing. The cold season was long, and the snow was deep.

An unusual windstorm brought the final loss. It came from out of the west and took down my lonely fir tree. We had always known that if it ever went down, it would take the front half of the cabin with it. Even so, we couldn't make ourselves cut it down. It had been part of my life since I first saw the cabin as a child.

I heard the popping of roots first, and it leaned further down-hill, trying to hang on with its remaining roots. I yelled, "It's going down!" and got back toward the center of the cabin. The remaining roots popped, and the tree slammed to the ground, its roots flipping the front support beam under the cabin and everything stored in the cellar through the air and down the hill. The cabin rested on the tree's root ball only 1½ inches lower than before. No windows were broken, no floor or ceiling or walls were cracked. There was no damage whatsoever other than the missing beam—a gift. Dennis had the front of the cabin reinforced within the hour.

My skinny red fir tree had become six feet in circumference and 175 feet tall. On the ground, it stretched toward the water at an angle across our property and across the neighbor's property and touched the water's edge of the next property. From the beginning, it had stood sentry outside the dangerous door and protected us from too much sun. It had framed my water view, had been my consistent anchor, a symbol of stability. In the end, it protected the cabin from breaking in half, returning the favor of our love; and I mourned its loss.

What is a legacy? The results of our good and bad deeds? Our children, perhaps? Might it be a lake cabin? For my family, it certainly wasn't money. It's remarkable that Dad was able to purchase the lake cabin even though the mortgage wasn't paid until after his death.

The lake cabin was always there when we needed it, like going back home, like going back in time. We'd go for fun or for refuge. It was resolute with our precious memories, a constant in my life.

I dig up a shovelful of gladiola bulbs, yellow blooms that had been planted along the property line by Mom and Aunt Freda. I'm still un-able to grip the fact that I am leaving forever. It's late afternoon. The sun skims the tops of the pines above the cabin. The water begins to darken. It's my last chance for a final trip down the hill.

My kayak cuts into the sunlight out on the water. I'm headed south along the string of plastic ski docks, hoping to remember every moment. It's quiet, nothing's stirring, no people or boats to be seen or heard. A fragile looking heron stands one-legged on one of the docks as I pass. I suppose he's fishing. He watches me as I paddle by, evidently curious.

I concentrate on paddling efficiently, the most force with the least waisted movement, silently slicing my paddle into the reflection of the lake without disturbance, pulling hard with control for maximum movement, bringing the paddle out cleanly without a bump or ruffle in the mirror. It's a lovely meditation, the idea of perfection, no matter how impossible.

I remember my sister Cathie saying that the water here is magic. It floats away anything that could trouble a person. It seems like magic to me, too, right now.

The heron flies alongside my boat, nearly touching the water as if we share the same dream and continues on, his stretched, skeletal wings propelling him to a ski dock ahead. He's perched there again as I pass. I call him Dulth, his Tlingit name, thinking how their relationship was established long before ours. I watch his graceful launch into the air and appreciate his aloneness. I've got to do this parting alone as well, say goodbye to magical water.

Back up at the cabin, I walk barefoot across the old fir floor, paying attention to its familiarity under my feet, and leave a bottle of bourbon in the corner cupboard. It seems fitting. Someone might need to take refuge during a snowstorm or need a stiff shot to manage some emergency or loss or celebration.

Grandma's rocking chair has already been put into the truck. Out the door, I bend to pick the last zucchini from the patch of sun that survives beyond the shadow of the neighbor's cabin. It's below "Helen's Coffee Camp." I've got her rolling pin and the three fluted, pink glasses that came with the cabin. Depression glass it's called. I pick up Dad's tackle box and force myself to keep walking. The steps are blurred but I don't need to see them anyway. I know every inch of this place. I'm jealous of those who will come after me even knowing that the cabin will always live in my heart, and I will forever be the one who loved it most.

Epilogue

Willie and Feretti tried to keep an eye on Hank when he was released from prison. He seemed hard boiled, bent on self-destruction, drinking until he was unconscious or his money ran out. Without a home, he slept along the river every night until winter, despite offers of a couch. Then he cobbled a shack together for himself behind a distant cousin's tool shop in Dishman in exchange for his night guard duty. Being lost without Emily, he wasn't very good at guarding anything.

Emily had convinced Willie to write his letter about her death so Hank would be free when he got out of prison. Free to live his own life, not be stuck taking care of her and her braces. He had so much to give, and she wanted him to be able to give it. She hadn't understood the depth of his love for her; she *couldn't* understand it. She'd thought she was doing the right thing by him.

Later, when Willie saw the devastation it brought to Hank, and doubted that he would ever recover, he told Hank the truth, hoping he would understand Emily's reasons and he would get better.

After the staggering shock of it, Hank understood it as

rejection. He cried, thankful to know she was alive, and he didn't blame her. He knew that he had lived a life that Emily and her parents would not have agreed with. It wasn't surprising that they didn't want him around anymore. He didn't want himself around anymore either.

He blamed Willie for lying to him. Willie who had been with him through all those close calls, his partner who had never understood what Emily meant to him.

Feretti stopped checking on Hank since he refused help and never had much to say. When he read in the newspaper about a fire in a business in Dishman that Hank had put out in the night, he hoped for the return of "old" Hank.

Willie sold his lake cabin for a down payment on the gas station and repair shop in Clayton. He wasn't sure if drivers stopped for gas because his was a bit cheaper than in the city or if it was to get his free Depression glass that came with a fill-up. Either way, he loved to see their faces light up when they received their gift, especially Abby's face, the sheriff's daughter. The pink, fluted glasses with the cherries engraved on the bottom were her favorite.

Liz married Feretti at the church in Clayton. Always doing her own thing, she wore a tight satin and lace, pale lemon gown with a poof of matched netting and lace on the back of her head like a hat. She'd had to take up smoking to fit into it, the only way to curb her fondness for milk duds and peanut butter cups that had offset her boredom in jail. She carried three stalks of yellow gladiolas. To celebrate, there was a party at his family's house in Clayton. He and his mother continued to make wine, creating a little boutique blend that Feretti marketed under the table to high-end restaurants.

They sold their lake cabin and bought a little house in Hillyard so he would be closer to restaurants. Liz rented space in a building on Division where she gave dance lessons. It had been a roadhouse during Prohibition. Their daughter, Rosie, became a tap dancer. Her curls bounced and her ruffles fluffed as she tapped. People said she was better than Shirley Temple.

Hank languished in his shack in Dishman until a lawyer came one morning to tell him that he had inherited a farm. Ben and Meg Pearson's Last Will and Testament read, "We hereby bequeath all our property and entire estate to Hank O'Neill, whom we've known and loved as our son."

Hank sat down hard, his head in his hands. Emily was truly gone now, and he hadn't said goodbye. He hadn't been in any shape to go anywhere near her. He thought he'd been forgotten and had felt it was for the best, yet Ben and Meg had continued to love him despite his misdeeds, despite his flaws. *Known and loved as our son* repeated in his mind. He hadn't really believed it before, but now he guessed it must have been true. He shook with regret.

After a few days of soul-searching, he walked to Joe's house to ask for a ride to the farm, said he owed it to Ben and Meg to take care of the place. It was quiet in the car. One of the things he liked about Joe was that he was comfortable with silence; folks could be left alone with their own thoughts.

As they entered the driveway in Chewelah, he saw the old bull standing in the one field that remained with the farmhouse and barn, the rest set apart by a barbed wire fence. "That's sad," Hank said. "Ben must have sold off most of his land."

He noticed the electrical line overhead as they drove to the house which gave him a tiny feeling of satisfaction. They were greeted by a neighbor who shook Hank's hand and welcomed him back, saying he had heard good things about him and had been taking care of the place until he arrived. It felt odd to be greeted in such a fashion after being invisible, as if he made some kind of difference.

After Joe left, Hank half-expected Max to come bounding around the corner, tail wagging, as he walked to the barn. A white picket fence sat on the knoll above the property surrounding a small space filled with blue forget-me-nots in full bloom. He shied away from it as his heart squeezed. He'd need to fix the place up before he earned the right to visit up there.

In the barn, he found a surprise. His old Dodge was there, looking ready to go, and his reflection waited for him in the driver's side window. He had aged some during his rough living, but with his recent clean-up, he didn't look half bad. He smiled at himself for the first time since he could remember. Ben and Meg and Emily had given him his life back. He truly had a home and a family who loved him. Regret for not coming back on his own began to creep in, and he pushed it away. He would need to forgive himself.

The farm needed repair and Hank made mental notes as he walked, his hands itching for tools. It felt good to have projects. He'd bring life back to the place as it restored *him*. Maybe one day he would get a couple of horses, some goats maybe, definitely some chickens. And a dog, the place needed a dog.

The kitchen door was unlocked, and he let himself in, wiping his feet as he always did, nearly hearing Meg's voice telling him to do it as he dragged them across the mat. He stepped inside and looked up. Emily sat at the kitchen table.

A cry erupted as his legs gave out, crashing him to the floor. He looked again, wondering if she was really there.

"My sweet Hank," she said, reaching out her hand to him. "I knew you'd come home to me. I'm just so sorry for the shock of it. Please forgive me."

Hank could barely hear her words above his hammering heart. He needed to catch his breath. He blinked to clear his vision. "Are you alive then?"

"I've been waiting for you for such a very long time."

He got himself up on shaky legs and stepped toward the table to touch her hand. It was cool, like porcelain, and he held it between both of his hands to warm it up, and before he knew it, he pulled her up into his arms and held her tight, and together they sobbed until all their regrets were washed away.

Author's Notes

Our families who were born between 1901 and 1924 are known as the Greatest Generation, the epitome of perseverance. They arrived along with World War I in time to experience the Spanish Flu and Prohibition, and they developed a tremendous work ethic during the Great Depression. Though the economy was still in the tank during their 20s and 30s, they marched ahead and fought in World War II. They took responsibility for their own well-being and were known for their integrity, valuing honesty and doing what's right over personal gain. The goal of my parents' generation was to make a living; their biggest fear, to let their family down.

They also experienced the most rapid advancement in technology of all time "from outhouses to outer space, from kerosene lamps to computers." (Quote is from Clancy Strock's prologue in *We Had Everything but Money*).

By excavating my childhood, I learned that we are influenced more than we know by those who raise us. I had no idea that my father had been a cowboy, though I remember him riding a horse without a bridle or saddle, turning and directing the horse with just his voice, knees and body. I thought he was doing me a favor by taking me horseback riding; now I wonder if I was doing something for *him* when I asked.

My parents taught me that family comes first, that there is value in hard work and honesty, and that a reputation is worth protecting. We were taught that we can accomplish anything if we believe we can and work hard enough for it; that perseverance, optimism and faith are the ways to get through difficult times.

Our grandmothers were wise. I met my maternal grandmother through an old letter to my mother, "cheer up, laugh, be gay. . . If we only have love, love and a home and family, we'll be alright." My paternal grandmother often said to "kill 'em with kindness." She taught that a relationship with God will sustain us, that faith delivers peace.

Those who experienced the Great Depression felt the experience helped them think of others beyond themselves, and that they didn't feel poor because everyone was in the same situation. "I didn't know we were poor; I thought we were just broke." There were endless examples of selfless, noble acts, like the man who cut all the trees on his property to provide wood for heat and cooking for his neighbors, and the man who funded the only gas station in his town to enable his small community to function.

Every "Joe" who survived had an inspirational story of perseverance. Today, when people complain about their economic challenges, even during years of strong economy and low unemployment and more assistance programs than ever before, I think of our families who made do when there was only the help of friends and neighbors.

Ultimately, the purpose of this book is for encouragement. Life could always get harder and knowing about others who struggled in the past could help us be strong.

Pictures:

PART ONE: Clarence in the Palouse Dairy Truck

PART TWO: Helen

PART THREE: Tommy, Mickie, Joe

Facts within the Fiction

In the 1920s, people just wanted to have fun. World War I was over, and the scrimping, saving and sacrificing for the war effort should have been over too, but flapper fun was only for those who had at least *some* money and was short-lived.

Our economy changed from agricultural households in small, self-sufficient towns to an industrial economy centered in cities connected with rail; and people followed the work into the cities.

Prior to Prohibition, liquor sales had been the fifth largest industry in our country, providing one-third of the federal government's revenue. Individual and corporate income taxes needed to be increased to replace it, and citizens were squeezed from every direction even though they'd been promised that the taxes would "only apply to the very wealthy."

Sometimes, breaking the law was the only way to put food on the table. Economic suffering during Prohibition enticed enforcement authorities to take bribes; and over time, they became corrupt as evidenced by eighty percent of the whiskey produced in Canada illegally ending up in the United States.

344 - VICTORIA VENTRIS SHEA

This story is fiction, though some parts are true:

Memoir chapters in italics are true, including the inscription on the beam in the cellar, "Hail Hail The Gang's All Here 1928." I should clarify that my father did not take his last breath at the cabin lest some new owners of the cabin might be queasy about that.

Part I is mostly true although a few events have been combined or slightly altered and some details have been imagined. For example, there is no evidence that Clarence sold snake oil. For clarity regarding the family, please contact me and I will email the details to you. If you need contact information, please use my website https://VictoriaVentrisShea.com

Alice's father, Elwood Harold, was a Christian minister, the son of Quakers. He organized numerous churches in Oklahoma where "Mother Younger" came to him with worries about her boys running with the wrong crowd. Her sons were the Younger Brothers, and the wrong crowd was the Jesse James gang. He was called to pastor a church in Genesee, Idaho, and then in St. John, Washington, where he baptized 28 converts in a single revival. At his death in 1932, the *Christian Standard* described him as "an outstanding Christian leader and minister of the Northwest."

The letters are actual letters. It is interesting that the envelopes were addressed to the recipient's name and town with no numbers. It was a time when folks really did know everyone in and around town. Note: Please date your letters.

Joe and Helen's first date when her father's jugs of moonshine broke in a borrowed car are true, as is the last scene at the end of the book on the Jack Rabbit.

Parts II and III are fictional characters set in authenticity. Oral legend tells us that many of the cabins built on Loon Lake during Prohibition were built as private drinking cabins where people could be ferried from their own cabins to dancehalls on the lake and back to their cabins for a drink. It was never a business that I know of. The Brick and Lime Club and the gang are fiction. Otherwise, the names, places, businesses, and events of this section are true including the artist Leno Prestini.

The size of the physical plant of Washington Brick and Lime Company in Clayton was estimated, but it looked like a city in the pictures. It was dismantled in the 1950s.

Leno Prestini and crew blasted the smaller smokestacks at the brickyard and took the others down with a bulldozer. The terra cotta building was torched. The boilers were turned into scrap metal. The main plant was burned and pushed into the clay pits and covered with clay. Not a single brick remained on site as evidence of that huge, industrious, life-giving plant that had built and decorated cities except for the main smokestack which fell on April 24, 1961.

Time on Loon Lake was somewhat collapsed. For example, it is uncertain if the steamboat *The Gwen* was still in operation in 1928.

The events of smuggling liquor over the Canadian border are based on Edmund Fahey's personal account in his book, *Rum Road to Spokane: A Story of Prohibition*. According to Fahey, since liquor coming into Spokane was the real thing, or close enough with less aging, Spokane became a large distribution area. "Haulers came from half-way across the country and paid retail." There wasn't any mob activity, each rumrunner hauled for himself.

Felts Field in the Spokane Valley served as the Spokane airport during Prohibition. It's likely that some illegal liquor came through there, although I didn't find specific evidence of it. Perhaps the Washington Air National Guard which set up at the airport in 1924 was a deterrent.

Resources

Abbott, Karen. 2019. *The Ghosts of Eden Park*, Broadway Books:NY.

Bamonte, Tony and Schaeffer, Suzanne. 1996. *History of Pend Oreille County*, Toronto Creek Publications, Spokane:WA.

Bell, Jessica L. *Mica Peak and Prohibition*, https://spokane-historical.org/items/show/527

*Clayton, Deer Park, Loon Lake Historical Society, www.cdphs.org/mortarboard-newsletters.html.

Egan, Timothy. 2006. *The Worst Hard Time*, Houghton Mifflin Company:NY.

*Fahey, Edmund. 1972. *Rum Road to Spokane: A Story of Prohibition*, University of Montana Press, Missoula:Montana.

Lusted, Lucia Amidon. 2014. *The Roaring Twenties*, Nomad Press, White River Junction:VT.

Mackrell, Judith. 2014. *Flappers: Six Women of a Dangerous Generation*, Sarah Crichton Books,:NY.

Meyers, Donald W. "It Happened Here: Prohibition came to Washington before the rest of the nation." *Yakima*

Herald-Republic, January 7, 2018, updated October 8, 2018.

Moore, Stephen T. 2014. *Bootleggers and Borders: The Paradox of Prohibition on a Canada-U.S. Borderland,* University of Nebraska Press, Lincoln:Nebraska.

Mulvey, Deb et.al. editors. 1992. *We Had Everything but Money,* Reiman Publications, Greendale:WI.

Nisbet, Jack & Claire. *Prestini, Leno (1906-1963).* Posted 10/03/2010. www.historylink.org/File/9571

Nisbet, Jack. April 25, 2002. "The Washington Brick & Lime Company," *The Inlander.*

Okrent, Daniel. 2010. *Last Call: The Rise and Fall of Prohibition,* Scribner:NY.

Parker, Wally Lee. July 2018. "Clayton's Moose Temple--The Early Years." *The Clayton/Deer Park Historical Society Mortarboard Newsletter,* Issue #123. www.cdphs.org/mortarboard-newsletters.html.

Simon, Linda. 2017. *Lost Girls: The Invention of the Flapper,* Reaktion Books, London:UK.

Walter, Jess. 1920. *The Cold Millions,* Harper:NY.

Walters, Daniel. "In Spokane, Prohibition meant the poor got jailed while the rich got drunk." *The Inlander,* February 27, 2020.

Wilson, Gary A. 2005. *Long George Francis: Gentleman Outlaw of Montana,* TwoDot Books, Imprint of Rowman & Littlefield:Blue Ridge Summit, PA

Wilson, Gary A. 2006. *Honky-Tonk Town: Havre, Montana's Lawless Era,* Twodot:Helena, Montana.

Acknowledgments

First, thank you to Edmund Fahey for his book *Rum Road to Spokane: A Story of Prohibition*. I would have had trouble imagining the details of smuggling without his account. And thank you to my historical consultant and number one reader, my husband, and to family encouragers, especially sisters, cousins and nieces. I could feel them hovering over this story more than they knew.

Thank you to family record-keepers: My Aunt Grace and Uncle Tom who wrote their memories for our family reunion in 1980; my sisters Barbara and Cathie, who helped fill in the gaps; my mother who saved some of her letters; my cousins Karyne, Ann, Ida Mae and Bobby who shared their family stories.

Thank you to Karen Meyer of Clayton, niece of Bud Schonfeld. She met with me and mailed family information. Thanks also to the Clayton, Deer Park, Loon Lake Historical Society of which Karen is a member. Their records include original posts regarding Moose Lodge activities as well as recollections from residents such as Peter Berg and Robert A. Clouse who wrote about the brickyard setting crew and the use of dynamite to create a well when the winch jammed.

Heartfelt thanks to my hairdresser extraordinaire, Janine,

who burst my false memory that Dad had offered to buy me a horse, but it was a three-legged colt; and to my brother-in-law Sam, vintage cars expert.

Thank you to early readers Sheryl Shearer, Crystal Eddy and Ann O'Mohondro and to my sister Cathie who found readers among her Zumba and church friends.

Finally, I'd like to thank future readers. Your reviews, especially on Amazon and/or Goodreads, are always appreciated. Mahalo!

SHAGOON

Historical fiction by Victoria Ventris Shea

Ana was meant to die in the Alaskan forest, a naked new-born left with moss in her mouth to keep her quiet while her mother lay screaming and fighting to keep Ana's brother. The babies were born with a deadly condition; they were twins.

Because of greed, Ana is secretly sold and raised in a Spanish California mission where she longs for someone like a mother. When she bonds with a native Ohlone healer who saves her life, the mission sends her back to her homeland, not knowing the dangers that wait for her there. Shocked by everything, she sails with Captain George Vancouver on *Discovery* and finds love in Hawaii where they winter. Now she must decide if she will perform her duty for the mission and possibly find her family or stay in Hawaii.

This 18th century, multi-cultural historical novel begins with Ana's young Tlingit mother whose fierce love for her warrior husband and son launches a change for future generations.

Praise for Shagoon

A wild ride . . . one of the strongest pieces of historical fiction I've ever encountered . . . a brand-new aspect of the world. Ana is a bold, brilliant character . . . so many gorgeous, literary aspects . . . it warrants multiple reads to understand the depth and level of work that Shea has created here. –**Writer's Digest**: *Judge, 29th Annual Self-Published Book Awards*

A wonderfully complete and beautiful picture of a society that was uncompromising and tough . . . that functioned perfectly well before the arrival of the "civilizing" Europeans. A powerful tale I truly appreciate because it is told through the eyes of the indigenous people. I can highly recommend this read. –**Readers' Favorite**: *Grant Leishman*

A wonderful discovery . . . I loved the characters. It reminded me how important it is for everyone to try to be a hero in life. –*Mrs. Bea Ticked, UK (from Amazon)*

Rarely do I come across a book that makes me feel like I'm a part of a major discovery. Check out Shagoon. --*A.J. Wells, reader for Writer's Digest.*

An exceptional read . . . the heartfelt plotline is dramatic and moving, involving struggle, loss, braveness, love, determination and hope; everything needed to make the story superb. Definitely recommended. --*Schmuel Yaccoby, author of Kumaz (from Amazon)*

Victoria Ventris Shea proudly presents this, her second book, as encouragement during hard times. In this 20th century historical fiction romance, which is part family history and memoir, her focus remains on the importance of family and appreciation of nature. She hopes that readers will be inspired by the industriousness and ingenuity of those who came before us, those who lived through hard times during Prohibition.

Although she grew up in the Spokane area and taught there for most of her career, she also lived and taught for many years in Sequim on the Olympic Peninsula and one year in Hawaii where she continues to visit. She currently lives with her husband on Whidbey Island in Washington state. Her adult children and grandbaby live nearby.